The Illusion of Honour

Pandey Surendra Prasad

Vitasta
Let Knowledge Spread

Times Group Books

Published by
Vitasta Publishing Pvt. Ltd.
2/15, Ansari Road, Daryaganj,
New Delhi - 110 002
info@vitastapublishing.com

ISBN 978-93-80828-92-3

Cover & Layout Design by Vitasta Publishing Pvt. Ltd.
Printed by Vits Press, New Delhi

To

My father, the late Pandey Ashtbhuja Prasad, and
to my mother, Smt. Jaishree Prasad

Acknowledgements

After the book is written it takes a friend to help find a publisher. My thanks to Sunil Patki for bringing a swift end to my despair at ever finding a platform for my outpourings.

To Yashovardhan Singh, whose eagle eye for detail and encyclopedic knowledge of everything under the sun, came to the rescue time and again in the polishing of the manuscript.

To my family whose deeds ensure that I will never be in want for stories, suffused with the multi-hued colours of life.

To my publisher Renu Kaul Verma of Vitasta Publishing for her professionalism, to Veena Batra for her editorial competence. Above all to the Vitasta team for their passion for what they do.

Contents

Foreword ix

1. A Party at the Modys 1
2. Rasulabad 22
3. Samir's Secret 70
4. Sita's Turmoil 112
5. Rahul's Trial by Fire 143
6. Matters of the Heart 155
7. The Defeat of Gayatri Devi 175
8. New Beginnings 207

Foreword

The Illusion of Honour is a compelling deconstruction of our times. It explores the hypocrisy, heartbreaks, and violence perpetrated by those who, in some form or another, seek to be 'the most honourable of them all.' The voice of sanity emerges from the lips of an outsider – one who renounces the pursuit of honour by lesser means till she finds that an obsession with honour, even through a life of virtue, is ultimately a trap. Essential reading for all those who are interested in knowing how India's judiciary and the government interact and the social milieu in which they mix.

Khushwant Singh
New Delhi
October, 2012

A Party at the Modys

A party at this time of the year was a regular feature in the Mody household. The guest list was like the who's who of the country. The party had ostensibly been thrown to usher in the forthcoming festive season but every guest was given the impression that the party was in his or her honour.

The drive way on the periphery of the huge lawns facing the mansion had been lit up with ornate designs, some emanating from electricity, others from wax and oil. The flower beds and flowering trees were all visible to the guests, their vivid colours gleaming under the light. Shining limousines entering the huge gate of the mansion were shown in by liveried men and the guests were received in the spacious portico in front of the large verandah by a retinue of attendants, courteously opening the back doors of cars to facilitate guests alighting and entering.

The hosts stood in the center of the verandah, which had been decorated with rare items of art and opulence besides the implanted greenery. B. Prabha and Anjoli Ila Menon's creations were presiding on either side and B. C. Sanyal was dominating the center stage in his undershirt and *lungi*, through a brilliant self portrait. Silver, brass and crystal items were scattered all over and the scene was further garnished by silken Persian rugs on the floor.

Rustom Mody was tall and well built. He looked impressive in his midnight blue suit, magenta tie and pink shirt. The scion of a very distinguished family known to be wealthy, he was broad minded and liberal in outlook. Nothing gave him greater pleasure than being of use to those who needed it. His Harrow and Cambridge education did not come in the way of his feeling one with the lesser privileged segments of the society in general, and those belonging to his community in particular. Along with his vast business empire, he ran several orphanages and charitable institutions. As a host, he was charm personified.

Rustom's wife Zaroo was beautiful and had the grace of a First Lady. Similar to her husband in all respects, there was seldom a difference of opinion among them. Humility was writ large on her face and her very bright eyes reflected the level of intelligence and wisdom stored inside her. She belied the belief that beauty and wisdom were sworn enemies.

She sported a fawn *gadwal* saree with a wide purple border and a purple *gadwal* blouse to go with it. In her ears and nose she had very delicate diamond studs, and one around her neck. The old Rolex on her wrist glinted with the diamond bangles. Standing in the porch with Rustom, she completed the picture of grace and dignity. Rustom and Zaroo had met in Cambridge, where they had completed their higher education. They made a very loving couple but the seed of the women's liberation movement, hidden in some remote corner of her personality, made it difficult for Zaroo to digest that in their inner circle she was called the 'clone of her husband.' "After all, one has to pay in some form or the other for marrying someone who is so much better than herself in every respect," they said. Unconfirmed rumours had it that Zaroo's father had been working for Rustom's father and that Rustom's family had identified her to be his bride after the two were through with their education. They even suspected that Rustom's family had borne the expenses of Zaroo's overseas education.

The only daughter of the family, Shahnaz, was a picture of beauty. She was a tall, slim storehouse of energy. She had returned home after finishing her course from the School of Arts in Paris. Her beautiful eyes and perfect set of teeth did justice to her milky complexion. She did not agree with her mother's latent and seldom expressed view that Indian women had been suppressed for a long time and that they needed to be liberated. Sporting a long, pink skirt and a black, sleeveless blouse, a string of pearls around the neck and an ornate watch, she cut a fine figure as she received the guests with her parents.

Neha, looking defiantly gorgeous and already in high spirits, entered the porch with her paramour, Ranjit, and was received with a peck on her cheek by Rustom. "Hello my dear girl, you look as beautiful as ever." He shook Ranjit's hand and directed them towards the hall.

Ranjit had managed to reach the top of the corporate ladder at a very young age. He had been gifted with good looks and all the worldly possessions but was said to be running from pillar to post in search of happiness without really settling into a groove. He had separated from his wife and now Neha was his live-in partner. They were known to fight like cats and dogs, totally oblivious of their surroundings.

Neha was a fresh product of IIM, Ahmedabad. She hailed from a well-to-do middle class family of a small town. The family had fixed her marriage with an IAS officer. But having come to Delhi, the ambitious girl had developed other ideas. She wanted to conquer the world and was determined to do so at any cost. Ranjit was convenient eye candy for the moment but she was open to better possibilities.

Rahul — tall, dark and very handsome walked in like a winner, dressed in his most funky attire. He walked up to Rustom and said with a bow, "Good evening sir, seems like a great evening is in store!"

"Ah, the Raibahadur of Rasulabad," Rustom gave his latest visitor a kingly welcome. "How is it going in your estates, young man?"

Rahul grimaced at the flourish with which he had been greeted, but only in mock disgust. Before he could respond, Zaroo rushed towards him and embraced him, saying, "My evening is made! I wasn't sure that you'd be able to make it. Please join us."

Shahnaz also received Rahul with a warm hug and told her mother, "How can he not be here? How could squash get precedence over a family party? He was only acting funny." Rahul joined the hosts in receiving the guests with aplomb.

He had just returned from England after acquiring a degree in law. He was a multi-faceted personality and appeared to be the master of anything he pursued. He could wield his pen effectively and with the melody of his voice, enthral his audience for hours. Hearing him speak in public, people found themselves spellbound. To top it all he was equally distinguished in the world of sports, having represented the country in golf and squash. He belonged to an old aristocratic family which was still quite respected, but had lost its sheen over the years. Money had yet to come his way but he was confident that he would have it one day and in abundance. But the respect his family name commanded was important to him, and Rahul was not one to compromise on his values to reach his goals.

Neha, having minutely observed the effusiveness with which he had been welcomed could not contain herself. "This *chamchi* Zaroo seems to have her eyes on Rahul for her daughter. Little does she know that there are any number of girls chasing him and he won't even look at Shahnaz."

Ranjit found Neha's observation irritating. "Why are you getting so upset? I hope you too aren't chasing him."

Pat came the answer from Neha, "I hope you're aware that it's the millstone around my neck that stops me from chasing him!"

"Any commitment can only be a millstone for a social climber like you. I'm sure that wouldn't change even if you got a Rahul for your husband." Ranjit moved aside as he said this, making way for the fresh batch of guests walking in.

The Army Chief, a few senior officers of the Navy and Air Force and their wives walked in, their bearing commanding and dignified. Rustom walked up to them and shaking their hands he said, "The Services do have the best looking men and women."

Zaroo walked in and said, "That's not fair. They're not only the best looking, they're actually the best in every way!"

The Chief's wife was equally gracious. "One has to put one's best foot forward for coming to such a grand party." They all entered the hall and found their preferred spots.

In a short time a stream of visitors sporting Versaces, Birkins, Jimmy Choos, Rolexes, Omegas, Cartiers and Pierre Cardins walked into the hall and filled it with joy and fun. Booze flowed like a fountain and exotic foods were being served all around. Ladies and gentlemen from all hues of the rich life seemed so relaxed together that it was unimaginable that they could have different objectives and goals. Merry making seemed to be the sole objective!

The chandeliers in the hall, in their benevolence, lit up even those faces that normally did not look too bright. So enormous were they in size that they covered almost all the guests at the party. M. F. Hussain, from his perch in *jannat*, on seeing so many of his creations on the walls would have been inclined to feel humble. The wood of the floor could be scarcely seen through the gaps between the Persian rugs. The eight feet tall Ming porcelain vases stood in their glory with loads of flowers hanging around them — as if competing with each other to kiss their feet. They looked grand and their fragrance permeated the atmosphere, tickling the romantic instincts of the guests. The heavily carved wooden tables with their three legs stretching out were attached to the walls, and all kinds of curios and antiques — crystal, lilac, silver — were tastefully arranged on them. The enormous furniture in the hall did not seem to come in the way of space, which appeared to be in plenty for everyone to walk around or sit to make themselves comfortable. The bar in the corner was stacked with all conceivable forms of alcohol, wines and liquors. Varieties of exotic snacks were placed at different places and the bearers were serving them in silver containers with an array of drinks.

An adjoining room with a dance floor and a DJ in attendance had been earmarked for those who wanted to shake a leg. The DJ had the best mix of music and was eagerly awaiting his commands.

The professional bearers, who are generally common in all big parties, are a class by themselves. They know a large number of the guests, their likes and dislikes and, more than anything else, the intricate details of their personal lives. They get the opportunity of watching and listening to the elite from very close quarters at their most unguarded moments—an opportunity no one else gets.

Seeing the local MP, Rajeshwar, walking in with his wife, one bearer said to another, "I hope there is no *maar-peet* and *gaali-gufta* this evening. I hope this politician's entry doesn't mean the night takes an ugly turn." The other replied, "You don't know how scared he is of his wife. With her around, there is no likelihood of any kind of aggression on his part."

The first bearer enquired, "I realise that being who he is, he gets invited to all parties. So why does his wife not accompany him to all parties to ensure that no unpleasantness takes place? After all, she must be aware of the happenings and surely she could not be relishing them."

The other bearer replied with a wise look on his face, "His wife has no problem in accompanying him. But generally, after every party he does not go home directly and so on some pretext or the other he avoids taking his wife along." They both shared a knowing smile and proceeded with their work, which had only warmed up for the long night of revelry.

It was too early for guests to crowd the dance floor but a few youngsters entered the room and the DJ started playing his music, happy to get his show on the road. The stimulants were playing their role and the party started swinging. Music, alcohol and conversation began to flow. Matters mundane, philosophical and frivolous received equal billing in the evening's fare.

❖❖

Rajeshwar and his wife Alka walked up to Vinay Khosla and his wife Vineeta who were both lawyers by profession. Besides being very successful in their careers, they were known to be very warm human beings. They were quiet by temperament but had firm views on the state of the society. Spending the evening socialising with the Rajeshwars was not a pleasant thought, but for the sake of politeness they put on gracious smiles. Enveloping Vinay in a bear hug, Rajeshwar asked ebulliently, "So when are you going to be elevated to the bench?"

Vinay felt a bit embarrassed at the directness of the question and replied diplomatically, "Not unless you become the Law Minister."

Rajeshwar boasted, "What to talk of a High Court judge, I can make you the Prime Minister also! Do let me know if you want any help. The Law Minister can't say no to me." There was a greasy-slick grin on his face.

Vinay replied politely, "I'll certainly let you know." And they walked on to another group.

This group was engrossed in taking stock of the politicians and the political situation in the country. It comprised some bureaucrats, some university professors and some lawyers. They were unanimous that unless the class of politicians changed and good people entered politics, there was no hope for the country. The problem, they opined, was not dearth of good people per se. It was just that the game had become so murky that good people did not want to join politics. A professor suggested that a minimum level of education must be made compulsory for everyone entering public life and contesting elections. He cited the examples of some lawmakers who could hardly even read and write.

"Even that wouldn't help," countered a lawyer. "Some of the

lawmakers have a law degree as well as criminal records. Swindlers in suits are swindlers after all."

One of the bureaucrats, who had helped himself generously to the abundant scotch in the party, commented dryly, "People get the government they deserve, so why worry about it?"

The professor, who was slowly nursing his drink and looking gravely concerned with the sad state of affairs in the country, could not contain himself. He said, "It's very easy to be smug. One has to go out of one's shell to see what's happening outside. It's not only the politicians who are raping the country; those who assist them are equally guilty."

The bureaucrat, not used to being contradicted, looked piqued and said, "I suggest you join politics and set things right then! I'm doing my job very well. And no thanks to you." He leaned back on the couch, satisfied with his response.

The professor by now had got into a combative mood. He said, barely keeping his volume down, "A discussion that was supposed to be of a general nature has been made into a personal one. I would've certainly joined politics if I had the means and the muscle which are imperatives for contesting elections these days!"

One of the lawyers interjected, "If you too have to use money and muscle for the election, then what would be the difference between you and the present day politicos?"

Another lawyer butted in, "It may not be necessary to have muscle and money to win an election. If the people are convinced that the candidate is good, then they will vote for him."

The professor, now officially in combat mode, asked, "Does the electorate not know what kind of person someone with a criminal record is likely to be, and is it not true that a sizeable number of our legislators have criminal records—some of them contesting the elections while serving their sentence and even getting elected?"

The wife of a leading industrialist who had been overhearing the conversation from a distance now came closer and joined the group. She had a glass of sherry in her hand and it seemed like she had been enjoying herself all evening. She was exquisitely dressed and the diamonds around her neck were lighting up her face which looked beautiful even with hardly any make up on. Everybody in the group seemed to know her and accepted her entry when she began airing her view on the 'very serious topic.'

She was not particularly keen on changing the shape and direction of present day politics. A dutiful wife, used to the luxuries her husband's business ventures brought, she was of the view that the present government should continue in power in order to ensure the continued success of her husband's group of industries. She said, "The present government seems to be doing quite well. The rate of growth of GDP is touching almost ten percent, the stock market is booming and we are now looked upon as one of the world's leading economies. I think we should rejoice over these positive events rather than taking a negative approach."

The bureaucrat took his cue from the lady and said, "With the finest scotch in hand, strolling over Persian carpets, the pseudos affect great concern for the affairs of the masses. When it comes to facing the music they withdraw in obscurity. And whenever they have to seek a personal favour, they don't hesitate to approach the same politicians and bureaucrats they incriminate in the privacy of their lavish homes."

Sensing the likelihood of an altercation, Vinay Khosla tried to bring about some order in the discussion. He said, "It won't serve any purpose blaming anybody. The fact is that politicians, bureaucrats, lawyers, judges, police, doctors, engineers — all are thrown up by the same society, and the basic culture of the society is reflected in the working of all who come out of it. There are some very highly educated and cultured ministers in the government but at the end of the day they are also found guilty of the same follies as those who have not had such advantages. Experience proves that those who come from under-privileged segments of society take some time to learn the ways of transacting big business and turning them to their personal advantage, whereas the privileged ones have to just dial a telephone number and everything falls in place. It has been seen that royalty too, after entering politics, behaves in the same manner as those devoid of the benefit of education and an illustrious background." It was clear that the most articulate view on the topic had been shared.

Rajeshwar, sensing an opportunity to redeem his profession, decided to join the discussion. He said, "Vinay is right. It's very easy to blame the politicians but tell me honestly if any wing of the society is clean. The judiciary is the most corruptible because they have no accountability and even an innocuous favour doled out by them can make a difference of crores of rupees to the litigants. An adjournment of the date on which a matter is to be heard, for example, is apparently the most harmless favour that a judge can extend, but it may mean a fortune to the litigant. Can the lawyers who have been manipulating their cases with the help of their colleagues, sever their relations with them overnight after being elevated to the Bench?"

An MP supporting Rajeshwar said, "The judges shout from the roof tops that they're overworked, but the fact is that they don't work honestly. Isn't it true that half the lawyers at all levels are busy trying to delay matters to the advantage of their clients, and they can't succeed in their objective without the active cooperation of the judges? A visit to the High Court leaves no doubt in the mind of the visitor that a full-fledged picnic is in process. '*Tareekh* after *tareekh*' is the order of the day, and the judges delude themselves by thinking that people are convinced about their being overworked. Sure, there are no-nonsense judges with a very fast rate of disposal but they're a rare breed." He further added, "Look at the prevailing system of arbitration; it's a part of the picnic. The retired judges are appointed arbitrators by the judges junior to them on the Bench, ensuring that the retiring judges continue to have employment. The rate of disposal of matters in arbitration is slow, as the arbitrators are intent on maximizing their personal incomes."

Rajeshwar, who had a bee in his bonnet about the judiciary, was buoyed. He said, "I know of a judge who delivers judicious judgements but sends word to the winning litigants before delivering the orders that they must pay him a certain amount of money. The litigants are so desperate to avoid rounds of the courts that they gladly part with the money asked for. The concerned lawyers are only too happy to liaise between the litigants and the judge because that helps in establishing their rapport with him. Explaining his conduct to his friends, the judge said that someone had to reward him for his intellectual integrity. After all he ensured that his judgements were honest and fair." Everyone laughed, saying "Rajeshwar, you're impossible."

Rahul, who had been quietly listening to the discussion for some time, came forward with his observations. "The corroding values of society have affected all its segments and only a few have remained unscathed. Irrespective of one's vocation in life there is hardly any difference in the ultimate objective — to derive maximum benefit for oneself. Most people remain clean because, much as they want to, they don't get the opportunity to line their pockets."

❖❖

The dance floor was pulsating with music. Youngsters were dancing with gay abandon and those in love were lost in close embrace, exchanging sweet nothings like 'Can't we dance like this all night?' or 'What you can do to me is beyond my dreams.' The answers to such questions were as ethereal as the questions. 'I have other plans after the party' or 'I can well imagine.' A husband who was dancing with his wife got emotional and whispered into her ears, "Do you realise what Mumtaz

Mahal must have missed in the seventeenth century, when there was no dancing like this here?" That was an unfortunate selection of a historical character, for the lady replied, "How would I know? All I know is that she had all the world's wealth at her feet." The man's pace slowed down but he said, "I would place the whole world at your feet." Pat came the retort, "Since when have you started calling yourself the whole world?"

The DJ was consistently receiving requests, from the good old waltz to the latest in hip hop. Alcohol, most diligently and honestly, was playing its part. Those who were helping themselves with higher forms of supplements needed nothing more than what they already had. They were well ensconced on cloud nine.

Something happened and Neha and Ranjit, who had been on the floor for some time, suddenly disentangled themselves. Neha walked out in a huff and Rahul, who had joined the floor with a European blond, overheard her saying, "A man is nothing but a chauvinist pig."

Ranjit, abashed, followed muttering under his breath, "Neha, please don't make a scene; please understand."

Rustom had made a big circle around him and was narrating a story to a happy and appreciative audience. He said that he had a friend who had a heart of gold and was full of virtues but he was a champion fibber — so much so that it became a constant source of embarrassment for Rustom. No amount of advice or reprimanding made any difference to him and he happily continued with his highly exaggerated and fanciful narratives. Ultimately when Rustom warned him that he could not continue with his habit without risking his friendship with him, he realised that the matter had taken a serious turn. He conceded, "I have done all that is possible to make amends but I've failed miserably. I get swayed by emotions and cannot help it."

After a great deal of planning, and deliberation, narrated Rustom to his audience, it was decided that whenever he found his friend getting out of control he would cough, and that would be the signal for the friend to stop. This arrangement worked out very well for some time till the day when the friend's habit got the better of him once again. This happened when they had just taken up their first jobs. To celebrate they went to a party together. The spirit of a party they were attending was high and the spirits, in material form, were flowing copiously as well. Kapil Dev along with some other cricketers was adorning the party and people surrounded him, competing in showering praises on India's pride. They were unanimous in their view that Dev and Co. had done the country proud, for winning the World cup was no mean achievement. Among such illustrious company, Rustom's friend felt left out and could not contain himself. He decided to do something to get noticed and steal the thunder. He said to himself that a little exaggeration in narrating a story, especially when it was harmless, would only add spice to the mood of the party. He justified to himself that social gatherings were meant to be enjoyed and anything done for the sake of the recreation of the guests at the party would only be appreciated.

He pulled his seat a little forward and said, "Any talk of cricket takes me down the memory lane when good old C.K. uncle, who was a great friend of my father, used to visit my home."

Fali, who was a young member of the IAS, shared Rustom's friend's uneasiness at the limelight on the cricketers. Not knowing of the great Col. C.K. Naidu, he asked Rustom's friend, "And who is this C.K. uncle of yours?"

Rustom's friend replied with an air of authority, "Col. C.K. Naidu was the greatest cricketer of yesteryear. He was a contemporary of Sir Donald Bradman and Sir Don held him in very high esteem."

Fali nodded his head and said, "Oh, *that* C.K. Naidu! Anyone who knows anything about cricket should have at least heard of Col. Naidu, but it's interesting to know that you knew him personally."

Noting Fali's interest in the subject, Rustom's friend realised that he was not far from taking the floor. He said, "Knew him personally?

As children, my brothers and I used to play with his *shikaar* trophies as well as those that he won in cricket. Did you know that besides being a great cricketer, he was also a formidable *shikaari*? And he was a crack shot. He and my father often used to go for *shikaars*"

Fali enquired, "By *shikaar* trophies you mean the heads of the animals he killed?"

"Exactly! And seeing the heads of those real animals from such close quarters used to be indeed very exciting. Father told me that C.K. Uncle once killed a tiger that appeared to be about fifteen feet long."

This was the cue for Rustom that his friend was getting out of control, and he coughed. His friend took the hint and said, "When they went near the animal they found it to be about twelve feet in length." Rustom again coughed. His friend, taking the hint, further corrected himself and said, "But when they finally measured the animal they found it to be exactly ten feet long." Rustom found the statement still beyond the realms of reality and coughed yet again. This time the friend lost his cool and said, "Keep coughing for the rest of your life, but the length of the tiger cannot change once it has been measured!" Everybody went into splits of laughter — some even clapped, both at the narrative and at Rustom's brave attempt to muzzle it.

Listening to Rustom's tale, no one in the audience noticed the entry of a gentleman looking stately and graceful, attired in a dark *achkan* and *churidar*, supported by a pair of shining pump shoes. His high cap matched the *achkan* and the trimmed beard and flowing moustache, creating an aura of distinction and style around him. Since Rustom was in the midst of narrating the story, the new entrant stood by with a mischievous smile. When Rustom's eye fell on him, he rose from his seat and advanced towards the gentleman, saying "Hello, *Nawab Saheb*! How wonderful that you're here. I'd almost given up on you as I was told that you were away to Lucknow."

The Nawab came forward and embraced Rustom, his tone

mischievous. "I have no doubt about it, because if you knew I was coming to the party you wouldn't have been narrating the story that you were!"

Rustom released himself from the embrace and threw up both his hands. "You've given out that the main character of the story is none other than you!"

"Nonsense!" the Nawab countered. He turned towards the conglomeration around them. "In fact it's Rustom who has no equal in storytelling. There was a time when his family had to employ a retainer with the specific task of modifying and making plausible Rustom's many splendoured tall tales."

"Of course, my friend," said Rustom leading *Nawab Saheb* to the bar.

By this time another individual, Prem Dutt, had entered this party at the Modys. He was an old friend of the Nawab and he walked up to him with a glass of wine and put his hand around the Nawab's shoulders. "*Nawab Saheb*," he said, "the gusto with which you've attacked the bar is a sure pointer to the fact that *Begum Saheba* is not here."

The Nawab immediately shot back, "If I had one *Begum Saheba*, I would have taken her to all the parties as you do. But I have four and it's not easy for them to decide who will accompany me for an outing."

While the Nawab and his friend Prem Dutt were laughing away with their hands around each other's shoulders, there walked in a beautiful lady and whispered into the Nawab's ears, "And who is this Don Casanova with four wives, may I know?"

The Nawab was startled and could not believe his eyes. He disengaged himself and assuming his usual poise said, "*Begum*, may God, give you a long life, how have you appeared here? We've been joking and narrating imaginary tales. Now that you're here it would be more fun."

Prem Dutt approached the *Begum* and said, "*Bhabhi jaan*, women don't have to do anything to tame men, for we are born henpecked. Those who try to be domineering do so only with the concurrence of their wives. The good wives allow the husbands their bravado and the good husbands put up with even the difficult demands of the wives in the name of chivalry, knowing well that they have no choice but to adhere to the wishes of the ladies. Take it or leave it, the lady of the house always reigns supreme."

Though everyone was smiling Neha did not find the conversation funny. She said to Rajeshwar's wife Alka and some other ladies sitting with her in a corner, "The male chauvinists are always the ones with the best stories about the women's so-called domination. All this party talk gives them the excuse they need to do as they will."

For support Neha pointed towards the *Begum's* daughter and said, "You live abroad and after obtaining a Master's degree and you've had the experience of working overseas. Do you agree with what is being said?"

Nikhat had not bargained with having to join the discussion. She laughed and said, "I have a Master's degree in Home Science but I can't afford to take up a job. I can earn as much if not more than my husband. My husband earns our livelihood but he's dependent on me as much as I'm on him. If I work, my home and my child would suffer and I can't earn enough to compensate for the agony my family will have to undergo with me away from home." Neha was disappointed.

Rahul, who had also strayed into this group, had heard only the observations made by the *Begum*. Neha saw a ray of hope in Rahul and, giving him a very friendly smile said, "Here comes the ladies' man. He has yet to start a family. Let us hear what he has to say about the movement for women's liberation." Rahul was aware that Neha had a soft spot for him, the wide gap in age notwithstanding, and was keen on making himself scarce.

He said laughingly, "Girls should be kept on a tight leash and the ladies should be given all the respect under the sun," and walked away.

Neha blushed and was searching for a retort when Zaroo walked in with a smile and said, "And what equation can develop if the two are hell bent upon proving their respective superiority?" With mock grandeur she announced, "Ladies and gentlemen, the dinner is served but this erudite discussion may continue while eating. You need to replenish the calories you have burnt."

The orchestra on the dance floor was playing Beethoven, which could be heard from the main hall and the dining space. All the guests started moving towards the food, lifted with the sound of music outside and the invigorating liquid inside. They all seemed to be very happy. The bearers were busy laying the food in beautiful containers, spreading an appetising aroma. The main bar was very active. One corner was buzzing with Urdu poetry, discussing life in this world and after it, and the other with jokes and pranks and in yet another corner people were discussing the governance of the country. The world seemed to be an ideal place to live in. The guests weren't in any hurry to call it a day. There was amity and camaraderie all over.

Sunita was telling Asha, "Do you know what the height of ego is?" And without waiting for her reply she continued, "A parrot hit a bicycle and got hurt. The owner of the bicycle took the parrot home and, after medicating and bandaging him put him, in a cage. When the parrot came to his senses, finding himself in the cage he asked, "What have I done to deserve this imprisonment. Did the cyclist die?"

Asha reacted, "Very good! But too clean."

Rahul, who had been deputed to announce at the bar that dinner had been laid, overheard the conversation and, putting his hands on the shoulders of the two girls said, "Alright, if you must hear something smutty, I'll oblige. Someone told my friend that he had fallen in love with a Brazilian girl and that he was going to marry her. This friend enquired with a straight face—Brazil is known for hookers and football, which team does she play for?" The two girls started giggling as if they had not heard anything funnier before. They were both soft on Rahul.

At the other end of the room, Qumar *Saheb* was engrossed in a philosophical discussion with Prof. Triloknath. He was of the view that life ended in this world only and there was no other world beyond, while Prof. Triloknath was hell bent upon insisting that this world was just an illusion. Fine Urdu poetry and Upanishadic extracts were being brandished in support of the two points of view.

Rustom personally went to this group said, in the same vein,

"Drinking must go on till dawn,
But it is time for swords to be withdrawn;
The food is on the table;
Please do join us when you are able."

❖❖

The food was sumptuous indeed. After the controversies of the evening, the guests were unanimous in their praise for the cooks and the hosts. All kinds of wines were being served with the food and the guests were taking their pick, based on what they were planning to eat. Beer was flowing in plenty too. Rustom, Zaroo, Shahnaz and Rahul were going around ensuring that all the guests were being looked after. The world seemed to be without any sorrow or suffering.

Dinner being over, the guests assembled in the hall where liquors and wines were flowing in trolleys. A fountain of champagne was fizzing out of the bottles taken out of the ice containers and wrapped in white cloths. The bearers were pouring out the champagne. Cigar humidors containing the best of cigars were placed on the trolleys for the guests to help themselves. The air itself seemed intoxicated.

Zaroo, pointing towards *Nawab Saheb* and the *Begum* said, "The two of you enlivened the party. Besides the stories and the jokes you narrated, your best gift to us for the evening was Nikhat. I had no idea that she was in town. I wish Azhar was also here." After a pause she signalled for the bearer carrying the liquor trolley to come over and said, "In the process of listening to your jokes I could not pay enough attention to you. *Nawab Saheb*, you must take a shot at Benedictine and cognac and *Begum Saheba*, you must try some champagne. Lason is good!" The bearer was all attention.

Nawab Saheb, who was helping himself to a glass of liquor suggested by the *Begum*, said "*Bhabhi jaan*, this is my own house; you don't have to look after me. It is a great party and we have thoroughly enjoyed ourselves."

Begum Saheba said, "Nikhat arrived here with me only this evening and she could not help visiting her best friends, Shahnaz and Zaroo Ma. Azhar and Nikhat both consider the Modys as an extension of their own family."

Zaroo affectionately put her arm around Nikhat and said, "We are indeed one family!"

It was well past midnight and people had started leaving. The family stood near the exit door and the guests slowly departed, after registering their grateful thanks and good wishes for the hosts. Rahul was personally ensuring that everything passed off smoothly.

After the party, the cooks and bearers departed in the catering van. They had been tipped well by the hosts and had fortified themselves enough with the spills of the party to feel elated and happy. The small, medicine bottles that they had deftly tucked into their inner pockets had in them enough material to enable them to continue the good mood for some time.

One bearer said to his friend, "It is a pleasure to come to the Mody household. They dole out tips as lavish as their parties, and they're happy that we also enjoy themselves. They have everything under the sun- health, wealth, happiness and respect. The only thing they don't have is a son but I suppose God, in his mercy, will give them a son-in-law who will fill the void."

The friend replied, "I understand, Shahnaz baby and Rahul *Saheb* are madly in love with each other, but Rahul *Saheb* is not keen on marriage until he is satisfied that he has arrived in life."

The bearer said, "I don't know where you get these rumours from. Rahul *Saheb* is at least ten years older than Shahnaz baby; there's no question of the two marrying each other. And what do you mean by saying that he has yet to arrive. Do you know that Rahul *Saheb's* father was a very big Zamindar and that he has left behind enough property for the next seven generations to live comfortably without working? Do you know my father worked as one of the cooks in his family?"

Another bearer, who was overhearing the conversation, butted in. He said, "What nonsense are you talking? The Modys will never give their daughter to Rahul. He's nothing but a playboy and all the façade of idealism he has around himself is a sham. Did you not see how he embraced the two young girls at the bar? And he's been having an affair with Neha. In fact he is responsible for the wedge between Ranjit *Saheb* and Neha."

The head cook, who by virtue of his position in the group had an air of superiority about him, joined the conversation and said with an authoritative tone "You fellows don't know anything about these *Sahebs* and *Mem Sahebs*. I've been watching them for a very long time. Someone paying a little attention to the other means nothing. It does not take a Rahul to drive a wedge between Neha and her partner. Neha's sole desire is to dominate any situation and bully men. It isn't beyond comprehension that she deliberately gives the impression of having an affair with younger and more eligible people, just to spite Ranjit *Saheb*. Rahul is too smart to fall for her. The other day, in Rajeshwar *Saheb's* party, she was playing up to his son Gyaneshwar who has just returned from America. When her friend Rita caught her holding Gyaneshwar by his waist and giggling away cheek to cheek, Neha whispered into her ears, 'It's just for a little fun.' Gyaneshwar is a nice young lad. I understand that he has done his Ph.D from Harvard and is planning to join his father in politics."

The head cook continued. "Her friend even warned her, 'Don't have ideas about him. He's known to be a very balanced and steady boy. And unlike his father he abhors politics.' And do you know what Neha's reply was? She walked away, saying that is all the more reason for him to learn the other things of life!"

The cook continued, "The boy in Mody *Saheb's* mind for Shahnaz baby is Azhar Mian, the son of *Nawab Saheb*, who's doing something in America and is scheduled to return shortly. Didn't you observe Mody paying special attention to *Nawab Saheb* and the *Begum*?"

One of the senior bearers who had been listening to the conversation quietly without commenting, just nodding his head in agreement, came forward and said, "How does it make a difference to us whether X marries Y or not? What is most important is that the Modys and the Nawabs are very generous in their tips to us and they're happy to see us happy. They're not like the miser, Rajeshwar. I understand that he was just a bus conductor before joining politics and now he isn't aware himself of how much wealth he possesses."

The van stopped with a jerk and the bearers set out for their respective homes.

Rasulabad

Rahul's mother, Shrimati Gayatri Devi, lived in a town called Rasulabad which, prior to the abolition of the Zamindari system in nineteen-fifty two, had been part of the grand Rasulabad Estate. Rahul's family was still very highly respected in the area. Gayatri Devi had been elected to the Legislative Assembly of U.P. for the fifth term in succession. It was said that she never went out to canvass for votes during the elections because nobody ever opposed her. Rahul's family traced its ancestry from the pre-Mughal period.

The Mughals had awarded large estates to them and bestowed upon them titles of respect, which some of the members of the family still held. The family continued to flourish during the British Raj and the Rasulabad Estate came into being when Lord Cornwallis established the Zamindari system in year eighteen-hundred and five. Originally, the Estate comprised one hundred and one villages but with the passage of time it had broken up into fragments. The Zamindars of Rasulabad arrogated wide influence and power and made sure that their writ ran large in the area. Unlike others of their ilk, they were well educated and took passionate interest in sports. Their attitude was highly egoistic and even their philanthropy emanated largely from their ego. Mercifully, they were absolutely clear in their minds that helpfulness and public influence were two sides of the same coin and since the prime aim of their existence was to attain power, they had to be helpful to the needy.

They extended their patronage to those who went to them for it but if someone ever dared to show them down, they left no stone unturned to ensure that he was reduced to smithereens. One-upmanship was the game in which they excelled.

Once a relative, who was also a big Zamindar of a neighbouring estate, invited the Zamindar of Rasulabad to his son's wedding. In those days wedding festivals carried on for days and the invitation was always understood to include friends and relatives. When the Zamindar of Rasulabad received an invitation to attend the wedding, he thought it would be a good opportunity to put down his relative. He accepted the invitation and arrived for the wedding with half a dozen elephants, scores of horsemen and almost a hundred friends and relatives with their attendants and horse drawn buggies. The relative was surprised to see the crowd of over two hundred people and the animals; but being familiar with the pranks of Rasulabad, he kept his cool and welcomed them with open arms. He took the entire party to a *shamiana* nearby where very elaborate refreshments and drinks had been laid out for the entertainment of the arriving guests, and requested them to relax there while arrangements were being made for their stay. He ordered his men to make the arrangements in the vast expanse of his mango orchards.

Before the sun could set in the western horizon, an adequate number of tents were pitched in the orchards and the entire place was lit with gasoline lamps. The weather was kind and no effort was required to beat down the heat. A bare minimum of furniture was placed in the tents, commensurate with the status of the occupants. Refreshments, drinks and various forms of entertainment were provided in abundance.

While the relative was laughing under his breath at the Zamindar not succeeding in his earnest efforts to cause offense, the Zamindar was seething at his failure. He had not imagined that his relative would be able to make all the necessary arrangements at such a short notice. His think tank deliberated over the matter for some time. It then decided to find out from the hosts if proper arrangements for feeding the accompanying animals had been made. An emissary was appointed to go and personally inspect the food earmarked for the animals. The expectation was that because of the very large number of guests for the wedding, no fine tuning could have been done for the food of the animals.

The emissary came back disappointed. He said, "Hundreds of buckets full of boiled rice and large quantities of gram soaked in water have been provided for the elephants and the horses. Besides this, tree leaves and branches have also been provided in abundance."

The Zamindar of Rasulabad went into depression. He shouted at his cronies, "Can't you idiots think of a way to show the host his place? I had thought of having some fun but here the host seems to be getting the better of me ." After a pause he continued, "Well, he has better people to advise him so he's bound to win!"

He had hardly finished his rebuke, when one of his cronies came forward with a sly smile on his face and said, "Sir, we must find out if the rice made for the elephants is of *Basmati* quality, because our elephants are used to eating only that quality of rice."

The eyes of the Zamindar lit up. He patted the crony on his back and said, "Great! That's why I like you. If your idea works you will be rewarded suitably." He asked him to go and make the necessary enquiries on his behalf. The melancholia of the camp was overtaken by exuberance and expectation.

The host was very upset to hear the most unreasonable demand that the elephants should be fed on *Basmati* rice. He told the emissary rather curtly that their elephants were not any different from those he possessed, and that there was no need for them to be fed on *Basmati* when his elephants lived on ordinary rice. He said that it was the first time he had heard that elephants were fed on *Basmati* rice. The man, with head bowed, said in a meek voice, "Sir, I'm only a servant. I'm conveying to you what my master has wished me to do. I will convey your views to him but please do forgive me if I have offended you in any way." The host reassured him that it was no fault of his and asked to be taken to the Zamindar.

The Zamindar, puffing a hookah, was relaxing in his tent surrounded by his sycophants. Seeing the host he said, "What wonderful arrangements you have made for our stay. Let me tell you that we're very comfortable. And I've decided to come for the wedding of your second son also."

The host smiled and said, "*Bhai Saheb*, how can a wedding be performed in my family without your blessings. It's our privilege to have you in our midst."

He sat down and continued very apologetically, "*Bhai Saheb*, your men seem to be under the impression that the elephants eat *Basmati* rice. There is plenty of rice for them but the *Basmati* is only for the guests. You know, more than one thousand guests have already arrived, and by the grace of God some more may arrive. The rice for the elephants is of good quality but it's certainly not *Basmati*."

The Zamindar looked sternly at his man and enquired, "Who has had the temerity to inconvenience our hosts about the food for our elephants? If I want to feed my elephants on *Basmati* rice, I should be able to provide for it and not go about with a begging bowl." After a pause, he looked at his host and said, "Please ignore the insolence of my staff, I have brought enough *Basmati* rice for my elephants to eat. I'm aware that on occasion, when thousands of guests are to be entertained, animals tend to be ignored." In a calm voice he told his man, "You should look after these arrangements personally. Please have the rice for the elephants delivered to the person who is looking after their food."

He got up and gave a hug to his host, saying, "Although I'm older than you in age, I apologise for the bad conduct of my men. Your honour is my honour." He released him with a hearty laugh, and the embarrassed host walked away.

❖❖

By the time Rahul's grandfather inherited the Estate along with his younger brother, its size had shrunk to twenty one villages, but the glory of the family was still intact. Rahul's grandfather had been decorated with the British title of the Rai Bahadur and his brother had been appointed Honorary Magistrate with first class powers. In fact, traditionally during the British Raj, for every generation of the Rasulabad family the title of the Rai Bahadur was bestowed upon the eldest member of the family and the others were made Honorary Magistrates. The peculiarity of the Estate was that in spite of its size being quite modest, it produced almost all human necessities. It had a flourishing handloom industry producing cotton material. The *Khandsari* mills situated in the Estate ensured that there was no dearth of sugar and the river flowing through provided employment to the fishermen as well as an abundant supply of fish to the inhabitants. There were mango orchards in almost every village of the Estate and a very large area was covered by forests. The lands were fertile and yielded all kinds of cash crops along with the conventional produce of vegetables, wheat and rice.

The Estate was the common property of Rahul's grandfather and his brother but they were both individually referred to as the Zamindars of twenty one villages. They were high livers and in spite of the dwindling income of the Estate they did not change their life style — *Haveli*, servants, horses, cars, *shikaars*, parties, sports — everything remained intact as before. As a result, their resources started depleting. The abolition of the Zamindari system in nineteen fifty two was the last straw. Rahul's grandfather and his brother died soon after, leaving behind a large family.

The family ran into debt but was still respected. No debtor ever harassed them and on their part they cleared their debts in the shortest possible time by liquidating their assets. The family was soon left with very meagre means but their influence and prestige remained intact.

When Rahul's mother was approached by the Congress party to stand for the Legislative Assembly as their candidate, she was surprised. She told those who had approached her that she had no experience in public life and that she certainly would not be able to put up with the rigors of campaigning and electioneering. They requested her to accept the proposal and leave the rest to them. They assured her that she would not have to step out of the house for campaigning.

And, indeed, so it happened. She won the election hands down without personally even opening her mouth for votes and support. This unique process of winning elections without canvassing has been continuing in Rahul's family for the last couple of decades. Initially it was the help from the Congress, supported by the high status and reputation of the family, that helped Gayatri Devi succeed; but later it was her work in the constituency that did the talking. She had been offered a seat in the state cabinet several times but had declined, saying that she wanted to serve the people living around the precincts of her ancestral *Haveli*.

Every morning the large compound received a large crowd of men and women with their myriad problems and they all went back with the satisfaction that the best effort would be deployed for their cause. Such was the confidence her constituents had in her integrity.

Her only weakness in life was her son Rahul. For his happiness she was willing to take any pains or sacrifice anything. Like any mother, she was anxious that her son marry and start a family. In fact she already had a girl in mind for him, and Rahul and this girl–Sita–had been friends for a long time. Sita had the benefit of education overseas and had the gift of numerous accomplishments. In spite of her high education and wide exposure, she was greatly interested in the Indian villages. She was convinced that the future of the country lay in the development of these villages.

Sita was conscious of Gayatri Devi's desire to draw her into a closer relationship, as her daughter in law, and was herself quite fond of Rahul. However all was under wraps and nothing had been spoken. After finishing her education she had worked for the U.N. for a while but, not finding satisfaction in her work, she had decided to work alongside Gayatri Devi.

Gayatri Devi had known Sita from the time she had been adopted by Diwan Mithai Lal who was the Rasulabad Estate's steward. She had already found out Sita's views on marriage. In the course of their interactions, she had shared with Gayatri Devi her view that life was meant to be shared with a companion. She had also confided that, while she hadn't found a man for herself, she did not mind an arranged marriage provided the boy respected her values. Gayatri Devi was appreciative of Sita's values and views on life and volunteered to find a match for her, assuring her that she would be at complete liberty to reject any proposal that was brought to her.

Diwan Mithai Lal's ancestors had been managing the Rasulabad Estate for the Rai Bahadurs right from its inception. He was a sensitive and kind man and his commitment to his masters received precedence over anything else.

The lack of a child had been a cause of great heartache in the early years of his marriage. One day, while returning from the *Shiva* temple he had stumbled against a small bundle, and found to his utter surprise that it had a beautiful baby girl in it. After the momentary shock, the humble man had realised that the Almighty, in His mercy, had blessed him with a child. He had picked up the baby and brought her home. His wife, who was known to be goodness personified, was delighted at the development. She had said, "Miracles will never cease!" Then her tone had become conspiratorial. "Let no one know about it. We'll keep it a secret for some time and then tell people that she is the daughter of a relative who passed away." Diwan Mithai Lal had joined his wife in her delight but had refused to go along with her plan without the blessings of his masters, Rai Ravi Prakash Bahadur and his wife Gayatri Devi.

Gayatri Devi, on her part, was delighted to hear the news and had said that there was no need to keep it a secret. She had jokingly added, "How can you keep it a secret? Who will believe that the two of you have produced this beautiful doll?"

"I'm very nervous. What if someone comes claiming the baby at a later date?" Diwan Mithai Lal's wife had asked. Gayatri Devi had explained that if someone wanted to stake a claim on the girl, she would not have been left on the steps of the temple, unattended and forsaken. She had further suggested that not only should the news not be kept a secret, but that a function should be held and the girl should legally be adopted by them.

This girl was given the name of Sita because she had appeared from nowhere, almost as if out of the Earth, just as the mythological Sita had done. Gayatri Devi told the parents that she would bear all the expenses necessary to bring their daughter up in the same manner as Rahul. Rahul was at the time nine years old and had just started going to school.

Rahul's father, Rai Ravi Prakash Bahadur was equal to the high stature of his family in every respect. His uniqueness lay in the fact that he had remained untouched by the signature family trait of arrogance. He was a lawyer by profession and had been a great sportsman in his time, having been awarded three university colours and university captaincies of three games.

He commanded enormous respect in society. He too was offered the Congress party ticket for the Assembly seat, but before entering public life he was keen on consolidating his financial position and therefore had declined the offer. Gayatri Devi and Diwan Mithai Lal had taken charge of the family Estate, relieving him of all anxiety on that front and he had already made a dent at the High Court Bar with his legal acumen and powerful advocacy.

He was known for his presence of mind and wit. Once, he sought an adjournment in a matter on the plea that, due to the late arrival of the aircraft the previous evening, he could not prepare his case. The lawyer from the other side, Mr. Javed Khan, who was a great friend, had objected to the request saying that a brilliant counsel like the Rai Bahadur did not need any preparation for arguing a matter. The judge, who had just been elevated to the Bench, suggested to Mr. Javed Khan, "Let's agree to Rai *Saheb*'s request for adjournment."

Then he had looked at the Rai Bahadur and said, "If the clients find you unprepared they will all go to Khan *Saheb* and you will be left with no work."

The Rai Bahadur had bowed and replied, "God forbid! But if that happens, I'm sure your lordship will be indulgent enough to elevate me to the Bench." Everyone in the court, including the judge, had laughed uproariously.

The Rai Bahadur and Gayatri Devi made a happy and friendly couple. Their mutual affection was tinged with a healthy dose of humour. Rai Ravi Prakash used to personally handle the cases related to his property in the High Court and due to the usual labyrinthine legal procedure the matters used to take their own time to reach a resolution. Each time Gayatri Devi asked her husband about the progress of the cases she got the same reply, "The next date for the matter to come up in the court is such and such." Getting the same answer every time, she remarked in exasperation, "Why don't you engage a good lawyer to handle our matters?"

Pat came the reply, "I'll certainly do that once I come to know of the existence of a better lawyer!"

Gayatri Devi was not one to be put down. She said, "I don't know if there's someone better than you but I understand that very soon the best lawyer is going to be elevated to the Bench, depriving the Bar of his contributions."

Gayatri Devi lost her husband to cancer. He was in the pink of health, and no one could have imagined that he would fall prey to the dreaded disease. In those days there was no cure for cancer and all that Sloan Kettering Memorial Hospital in New York could do was to prolong the agony.

The sad demise of the Rai Bahadur was widely mourned and as far as Gayatri Devi was concerned, the heavens may as well have fallen. Her husband was the embodiment of love besides being her friend, philosopher, and guide. She was at her wits end when, early one morning, her husband had appeared in a dream and told her that she had nothing to worry about, and that he would reach out to her whenever she needed his help. He had told her that there was enough property in the family for her to live on, and that her son would one day wipe off all her tears. The dream had rejuvenated her sapped energies and she had decided to stand up once again and fight. It is said that each time she found herself in a tight corner, she thought of her husband and he invariably appeared in her dreams and benefited her with the right advice.

Once a particular document connected with a legal dispute got misplaced and all efforts to locate it were in vain. The matter was to come up for hearing in the court and if this document was not traced, there was no hope for the matter to be resolved favourably. Gayatri Devi prayed to her husband and sought his help. He, as usual, appeared in her dream and told her that the document had been buried under a heap of old files in a particular corner of the room from where she transacted her business. He also assured her that the case would be decided in her favour. And lo and behold- things turned out exactly as she had been told!

One afternoon, while she was relaxing in the verandah in front of the inner courtyard of the *Haveli*, a maid servant appeared to announce that Diwan *Saheb* was waiting outside to see her. She instructed the servant to show him in. Diwan Mithai Lal walked in with folded hands and bent head. This, not being the usual posture of Diwan Mithai Lal while appearing before Shrimati Gayatri Devi, she surmised that something unusual had happened and, asking him to take his seat she said, "I hope all is well, Diwan *Saheb*?"

He took the seat but offered no response. His demeanour was tense and worried. She noticed the change, and in order to allow him time to settle down she asked the maid servant to get some refreshments. She again turned towards him and enquired if everything was all right. By now he had regained some of his composure and courage. He said, "For generations we have been living by the grace of your family, now the time has come for me to acknowledge it. My family has received enough property from you to live comfortably. I beseech you to allow me to continue working for you, as in the past, but without drawing any salary. All I have is yours in any case." Having said this he looked relieved, as if a burden was off his back.

Now it was the turn of Gayatri Devi to feel embarrassed. She knew that he was concerned about the Estate's depleting resources and this was a gesture to assure her that he was with her in her trying days. She said, "I appreciate your gesture but you're well aware that the situation is not so desperate, and things can comfortably continue to be as they are. In any case, you know that you're a member of our family and you draw from the resources of the Estate, as we all do, according to your need. The salary has always been a formality. I'll be very happy if the present system continues."

Diwan *Saheb* was a very intelligent man. He took the cue from what she stated and said, "So, shall I take it that your instruction is that I need not draw a fixed salary, and can take whatever I need with your permission." Gayatri Devi, not knowing what to say, kept silent and ever since then Diwan Mithai Lal did not draw a penny for himself. He lived in the house given to him by the Rai Bahadurs and made his ends meet from the property his predecessors had received from the Rasulabad estate.

Gayatri Devi drew enormous solace from the outstanding performance of her son. He was extraordinary in every respect. He was a silver tongued orator, a fine actor, and a versatile sportsman. He bore himself like a prince and was at ease with prince and pauper alike. All his friends thought that they had a special equation with him. He indeed appeared to be the master of all that he surveyed.

But, despite having all that one could ask for — education, health, talent and charm– Rahul was constantly haunted by the dream of restoring his family's honour to the time they had owned a hundred and one villages. He lived and moved in a society that had gone from strength to strength through a variety of means - entrepreneurship, will power, connections, and corruption, and was constantly agonizing over the methods he could adopt to come good in the new world.

The responsibility of being the scion of the Rai Bahadurs sat heavily on his shoulders. The values of his family made it impossible for him to stoop to conquer, as many others had done.

His academic achievements were good enough for him to make it to the IAS, but he did not want a 'middle class existence.' He set up an export house which had to close down because the U.S. dollar suddenly took a beating in the international market. He dabbled in a few other ventures but could not really make it big. He could have easily joined public life but, from his mother's experience, he knew that the process would require him to draw from the depleting resources of his family. Therefore he did not consider it worth his while. Having drawn a blank on all fronts he decided to step into his father's shoes, with his heart set on being a leader of the Bar one day. His plan was to amass wealth from the profession and then join public life to ultimately reign over the destiny of the country. And so Rahul joined Vinay Khosla at the Bar. Vinay Khosla was a leading lawyer and Rahul soon became his assistant and confidante.

Once he was well settled in practice Gayatri Devi, like all Indian mothers, began to think of his marriage. But Rahul was too preoccupied with his career and work to devote any time to the prospects of marriage. This was an area of sensitivity between her and Rahul. She believed that marriage might work as a spur to Rahul's endeavour to restore the status of the family, whereas he was of the view that marriage would hinder his efforts.

As he approached his thirtieth birthday, she decided she needed to broach the subject one more time. She waited for his next visit to Rasulabad which, according to his latest communication, was to be soon after the party at the Modys.

❖❖

Rahul's visit to Rasulabad was always a big occasion. There was no particular reason for it except tradition–the head of the Rasulabad Estate had always been welcomed with a lot of fanfare. The railway station master would inform Gayatri Devi immediately after the train carrying Rahul departed from the previous station and she would to go the station to receive him. The station master was pressed into service to ensure that no time was wasted if the train was late.

Gayatri Devi, Diwan Mithai Lal and two attendants entered the railway station just as Rahul's train was steaming in. Seeing her, many others joined her and the conglomeration of people formed a very impressive reception committee.

He soon appeared in a pair of blue jeans and a white t-shirt, waving to his mother from his compartment. Gayatri Devi waved back with a broad smile and so did the others who were standing with her on the platform. She was a bit surprised to see a very pretty girl standing behind Rahul in the door way. Gayatri Devi told herself that she could be just another passenger travelling in the train, but when she got down with Rahul and touched her feet along with him, she realised that the girl was accompanying her son.

Gayatri Devi embraced Rahul and asked him jovially, "Who is this beautiful girl with you?" Rahul introduced Shahnaz Mody to her and said that she was his very good friend who wanted to see rural India. Mindful of his status and the expectations from a Rai Bahadur, Rahul proceeded to greet Diwan Mithai Lal and the attendants with great cordiality.

Gayatri Devi embraced Shahnaz warmly and affectionately and said, "Good that you are here, but you must stay with me long enough to travel and experience the real life in this part of the world. There is no point in having just a bird's eye view of the villages if you really want to learn."

Shahnaz stood smiling and nodding her head politely. Rahul returned after greeting everybody and they all left for the *Haveli*. On the way, Gayatri Devi thought of nothing but Shahnaz. She conceded to herself that the girl was beautiful and had the stamp of good breeding on her face. Then another thought came to her mind–was she just a friend or something more than that? She answered herself–No, she could not be anything more. Rahul had always been quite open with his mother about his life and relationships.

While she was busy contemplating all this she heard him say, "Ma, you seem to be preoccupied, you are not even talking to me, let alone Shahnaz. She is Mr. Mody's daughter, and you know that the Mody household helps me survive in Delhi, without you and a home." And then he added, only half in jest, "In spite of her love for the piano and ballet dancing, Shahnaz is very concerned about the sad state of economy, especially our rural economies. She wants to make a contribution but first she wants to understand the ground realities."

Shahnaz, who was used to explaining things herself, interjected, "Besides what Rahul has said, another reason for my coming here is to meet you. From everything I have heard about you, I've decided to emulate your example–at home as well as outside it. My parents are all praise for you and I know that your association with them goes back many years."

The compliment came unexpectedly, and perhaps smacked of flattery. Gayatri Devi wondered yet again whether Rahul had chosen his life partner and felt dismayed that he had not shared this with her. But then she thought that it was not unlikely that he had brought Shahnaz to her only to seek her approval, and drew solace from this. She put her arm affectionately around Shahnaz's shoulders and said, "It's indeed laudable that youngsters like you spare time to think about the society and its well being. The fire within you is so strong, and you have already seen so much of this world that you don't have to learn anything from me. When your inner voice has propelled you to feel for others, it will also show you the direction that you have to follow. But all that can wait; at the moment you must relax and enjoy your new surroundings."

They had reached the *Haveli*. The cars stopped and while the servants were busy taking out the luggage, Gayatri Devi, Shahnaz and Rahul got out. Some people from the nearby villages had come to greet Rahul. He embraced them one after another, and enquired about their wellbeing and that of their families. Shahnaz struck everybody who saw her as poised and graceful and immediately they started hazarding guesses about her and the reasons for her presence in Rasulabad.

Rahul's visits always brought a lot of excitement to the household. The family retainers were bending over backwards to please him and the cook had prepared his favourite dishes. An old family retainer, Ram Lal, nearing eighty years in age, had produced a special preparation of meat, which it was believed only he could cook. It was said that he was in possession of sixty-five recipes of meat curries and *kababs*. But the *kheer* had been cooked by Gayatri Devi herself, for nothing but her *kheer* could satisfy Rahul after a hearty meal.

Sita had also joined the family for lunch and when she met Shahnaz the same thoughts that occurred to Gayatri Devi came to her as well. While she was pondering over the purpose of Shahnaz's visit to Rasulabad, she joined the others in her verdict that Shahnaz was indeed a beautiful girl. Seeking to strike a conversation, she asked her at the lunch table, "I hope you don't mind vegetarian food."

Shahnaz smiled, rolled her beautiful bright eyes and replied, "I prefer vegetarian food and I know that you are a cook par excellence."

Sita giggled, "Rahul seems to have updated you on everything!"

Shahnaz nodded. "Indeed. He also told me that you're indispensable to Ma in her work as well as here at home."

Sita replied, "Rahul has been exaggerating. The fact is that Ma is my friend, guide and philosopher and it is I who can't do without her. She is my idol and I'll be happy to end up being half as good as her."

Shahnaz smiled and said, "That makes two of us."

Gayatri Devi overheard the conversation and remarked that those who told lies were bitten by crows and those who ate quietly enjoyed their meal. Everyone decided that enjoying the meal was the better option.

❖❖

After lunch, Sita was entrusted with the responsibility of showing Shahnaz the room in which she was to stay. She took her to the large room, narrating the history of each of the areas of the *Haveli* that they had to pass through. The court yard inside the house was like a football field, covered by emerald colored grass and skirted by a wide flower bed with roses in different shades. At the center of the court yard there was a marble fountain with recycled water springing out of its different heads. The rooms were neighboured by verandahs where arrangements had been made to lounge and relax. She pointed out Gayatri Devi's meditation room in an isolated corner. The room was swept and maintained by Gayatri Devi herself. The room in which Shahnaz was to stay was located three rooms away from the meditation room, with a direct view of the fountain and the roses. A few chairs and a rose wood coffee table supporting a flower vase had been placed in front of the large room. Inside the room, the furnishing was sparse but elegant and the attached bathroom was as big as an ordinary bedroom. There was no air conditioning but the heat did not seem to get the better of the place. Fans hanging from the high ceiling seemed to see to that. When the two young ladies were inside the room, Sita thought it apt to familiarise Shahnaz with the lifestyle of Gayatri Devi and the ways of the *Haveli*.

"She wakes up at five in the morning and heads straight for a forty-five minute' walk followed by her morning bath. After she's through with her morning rituals she sits down for meditation and prayers, which last for one and a half hours, and she insists on being left alone at this time. She has her breakfast in the main dining hall at eight-thirty. At breakfast she encourages all residents of the *Haveli* to join her, but this isn't mandatory of course."

Sita informed Shahnaz that on her part she always had breakfast with her, and made use of that time for exchanging views and discussing important matters. She added that when Rahul was in town, he would join them at breakfast to update himself on the politics of the area and matters related to their personal properties. Shahnaz was not surprised to learn that Rahul was the apple of his mother's eyes, and that she was very proud of him. Sita continued, "After breakfast, she meets her constituents who visit her in large numbers every day. They all come with their problems with full faith that she will render whatever assistance is legitimately possible. Shrimati Gayatri Devi makes no bones about the fact that she won't do anything wrong even if it is to help others."

"On most days she makes it a point to visit a part of her constituency on foot to experience things first hand and to meet her constituents. The modality that she followed to achieve this end is to start from

Rasulabad on foot and walk to a distance that was convenient, returning home in the car. The next day she would drive to the place where she had concluded her walk the previous day and walk a further convenient distance, returning home from there in a car. The same system would be followed till the distance between her *Haveli* and the place she walked to on foot became so large, that returning to Rasulabad by car was not convenient. On such occasions she would go to some place where she could spend the night comfortably and follow the procedure again in the morning, making that place a temporary abode for her stay. This she did year in and year out and as a result kept in constant touch with her people."

The activities of Gayatri Devi, Shahnaz found, revolved around achieving five basic things. The first was to make drinking water available, the second to provide basic education to children, the third to provide road connectivity to the village, the fourth to provide basic medical facilities including family planning programs and the last was to run community development centres that focussed on developing communal harmony.

Gayatri Devi's modus operandi, to give a concrete shape to these plans, was to mobilise the constituents and prevail upon them that until they decided to solve their problems, they would not get rid of them. Groups comprising responsible and, wherever possible, knowledgeable people were constituted in different places to ensure that her programs were implemented. The groups would draw a plan of action and work out a budget for meeting the expenses. No project or budget was finalised without her direct approval. They would then ascertain from the government the amount of money that was available for such projects and prevail upon them to provide that amount. Those people for whose benefit the project was being launched would be motivated to contribute as much as possible and the remaining balance was covered by a trust run by her. This trust enjoyed the confidence of many philanthropic and charitable institutions, because the donors were sure that the money would be put to the best use. These projects received adequate support from the government because of her integrity and influence.

With her untiring efforts, she had been able to establish several water sheds responsible for harvesting water during the rainy season, primary educational institutions, primary nursing centers and also community development centers that provided employment to women who were involved in producing cottage industry products like pickles, paapads, jams, toys, sewing and stitching, making ropes of jute and straw etc. What was most laudable was that she oversaw everything personally, and was absolutely up to date with the state of affairs of all the projects. Sita was indeed her alter ego but Gayatri Devi had the final word in all matters.

She had her lunch on her way to the different destinations in the constituency and after a hard day's work when she returned home she bathed and sat for a relaxing dinner. The dinner was always light and she never missed out on a glass of milk before retiring to bed. She did not encourage any visitors in the evening unless there was a special occasion. Sita would accompany her on her daily tours and upon return proceed to have dinner with her parents, the Diwan *Saheb* and his wife.

Shahnaz listened to every detail carefully. She found the routine rather exciting and was tempted to join Gayatri Devi right away. But then she was struck by the thought that Sita might consider her an intrusion, or that Gayatri Devi might not find her to be equal to the job. There was no denying that she was totally ignorant of the ways of the rural masses with whom they both spent most of their time.

Sita interrupted her reverie to tell her that Gayatri Devi would be going to a nearby village in the afternoon, and would return by dinner time. She was not accompanying her for her tour so she could be with Shahnaz for the afternoon tea.

Shahnaz realised that she was not going out with Gayatri

Devi because she did not want to leave her alone in the unfamiliar surroundings of the *Haveli*. She said, "I appreciate your concern, but why don't you take me for a reconnaissance of the constituency? Believe me, I'm not tired. I'd like to get the feel of the villages at the earliest."

Sita was happy to see her enthusiasm but since Gayatri Devi's program had already been finalised, she suggested that instead of going to the constituency, they go to Sita's house instead. Shahnaz agreed to the suggestion and after a little while they arrived at Sita's house.

❖❖

The house was old but very large, with a sizeable compound and huge wrought-iron gates. Diwan Mithai Lal's family had been living there for over a hundred years. The original structure of the house was still intact, with some improvisation and repair work having been done over the years. Inside the compound there were patches of grass, unkempt flower beds and a few trees of mango, tamarind and neem. An old Maruti 800 and a scooter were parked under a gigantic neem tree near a large verandah, which had a few chairs, a table, a long wooden settee and a couple of benches. A pair of cross bred Alsatian dogs was quietly lying on the settee. They got up to welcome the visitors and on seeing Sita they leapt excitedly towards her. There was nobody else outside the house but once Sita and Shahnaz entered, through the elaborately carved old wooden entrance door, they saw Sita's mother Savitri Rani squatting on a *charpoy* in the inner courtyard with a couple of women sitting on the floor. One was cleaning the rice in a metallic vessel with her fingers and the other was chopping vegetables. There were some guava trees in the courtyard with a few cages hanging from them, inhabited by parrots. The inner courtyard had verandahs and rooms on all its four sides. The kitchen was located in a corner and outside it, bags full of grains had been stacked. There was a kitchen garden in which green pumpkins were seen hanging from a small pole. A few wooden chairs were lying in the verandah.

Seeing an unfamiliar face with Sita, Savitri Rani got up in excitement and said, "Who is this beautiful girl you've brought home today?" She walked up to Shahnaz, embraced her and said, "You must be knowing Sita from her college days!"

Sita introduced Shahnaz to her mother and said that she had come to the *Haveli* with Rahul to get a first hand idea about life in rural India.

Savitri Rani nodded. "You've come to the right place," she told *her*. " Nobody can surpass the *Malkin* (that was how Gayatri Devi was generally referred to by the people in Rasulabad) as far as the knowledge of rural India is concerned." She asked one of her maids to pull up a chair for Shahnaz but Shahnaz dissuaded her from doing so and said that she would much rather join them on the *charpoy*.

Savitri Devi was overwhelmed by Shahnaz's visit. She decided to go to the kitchen and make something special herself. Shahnaz caught her by the shoulder and said, "Ma, please don't take any trouble for me. Sita and I have eaten so much at lunch time that any more food will burst our tummies."

Sita came to her rescue and said, "Ma, please don't worry about anything. Just sit and talk to us. She is here for some time and I'll bring her home for lunch one day. Then you can treat her to your culinary prowess."

But Savitri Rani was not to be dissuaded. She disappeared into the kitchen and soon the aroma of *pakodas* started wafting from there.

Sita shook her head with a giggle and said, "You think Ma will listen to anybody? Now you're in trouble." She led Shahnaz to her room.

Sita's room was a replica of the room that had been earmarked for Shahnaz in the *Haveli*, except that it had a sizeable bookshelf that was jam packed with books. A *sitar*, a *tanpura* and a pair of *tablas* were lying on the carpet in one of the corners. A desktop computer and a few neatly stashed files were on the working table. As she took in the room Shahnaz said, "Besides social work, books and music seem to be a consuming interest of yours. How do you find so much time to do justice to all your interests?"

Sita replied, "You'll soon find out for yourself that in the process of doing so many things, I've ended up being good at nothing." Shahnaz knew that she was being modest, or Rahul would not have told her all that he had about her qualities.

They sat down, Sita on the bed and Shahnaz on the chair in front. Shahnaz told Sita, "Your reputation and achievements are far more than what you say. What you do passes my comprehension. And to top it all, I'm told that you bake a cake for your father every week."

Sita said with a straight face, "You truly seem to have the complete dossier on me. What else has Rahul told you?"

Shahnaz replied, "Rahul says that you're quite versatile, and that whatever you do, you do well. He says that you're very good at motivating people and that you're of immense help to Ma."

"That's not all true," Sita said defensively. "Rahul is so perfect himself that he does not see any flaw in anybody." Then she tried to change the topic. "You know so much about me, tell me something about yourself."

Shahnaz told Sita that she lived in Delhi with her parents, who had always doted on her. She said that anything she desired was made available to her at the drop of a hat. As result she had rarely had to exert herself in life. Working in her father's office also did not offer any challenge, because her father's name always preceded her wherever she went. She said she acted in plays, loved reading and met lots of well-heeled people at parties but, at the end of the day, found her existence to be quite hollow. Thus, she had a burning desire to find a stronger anchor in life. She felt that making herself useful to society could provide the moorings she sought. She seemed to share Rahul's disdain for the corrupt ways of the politicians. In Shahnaz's conversation it became obvious that she considered Rahul to be an outstanding person with exceptional talent, grit and character.

Sita was intrigued at Shahnaz's admiration for Rahul, but knowing Rahul's magnetic personality, was not surprised. She herself had always idolized Rahul but had kept her feelings to herself because things seemed to be working out favourably on their own. She only hoped that Shahnaz's admiration for Rahul was academic and nothing else. She asked her, "How do you know Rahul so well?"

Shahnaz told her that she had first met Rahul in London. She had finished her O-levels and had taken admission in The Christ Church College at Oxford while he had just been called to the inner temple for his Bar-at-Law. She told her that her father's friend, Vinay Khosla, had told him to meet her. He had a large circle of friends in London and he did all that was possible to ensure that she did not feel homesick. That legacy continued through his friends even after he left England. She said, "When I came back to India I found that he had become a close confidant of my father. Dad would seek Rahul's advice on all matters – legal and otherwise. He had become so entrenched in the family that even I started looking up to him for guidance and support, and I'm not sorry for it."

Sita had met Vinay Khosla while she had been working for the U.N. and had met him again with Rahul in Delhi. She said she had attended his swearing-in ceremony when he had been elevated to the Bench. She had noticed a lot of common traits between Rahul and Vinay. She told Shahnaz, "I know Vinay Khosla. I think he's Rahul's idol and they both have hit it off very well. I hope Rahul follows Vinay's footsteps to the Bench soon." But she added she was surprised that she hadn't met Shahnaz in London, because she too was there at almost the same time.

Shahnaz told her that she had left U.K. for U.S.A. in nineteen-ninety two, the year when Rahul had been called to the Bar, which was why they had not met. Sita said that he had spoken often about Shahnaz to her. On the basis of his account she had sketched a mental picture which she now found to be not very different from the original.

They found out that they had a lot of common friends in London. Sita told her that her life in England was mostly confined to the university campus, punctuated by occasional visits to an Indian restaurant run by a Pakistani. Shahnaz in turn said that her London was a whirl of activity ranging from visits to places steeped in history, to parties at the poshest clubs, and art galleries. She adored the theatres in London and caught every new play she could at West End. What she missed most about London, however, were the English pubs, where conversation ran in quicksilver fashion from football to philosophy and back again.

"But enough of all that," Shahnaz said. "Now I want to get to grips with the ground realities of the Indian villages. On this subject, Sita, you have to be my guide."

While the conversation was on, Savitri entered the room and Nepali, the major domo followed with a tray, carrying snacks and readymade tea in three glasses. He placed the tray on the table and disappeared. Looking at Shahnaz, Savitri said, "I've made delicious *pakodas* and *halwa* for you. And luckily there's some cake leftover from Sita's baking. It goes very well with the *masala* tea that Nepali makes."

Shahnaz was quite full given the heavy lunch at the *Haveli*, but seeing the enthusiasm of Savitri she decided to play along. She said, "I love *masala* tea."

Sita served *pakoda* and *halwa* in a plate and placed a small table in front of Shahnaz. Savitri Rani's effusive hospitality had yet to cease. She brought the plate of cake to Shahnaz and said, "You must have this. This has been baked by Sita and you will relish it."

Sita intervened, "Ma, don't be a heavy host. She will now be your regular visitor. Let her have what she wants."

"Alright, I'll say nothing but make sure that she helps herself well."

They sat sipping tea and nibbling at the snacks. Savitri had overheard the last part of the conversation between Shahnaz and Sita. She said, "*Beta*, I've not seen the English villages but I find a lot of peace and solace in our Indian villages. The people are simple and content and they've learnt to live within their frugal means."

Shahnaz kept quiet but Sita said, "Ma, that's alright. Indians are born with a philosophical bent of mind and perhaps they understand the meaning of life better, but the question is why can't they be provided with more facilities?"

Agreeing with her, Savitri said that more people should dedicate themselves to selfless service of the poor, like Gayatri Devi. She continued,

"Do you know, before I got married, Diwan *Saheb*'s family used to live in the back portion of this house. It was after our marriage that he was allotted the front portion also. Rahul ji's grandfather was an Honorary Magistrate and he used to hold his court in this building. When we got married, he vacated this house for us to live in. Where do you see such patronage and loyalty these days?"

Shahnaz said, "I would love to live here and help Ma along with Sita, provided there's enough work for both of us."

Sita said that there was so much work to be done that besides Shahnaz and her, many more were required to cope. They chatted for a while and then Shahnaz left for the *Haveli*. After she left, Savitri asked Sita if Shahnaz had a relationship with Rahul. Sita replied, "I don't know, and it's not important anyway."

❖❖

When Shahnaz reached the *Haveli*, Gayatri Devi was sitting with Rahul in the verandah. She had returned from her tour of the constituency and seemed very happy with the progress of the work. In any case, Rahul's visit always brought a lot of cheer in her life. She was telling him about the impediments that were deliberately planted by the government agencies to retard, or altogether hamper the work. She was of the view that obstructions were deliberately built into the system and until a concerted effort was made, no constructive work could be accomplished.

Seeing Shahnaz, Rahul got up and said, "You seem to have hit it off well with Sita. I'm sure that you've been gorging on the delicious snacks that Savitri *chaachi* cooks. The quality of the food in her household is assured, and her guests have no choice but to eat!"

Shahnaz acknowledged that she had had a wonderful time, and that she was totally sold out on Sita and her family. She said that they were affection, simplicity and loyalty rolled into one. She congratulated Gayatri Devi for having such an efficient and committed person like Sita as her assistant. Gayatri Devi said with a sense of triumph, "She's not just my assistant; she's like a daughter to me. I simply cannot do without her."

Rahul asked, with a grin, "And what happens when she gets married and goes away? You may not find another daughter."

Gayatri Devi got up to go inside the *Haveli*, saying gruffly, "Nothing happens, of course. I seem to have been banging my head against a wall."

Rahul realised his mistake and withdrew, while Shahnaz looked a bit confused. She asked Rahul if something had upset his mother. He brushed aside her query and said, "I hope you had a good time with Sita. You know, Savitri *chaachi* has nothing to her credit in the name of formal education, but she's as wise as they come."

She agreed with Rahul and told him all that Savitri Rani had told her about his mother's community development work and the strong bond between the two families. She asked Rahul, "Aunty's dedication to her work is indeed remarkable, but where does she get the money to finance her centers?"

He explained to her that she had been allotted fallow lands in different places by the government for establishing the centers. By dint of hard work done by the people of the area, the centers had assumed their present shape. He said that all the centers had several profit-making units like dairy, fishery, nursery, orchards, agricultural farms, pickle-making and other handicraft work to finance themselves. Besides making money for the centers, these units also served as model units for others that were interested in setting up their own cottage industry. He added that hundreds of people passed out of the centers every year, after taking training in small scale trades and skills. Besides the profits earned by the small scale units, the centers also got grants from the government as well as donations from philanthropic institutions and individuals.

Shahnaz seemed very interested in the work. She asked, "And who keeps the accounts of the money received and expended?"

Rahul told her that the accounts were properly maintained under very strict discipline by a Chartered Accountant, and his mother insisted on their being audited by the government agencies at the end of every financial year. He said that his mother insisted on complete transparency in her work. Looking at his watch, he said, "Time has flown. Ma sits for dinner at eight-thirty and she would be happy if we joined her."

Shahnaz politely protested that she had had too much to eat during the day and wanted no dinner. She enquired if there was a jogging route she could use. Rahul replied, "You have the entire compound to yourself. But you have to go through the motions of dinner nevertheless."

They both left for their rooms, Shahnaz to put on her jogging shoes and Rahul to wash and relax. They joined Gayatri Devi for dinner. The table had all the dishes that Rahul liked but the appetite to do justice to the spread was missing. Gayatri Devi was a very sparse eater in any case. Her dinner comprised a *roti* with vegetables and a glass of milk, so eating was reduced to a mere formality. She asked Shahnaz what she had done during the day. Shahnaz's response showed that she had been deeply moved by the work she had seen and wanted to participate in a deeper way.

Gayatri Devi was pleased to notice Shahnaz's grasp of her work. She said, "There's enough work in the centers for you and many others. You would be a great asset but you will have to acclimatise yourself to the environment here first and, more than anything else, you will have to live here."

"I realise that if I want to work with you I have to live here, but do I have your permission to do so?" she asked.

Gayatri Devi assured her that she would welcome her with open arms but cautioned her not to decide in haste. She suggested that she discuss the matter at length with her family, because relocation from Delhi to here could be trying and even disenchanting.

Rahul, who was listening to the conversation said, "This place is very good for a visit and joining Ma's work is a romantic thought, at best. The ground reality may be quite different, especially since there are no material rewards. You'll miss all that has been ingrained in your system – the friends, the clubs, the musical concerts and sports, the libraries and seminars and the comforts of an affluent household." And with a smile he concluded, "You will not even have the benefit of my company."

Gayatri Devi gave Rahul a curious look and got up, saying that no decision should be taken in a hurry and that Shahnaz should first stay for some time and watch the work. After this they retired for the day. The next morning when Shahnaz went to the dining room for breakfast, Gayatri Devi was already there along with Sita, Rahul and Diwan Mithai Lal. She wished everybody good morning and apologised for being late. Gayatri Devi assured her that she was not late and that they had all just taken their seats. She asked if her sleep had been comfortable and Shahnaz replied that she had slept like a log.

She told Shahnaz that she was not going out that day. But Shahnaz could visit the Bilaspur center with Sita, if she wanted. Shahnaz did want to visit the center. In fact that was one of the reasons for her visit, but she was disappointed that Gayatri Devi would not be accompanying them. She did not consider it proper to ask why she was not going, and agreed to go along with Sita.

Gayatri Devi told Sita to pack some lunch because the food at the center might be too coarse for Shahnaz. Shahnaz politely objected to the idea of carrying special lunch because she wanted to experience the real life in the work. Gayatri Devi appreciated Shahnaz's attitude, but insisted that it was not advisable to suddenly change one's pattern of life, especially the diet. Shahnaz would have none of that and said adamantly, "I shall be very happy if no special arrangement is made for my lunch. I want to make do with what the others eat, and in the unlikely event that I don't like it, I'll skip lunch and make up for it on my return in the evening."

Rahul said that he had not visited the Bilaspur center for a long time and that he also might accompany them. After a pause he said he was keen on going with them also because there were prospects of a good lunch being available. Gayatri Devi dissuaded him from going, saying that she had some urgent matters to discuss with him.

❖❖

After breakfast, Sita and Shahnaz left for the Bilaspur center. Diwan Mithai Lal had to attend to some contractors who had come to Rasulabad to negotiate the sale of the produce from the orchards. His suggestion that Rahul also participate in the negotiations was instantly shot down by Gayatri Devi who repeated what she had said earlier–she had some important matters to discuss with Rahul.

After everybody left and Gayatri Devi was alone with her son, she said, "You don't seem to have paid any attention to what I suggested last evening. If you have any particular objection about the girl, you may say so and I won't force her down your throat. But I'm very clear that your marriage can't wait any more. On my part I have always wanted you to marry Sita, who to my mind is your equal in all respects–looks, education, commitment and whatever else you may ask for. I always thought that the two of you were quite fond of each other too, but its ok if you are not. If you don't want to marry her then don't, but do marry someone of your choice."

Rahul took a deep breath and said, "Ma, have you talked this over with her? Does she also think along the same lines as you do?"

Gayatri Devi felt encouraged by this question. It occurred to her that perhaps he was hesitant because he wanted to know Sita's view on the matter first. She said, "You're right, her consent in the matter is of utmost importance and I must confess, I haven't sounded her out formally. But I've seen enough of this world to know that she would very gladly accept this proposal. Besides being extremely fond of you and me, she is also deeply entrenched in the community work here and marriage with you allows her to continue with it."

Rahul laughed and asked his mother if she had realised that even Shahnaz was interested in working with her. She took it as a hint and said, "If you're interested in marrying Shahnaz I have no objections. But marry you must, and that too as early as possible."

He dropped his nonchalance and said, "Ma, I haven't been considering marriage for the time being. I agree with all you say about Sita's enormous qualities of head and heart. But she and I are childhood buddies more than anything else. She used to make endless cups of coffee when I had to stay up before exams, stand up for me when I used to get into trouble with Dad. But I've never entertained the idea of marrying her. Is it not funny that while I've been looking for a suitable match for her, you have been looking at me as a match for her? In fact, I've been thinking of talking to her about a boy in Delhi who, to my mind, would fit Sita's idea of a husband. He is an idealist, well-educated, and totally committed to rural upliftment."

Gayatri Devi said, "That does not solve my problem. What I want is your marriage; you're running out of time. And what are you waiting for? Is there not enough at home to provide for a decent family life? In any case, what stops you from continuing to pursue your goal even after you get married? You do me proud with your achievements and your ability. Why can't you understand this simple thing? You're not getting any younger and there's always a right time for every thing." Rahul said with a hint of exasperation in his voice. "Ma, I would do anything to make you happy, except getting married just now. And the main impediment in achieving the goals I have set for myself is that I'm honour bound not to deviate from my scruples. Remember the word of honour you extorted from me when I was leaving for London?"

Gayatri Devi said slowly with great emphasis, "You mean, you would have compromised with the values that your forefathers held so dear to attain your ends, if you hadn't committed to me that you wouldn't do so? The fact that you even entertain such thoughts is enough for me to hang my head in shame."

Rahul stood up and with folded hands beseeched his mother not to get upset, just because he had spoken candidly to her. He said that times had changed and one had to pay a very heavy price for living with one's conscience. He added that he did not intend to change his ways but surely wanted to give himself a fair chance and arrive at the logical end of his endeavours.

Gayatri Devi told Rahul to sit down and said, "Your idea that marriage comes in the way of one's progress is wrong. In fact the relationship of companionship and trust you share with Sita is an excellent foundation for marriage. But I do appreciate your sentiment that you can't marry someone whom you are not romatically inclined toward. I have to make three requests to you. The first request is that you must restructure your idea of marriage and its likely impact on your progress, and when you realise that you've been on the wrong track, let me know whom you are marrying. The second request is to follow the straight and narrow path. Unless you uphold the banner of integrity that has been flying high in your family you will never be able to bring back its glory. And the third request is that if you have somebody in mind for Sita then please do discuss him with her, because by declining my suggestion, you have saddled me with the additional responsibility of finding a suitable match for her."

Rahul embraced his mother, saying that he would follow her instructions verbatim. Diwan Mithai Lal came and stood at a distance. Gayatri Devi asked him if he had finalised the deal of the orchard with the contractor. He replied that he had clinched the deal and taken an advance payment but that there was some other problem which called for her attention. He said that the same contractor had purchased the standing crop of paddy at a certain price and had paid the due advance, but after harvesting it he had found the yield to be poorer than what he had expected, and therefore he sought her intervention to reduce the contract price.

Rahul asked him, "Do you think he would have paid us more than the contracted price if the yield had been more than what he had anticipated?" When he replied in the negative he said, "There you are, why should we allow him any concession when we don't expect reciprocity from him? I don't think the matter deserves consideration."

Gayatri Devi asked Diwan *Saheb* about his view on the subject. He said that in principle Rahul was right, but since he was aware of her idea of equity, he had thought of bringing the matter to her notice. She thought for a while and asked him to check the records and find out the yield of crop on the lands that they had harvested themselves during the corresponding period. She decided that if the contractor had paid more than what would be recovered from the crop in the lands harvested by them, then he could be compensated. If not, then no notice was to be taken of his grievance. She told him to send for the contractor.

The contractor came with folded hands. She smiled at him and enquired about the welfare of his family, especially about his daughter who had got married the previous year. And then she said, "What is this? Diwan *Saheb* tells me that you do not want to pay the contracted price. How can you make such a preposterous proposal?"

The contractor bowed a little more and said, "*Malkin*, the contract is over. What I've brought to his attention is just a child's tantrum."

She laughed and said that she had made an appeal in his favour to Diwan *Saheb* and that he would soon be hearing from him. After the contractor and Diwan *Saheb* left the room Rahul said, "Ma, I'm most impressed. Although I must confess that I would not have deviated from the terms of the contract. That is why you are respected like a Goddess."

She said, "I don't do things to earn respect. I only follow the dictates of my conscience. And people are so kind – they give so much for so little."

Learning that Gayatri Devi had not gone out to the center, some people gathered in the verandah with their tales of woe. Rahul pointed towards them and asked her, "Ma, how have they come to know that you're here this afternoon?"

She didn't answer and asked him to go with her and talk to them. He, not being in a mood to mingle, excused himself and proceeded to his room while she joined her visitors.

A little after dusk, Sita and Shahnaz returned from their visit to Bilaspur. They found Rahul and Gayatri Devi sitting in the verandah, sipping tea. Gayatri Devi looked at them and said, "Good! You're back on time. Shahnaz, I hope you liked your outing and the new experience, and I do hope Sita made sure that you were not too uncomfortable."

Sita appeared a bit tired but Shahnaz was bubbling with enthusiasm. She stood in front of Gayatri Devi and said, "I salute you for all that you've achieved. If only a few more like you could dedicate themselves to serving the community, the country would be transformed. But I have to make a complaint about Sita. She hardly did any work there except for showing me around and looking after me."

She then declared that while she was there she would like to go with Gayatri Devi each time she went to the centers. Gayatri Devi told her that she was welcome to do so and asked her to join them for a cup of tea. Sita told them that Shahnaz had been a big hit with the people at Bilaspur, and that at the time of their leaving a large crowd had collected to greet Shahnaz and to tell her to visit them again. Rahul, who had been watching patiently, remarked that one day's visit was not the same as committing oneself to a complete metamorphosis in one's way of life. He told Shahnaz, "Madam, do you know that there is hardly any place here for the stilettos, Birkins and Jimmy Choos? Tennis and musical concerts are quite far away, and what you have for painting exhibitions are designs made from rice paste on cow dung. Sita is too busy and you won't have a readymade chaperone in me to escort you wherever you go."

Shahnaz laughed and replied, "Don't underestimate me. And don't overestimate your worth as a chaperone. I'm very excited about the venture and the work will keep me happily occupied. "

Gayatri Devi sternly told Rahul to keep away from the centers, because he had no interest in community work and his visit to the centers reminded her of the visits by British officers to the areas in their official charge. The actual work suffered while they visited their territories. She said that the British officers always included *shikaar* in their tour program and took a few friends with them. On one of the tours, Rahul's grandfather was accompanying the District Magistrate. The District Magistrate was a very strict officer but on the first day of the tour when he was boarding the car to go for inspection, Rahul's grandfather took him aside and said, "A mild inspection will make the *shikaar* more enjoyable because unless your officers work overtime for the arrangements, it could be a damp squib."

The Magistrate had a hearty laugh and said that he was fully aware of the rules of the game. The inspection was just a formality. The officers did not miss out on anything in the arrangements to make the *shikaar* a great success and received an excellent chit.

She continued, "When Rahul goes, everybody gets busy to please him and no actual work is done."

He reacted sarcastically and said, "That is why Rahul seldom goes there, and he's sure that today's welcome to Shahnaz was a spontaneous outpouring of gratitude for all the contributions she has made to the centers!"

Gayatri Devi said that one would have to wait and see how things worked out, and asked Sita if the new teacher had joined at the Bilaspur center. She replied, "She's joined and seems to be good too. The children took to her instantly."

After a pause she told Gayatri Devi that the report from Ramgarh had come and all was not well there. She said that she would discuss the report at dinner and asked to be excused to go freshen up. Gayatri Devi said that she also wanted to have a wash before dinner and got up, but before leaving she told Shahnaz, "You've had a very hectic day. You'll need to relax and wash before dinner."

The dinner was simple but Ram Lal's *parcha-kababs* were scandalously good. Rahul gorged on the *kababs* and even Shahnaz nibbled at them with great appreciation. She declared that she had not eaten such *kababs* before. Sita and Gayatri Devi were vegetarians and very sparse eaters.

Gayatri Devi asked Sita, "So what's happening in Ramgarh? You said that there was something disturbing going on."

Sita looked around to make sure that no servant was present and started in a low voice, "As you know, we've constructed a five kilometre long road to connect Ramgarh with the National Highway and it has been funded by the government and the residents of the area, besides your MLA fund and the resources of our center. The PWD department, on inspection, found that the specifications laid down for construction of such roads had not been adhered to, and now it has been found that the road has caved in at three places. Since the road has been constructed under our supervision, the PWD has put the entire blame on us and in their report they have recommended that no further assistance should be given to us, for any such project. They have further recommended that the money given to us for this project should be recovered."

Rahul interjected, "Well, the roads constructed by the government departments all over the country keep caving in all year round. Why should this project be singled out? Does the PWD pay back to the government the cost of building a road that they construct, in the event of the road getting washed out?"

Gayatri Devi realised that perhaps her talk with Rahul that afternoon about Sita was still disturbing his mind, and that a discussion on a serious issue like this was not really a good idea right now. She looked at Shahnaz and said, "Let us hear everyone's view on the subject and then decide what should be done. Rahul has expressed his opinion. Let us see what the new entrant to the team has to say."

Shahnaz looked around a bit sheepishly and started, "I think that the center must pay back the money to the government, because it has not performed its part of the contract. The government must get a justifiable account of the money it spends."

Gayatri Devi then looked at Sita who said, "Rahul is right, that there is no question of our refunding the money to the government. The trust has very limited resources and has hardly any surplus ever. But at the same time we can't brush aside the observations of the government department, for we have to deal with them all the time. I'm of the view that we may offer to repair the damages at our cost."

Gayatri Devi said, "And should somebody not find out who is responsible for this and why such incidents are being repeated of late?" She asked Rahul whether he would like to look into the matter but he shook his head and said that he had to return to Delhi in a day or two.

❖❖

Changing the topic, Gayatri Devi asked Rahul whether he had met Sam uncle of late. He answered in the affirmative and added that Uncle Sam had not been keeping good health. He said that each time he met him, he talked very fondly of his stay at Rasulabad and enquired about all his friends. He never forgot to convey his regards to Ma and Mithai Uncle and Savitri Aunty.

Gayatri Devi, remembering the old times, said that Samir Saxena had been posted at Rasulabad as an Addditional Collector and by sheer coincidence had stayed there for four years. She said that he was very popular as an officer and was like a family member to them. She asked Rahul to tell him that she had invited him to pay her a visit. She added that a change of climate may do him good.

Rahul asked, hesitatingly, "Ma, what is the truth about some people saying that Samir uncle had been transferred out of here under a cloud?"

She got into a contemplative mood, and after a while replied, "People may say whatever, but Samir is an epitome of gentlemanliness and a great friend."

He persisted, "But there must have been some reason that he was transferred." Gayatri Devi became serious. She said, "No reason was given for the transfer because the time for it had come in any case, but unfortunately Samir's name was somehow connected to a scandal and then people connected that to the transfer." After a pause she continued, "You know Haji *mian*? His sister Farah used to work as a cook in Samir's house. Her cooking was a rage. Even your father was a great admirer of her culinary prowess and each time there was a party at Samir's house, he didn't miss expressing his appreciation for the gourmet cook. Besides being a very fine cook, she was a very good-natured girl and had taken charge of Samir's housekeeping. This arrangement suited Samir – he was a bachelor and loved to entertain friends."

"One day Farah disappeared and no one including Samir had any idea as to where she had gone. An FIR was registered with the Police and Haji *Mian*, with the assistance of Samir, searched all over in vain for her, but ultimately they had to give up. The Muslim community, in the process of politicising the matter, tried to put the blame on Samir. The accusation was that he had kidnapped her and was now keeping her in captivity. They had nothing to substantiate their charges but Samir's transfer coincided with the agitation."

Rahul enquired from his mother, "What did Samir uncle have to say about it?" But Gayatri Devi had fallen into a melancholy mood. She said, "Poor chap, what could he say? He was flabbergasted himself."

Sita, who had been listening silently so far, did have some inkling about the rumour. She said, "I know Samir uncle is a lovable character, but under the circumstances the needle of suspicion does point towards him."

Gayatri Devi defended Samir. She said that, in the first place, Samir could not be connected with any act of criminality. Moreover she added, barring Farah's family, Samir was the only one who stood to lose by her death. He lost a house keeper and a great cook, who was like his family.

The lawyer in Rahul found the story puzzling. He asked, "What did the Police say before closing the case? She couldn't have evaporated into thin air!"

Shahnaz, who was listening to the conversation with rapt attention, asked if Farah had enjoyed a good reputation. She speculated whether Farah had eloped with someone, for if she had died the Police would have recovered a body. Gayatri Devi clarified that there was no question of there being anything of that sort because Farah's movements had been confined between her house and Samir's bungalow. She also told them that her family had fixed her *nikah* (marriage) with her uncle's son who lived in the same town.

Sita came up with a preposterous idea. She said, "From what you say about this lady, is it not likely that Samir uncle and she might have fallen in love? And before he was transferred out of Rasulabad, he could have sent her away to some place where she might be still living in anonymity – with the full knowledge of Samir uncle."

Gayatri Devi was appalled at this suggestion. She said, "Anything is possible, but Samir is a man of very high morals and this theory does not stick on him. He is so committed to his convictions that he remained unmarried, because in his younger days he fell in love with someone who died, and he took a vow to live the rest of his life with her memory. He was too sophisticated to fall for Farah, but even if he did what stopped him from marrying her? There might have been some token resistance in the beginning, but Farah's marriage to Samir would have been such a social boost for her family that they would have eventually succumbed. I don't see much force in your contention."

Sita asked her whether she knew the girl whom Samir uncle had fallen for but she shook her head. She added, "Each time the matter came up during our conversations with him, he became so emotional that the conversation had to be abandoned."

Looking at the wall clock, she said, "Time to retire, tomorrow is a busy day." Everybody got up to leave.

❖❖

The early morning was crisp and pleasant. Both the sun and the moon could be seen in the sky and the lack of pollution had created quite a contrast to the scenario Shahnaz and Rahul were used to in Delhi. Gayatri Devi, Sita, Shahnaz and Rahul got into an Ambassador car and some workers of the Trust followed them in a Jeep. They stopped at a *dhaba* for breakfast. The owner of the *dhaba* seemed very familiar with them. He touched Gayatri Devi's feet and bowed before the rest of them. He complained to Rahul that he was visiting after a very long time. Looking at Shahnaz, he made his own assessment and said, "You're visiting my humble establishment for the first time and therefore you are the guest of honour today."

They gorged on *aloo-paranthas*, pickles and curds with a light sprinkle of locally made sugar served in very neat, stainless steel containers, followed by *masala* tea and then proceeded with their journey. Shahnaz had not eaten such food before but her palate had accepted it with great aplomb. She was however surprised that no payment was made to the owner of the *dhaba*, and he seemed to be obliged to the group for the visit. She later came to know that the ancestors of the *dhaba* owner had been old retainers of Rahul's family and Gayatri Devi had donated to the owner, the land on which he had built the flourishing *dhaba*.

Kasya was the largest of the community centers run by her. The center was spread over an area of hundred acres of land. It had the unique distinction of having a large lake surrounded by small hillocks. While choosing the locations for the centers, she kept in mind the natural advantages of the place. Once she had told Sita that it was possible to build anything on the ground, but hills were not possible to build on, and therefore she had always preferred to build community centers in the proximity of hills or mountains. The center had a fishery, a dairy, a large orchard of fruit trees and agricultural farms to generate resources for its survival. On the service front, it ran a school, a dispensary and a women's polytechnic institute. The work force attached to the center comprised about 100 men and 20 women who lived on the center premises. The residential accommodation was quite spartan and the allowances given to the workers were need-based. Depending on the age and need of the workers, they were allotted single or shared accommodations. They all ate simple food together, in the common dining hall. Those who had to go out to the villages, to follow up the public projects undertaken by the center, used to leave the center in the wee hours of the morning.

Madhoji, who was in-charge of the center, used to assign each and every worker his work for the day. He also took stock of things periodically and maintained a record of developments. He enjoyed the complete confidence of Gayatri Devi and commanded a lot of respect among the people of the constituency. In his days Madhoji had been a force to reckon with. He had lived incognito for seven years during the freedom struggle and after Independence had never lost an election to the U.P. Legislative Assembly. Later, he got disenchanted with politics and decided to devote his time to social service.

They reached the center in the forenoon and Gayatri Devi and Sita got down at the gate to walk the rest of the distance on foot. They did that each time they visited the center, because that was the best way to meet the maximum number of people in the shortest time. Seeing them get down, Shahnaz too expressed a desire to get down and walk with them. Rahul was not too keen on accompanying them and requested Shahnaz to stay back and accompany him to the living quarters. He tried to tempt her, saying that the lawns and the beds of roses around the living quarters were very beautiful and more inviting than anything else at the center, but Shahnaz was insistent. She got down while Rahul proceeded to the living quarters.

The center was a world in itself. The roads were skirted by rows of fruit and flowering trees, providing enough shade to those walking around. The musical bird calls created the ambience of a symphonic glade. The water bodies served as reservoirs for the water saved through water harvesting during rainy seasons. Some were covered by lotus flowers while others had various fish in interesting colours. The fish in such water bodies were not meant for consumption. There was a *gobar-gas* plant near the dairy which took care of half the electricity requirement of the center.

They first visited the school and the dispensary that were situated side by side and spent some time talking to the students, teachers, patients and the doctors. Gayatri Devi was intimately familiar with whoever she talked to and whatever they did. Her visit seemed to have induced an atmosphere of happiness and optimism among the people. By the time she was through it was afternoon but she was not tired. She wanted to visit the fishery and the dairy but Madhoji pointed out that they had not had their lunch and that Rahul was waiting for them at the living quarters. Having gorged on a sumptuous breakfast, Gayatri Devi and Sita were not too keen on lunch. They only had fruits for lunch when on tours but were not sure about Shahnaz. Sita said to Shahnaz, "I always knew that you were interested in the work here but I couldn't imagine that you would get so engrossed that you would forget about lunch. I suggest you join Rahul for lunch. Ma and I prefer to make do with some fruits."

Shahnaz reiterated that she wanted to experience exactly the same life as they did at the center. Also, she added, she was not hungry.

The rest of the afternoon was spent touring the production units and listening to the concerns of the workers, ranging from poor working conditions to suspicions of marital infidelity. All concerns were given equal importance and handled with tact and perspicacity by Gayatri Devi.

The dinner was simple but tasty. The freshness of the farm vegetables was the main highlight. Madhoji mentioned that the farm-made ghee on the hot *rotis* and the jaggery in the curd were the specialities of the center. Shahnaz relished the ambience and the dinner alike. She asked him, "Uncle, tell us about your experiences of the freedom struggle. It must have been tough taking on the might of the British Empire. And opting for the struggle, in preference to a comfortable life, for a well-educated man hailing from an affluent background, must have been a very difficult decision."

He replied, "An obsession has no apparent reason. It is so well reasoned from within that it becomes immune to any counsel or advice from outside. The pleasure of defying falsehood and living with one's own convictions is something which one has to experience oneself." He smiled and said that he had been convicted for the first time by Shahnaz's grandfather, who was a member of the Indian Civil Service and was posted as a Magistrate. But after pronouncing the verdict, he had driven Madhoji in his car to the jail and asked the jailer to extend all facilities due to a political prisoner.

"But why did the jailor have to be told about providing you with all that was done for a political prisoner? Was it not your due?" she asked. Madhoji told her that nothing was due to anybody in those days of arbitrary laws.

She was anxious to know what the real situation was during the British Raj, because she had heard certain good things alongside the criticisms about the British from different sources. She had heard that they were good administrators and provided India with the modern systems and networks that ran even today. Railways and Postal Services were quoted as some of the several gifts given to India by them. She asked him, "There cannot be any justification in forcefully usurping control over the destiny of a nation, but some are of the view that the British ushered India into the modern world and contributed a great deal in developing new technologies and systems." After a pause she added, "The Mughals too were foreigners and ruled over India for a much longer period than the British, but nobody talks about the atrocities committed by them, whereas there is unanimity about the excesses of the British rule."

Madhoji, who had retained a very personable presence even at the age of 91, straightened himself and fixed a piercing gaze on Shahnaz. In his soft baritone he said, "*Beta*, you must learn to see things in the right perspective. The British did introduce some good systems in the working of the administration, but they did so in their own interest. They had to administer a large country and it wouldn't have been possible to do so without the aid of those systems. "

At this stage Rahul came up with the observation that now the Indians were doing the same thing that the British had done – transferring India's wealth to tax havens. Madhoji looked at Rahul and said, "You're right, values are changing so fast that it seems to be difficult to keep up with the times. I wonder if Gandhiji would have waged his titanic struggle if he knew that matters would come to such a pass after independence."

Gayatri Devi said, "The values are corroding very fast but one is likely to find happiness only in living with one's own values."

Rahul did not concur with her observation and said, "Living with one's own values is indeed laudable, but what does one do when one is surrounded by thieves and scoundrels? When the choice is between success and failure what do you choose?"

Fixing his gaze on Rahul, Madhoji remarked, "Without going into the desirability or otherwise of one's values, I would say that the best results are achieved only by abiding by the morals one believes in. Aping others can never bring out the best in a person. Chasing success at any cost may have disastrous results. "

Rahul shook his head in disagreement and said, "I have a lot of respect for all that has been said by Ma and Uncle, but time has proved that scruples and material success pull in opposite directions, and those seeking material success have to pursue a different way of life– a way where the end and not the means is of essence."

"Each one to himself, that is the best way to live life," chuckled Madhoji and while getting up he suggested that since they had to leave the next morning, they should all retire for the day.

The next morning at the center was extraordinary. The aromas of the pastoral idyll mingled with the chorus of the community prayer to create a scene that belonged to a bygone age. After the morning prayer, the group visited the dairy where cows and buffaloes were being milked. Debu, one of the workers at the dairy offered a glass of fresh milk to everyone and they accepted it with enthusiasm. Only Shahnaz had some reservations about drinking un-boiled milk, wondering if it would be unhygienic. But since Gayatri Devi herself had accepted the milk, Shahnaz could not muster enough courage to openly refuse to drink it. Under her breath though, she told Debu that she did not like raw milk. He was a bit puzzled but silence, he thought, was the better part of discretion.

They moved towards the pond by the side of which breakfast had been organised. This pond was a fishery of sorts. The plan was to convert it into a full-fledged fishery, but currently it was just a beautiful water body housing multiple varieties of colourful fish. The breakfast comprised of guavas, bananas, milk, roasted gram with jaggery and bread with dry vegetables, followed by tea. While the others were going through the motions of having their breakfast, Madhoji and Gayatri Devi used their time to discuss matters related to the centers.

The return journey was swift. They did not stop on the way and managed to reach home before dusk. Having missed lunch, everyone were famished and gorged on the goodies Mithai Lal had affectionately prepared for them.

Gayatri Devi told Rahul that before he left for Delhi the following day she wanted to have a chat with him. He replied that he too wanted to seek her advice on certain matters. They got up together and left for the study. Sita and Shahnaz left for their respective rooms. The study had old mahogany furniture and the racks along the walls had stacks of old books, not dusted for some time and looking rather unkempt. Looking at them, Rahul said, "Ma, these books deserve better treatment."

Gayatri Devi, as if she had been waiting for this observation from Rahul, said, "I wish to talk to you precisely about this." They sat down across each other and she was in no mood to waste any time. She said,

"I'm getting on in age and the social work I have undertaken has been multiplying manifold. It is not only this study, but the entire *Haveli* and the matters connected with it that have been suffering for want of personal care. Besides the consideration for my happiness, you need to get married to retain the legacy that your fore-fathers have bequeathed to you. Sita's marriage to you would have sorted out many things but you have shattered my hopes. Not only that, I shudder at the thought that very soon Sita too would not be by my side to share my work and responsibilities. She is not just my right hand but in fact both my hands and I will have to lose them when she marries somebody and goes away."

Rahul, trying to be reconciliatory, spoke in a low, soft voice, "Ma, I too have wanted to speak to you about your social work for a long time. I see your work taking a heavy toll on your health. You've done whatever you could and I must confess that you have achieved a lot, but this cannot go on forever. The time has come for you to nominate a successor and take life easy. One should bite only as much as one can chew. My marriage is a far cry and even if it takes place, what is the guarantee that the girl I marry would like to share your social responsibilities? About Sita, I have already made my position clear. "

Gayatri Devi looked piqued and said, "You don't seem to realise that I'm totally committed to the social work I've undertaken. It's not a recreation for me. If this collapses, I too would wither away with it. Also, it's not easy to find someone to take over the work from me. Social service has no meaning without incessant commitment and total dedication. Sita fits the bill but I find myself on the horns of a dilemma, because I'm as keen on Sita's marriage to a suitable boy as I am on continuing with my social commitment. Incidentally, you mentioned to me that you had someone in mind for Sita. Who is he?"

Rahul replied, "Ma, we're jumping the gun. We're making plans for someone without knowing her mind. For all you know, she may not want to get married just now and in any case, a proposal for an arranged marriage has to be handled with caution. The person I have in mind is perfectly eligible but all depends on whether she and he would be able to hit it off."

She nodded and said, "You're right, but before talking to her I would like to know about the boy you have in mind for her."

Rahul told her that the boy in question was the son of Shri Rajeshwar Singh, who was a Member of Parliament and owned a very large business establishment in Delhi. The boy, Gyaneshwar Singh had done his MBA from Harvard, had a very pleasant disposition and was looking for a girl like Sita. He said that Gyaneshwar was an idealist, committed to the philosophy of simple living and high thinking and had basic differences with his father's more material way of life.

Gayatri Devi's eyes lit up. She commented, "I see a ray of hope in this proposal. If Gyaneshwar and Sita like each other and decide to get married, he could join her here and do what he has wanted to do all his life."

Rahul got impatient. He said, "Ma, you're assuming that Gyaneshwar would like to come here and work on your project with Sita. You must realise, he has a family business and his father's constituency which need and rightly deserve his attention. Also, his mother would not be happy at the thought of his leaving his home and shifting to his wife's place after marriage. His father would certainly have reservations about his son getting married to the daughter of Diwan Mithai Lal ji."

Gayatri Devi nodded in agreement and said, "You're right, but do explore the possibility of this proposal further when you go back to Delhi. I will sound Sita about it and get her reaction. Also, Shahnaz is a good girl, why don't you try and make something out of your friendship with her?"

Rahul laughed at the prospect, and getting up to retire he said, "Ma, you are being pushy – if I may use the expression! Anyway, we are leaving early morning tomorrow and I must get some sleep before that."

Gayatri Devi reminded Rahul to call on Samir Saxena in Delhi and inform her how he was doing. He touched her feet and she blessed him and caressed his head as they parted.

The next morning when Rahul came out to depart, he found Shahnaz sitting with his mother, Sita and Dewan Mithai Lal on the main verandah of the house, sipping tea and looking very cheerful. He overheard Gayatri Devi saying that meeting Shahnaz was a great pleasure and that she was most welcome to come back to Rasulabad and join her in her work. From Sita's smile he could make out that she too was happy at the idea. He understood that Shahnaz had finally succeeded in her mission.

The next morning as the train left the railway station Mithai Lal watched it depart and wondered if the relationship between Rahul and Shahnaz was just friendship. He was a bit concerned, because Gayatri Devi had hinted to him that she would like Sita to marry Rahul.

Samir's Secret

Delhi was eight hours away from Rasulabad by train. Shahnaz took a couple of pillows and made a cosy corner for herself. She suggested to Rahul that he make a similar arrangement for himself, and they both settled down with a book each. Some time passed but neither of them could concentrate on reading. They were both thinking of the same person –Gayatri Devi. Shahnaz was in awe of her selfless and austere life, total dedication for the welfare of others and the enormous achievements to her credit. Rahul was wondering if she had been on the right track in their discussion of the night before. He was not sure if it was advisable to sacrifice all the comforts and luxuries of life, and engage oneself with something that was beyond the scope of an individual.

He put his book down. He looked at Shahnaz and found her too in a contemplative mood. She was looking up at the berth above her with a glazed look in her eyes. He told her, "I'm sure you're thinking of your holiday in the summer. Where do you plan to go? Rustom Uncle told me that he and Aunty would spend this summer in Europe, with the new villa they've acquired in Barcelona as their base. He told me that a mid-size yacht has also come along with the villa and that they are looking forward to a great time on it. About you, he said that you were at a liberty to go wherever you wanted ."

She replied, "You're totally off the mark. I'm thinking of your mother – what an incredible lady she is! In fact you've given me an idea; I may want to spend the summer with her at Rasulabad if it's alright with her."

Rahul laughed patronisingly and said, "You have no idea what Rasulabad is like in summer. You would feel like a fish out of water. Ma does not use air-conditioners and my dear girl, you cannot breathe without them during summers. I suggest you shake this idea off and plan your holiday as you have been doing every year."

Shahnaz could not hide her irritation at his suggestion. She said, "Rahul, have I not had enough of limousines, yachts and European villas? In fact, I'm embarrassed at being so far away from reality. What a satisfying life your mother has, and why can I not be a part of her life? It is so rewarding!"

Rahul spoke in a lighter vain. He said, "Ma is very keen to make you a part of her life as well as that of mine. She will be delighted to hear this from you."

"About you, I don't know, but I would certainly like to 'delight' her by joining her in her work," retorted Shahnaz.

"And what happens to the Rustomjee Empire so assiduously built over the years?" Rahul asked.

Shahnaz said with a sigh, "I'm not really cut out for it. It calls for very deft and astute handling by someone like you. I'm sure Dad would trust you more than me with that work. My parents know very well that that is not my cup of tea." There was silence for some time and then she started again. "Meeting Gayatri aunty was a great privilege and Sita is the icing on the cake. Aunty's grooming is writ large on her personality. Has the idea of proposing to her never occurred to you?"

She would have perhaps continued her monologue but Rahul stopped her and said, "In the first place, let me clarify that Sita is a childhood buddy, no more, and in any case I am not contemplating marriage in the near future. About your other observations, I may agree with you in parts but not with your general assessment of the situation. Don't you think that instead of concentrating on only the social projects, if they had devoted themselves to politics, Ma would have been the Chief Minister of the State? The family vaults would not have been empty, although I do realise that my mother is incapable of filling the family coffers."

Shahnaz said, "And the opposition would have lobbed charges of corruption against your mother and removed her from the position. She would have spent her entire life trying to stage a comeback with very little chance of success. And the high reputation established by the family over the years would have gone for a six. No Rahul, that is hardly a thing worth pursuing. Even the good ones who go there get charred and blackened. Look at Rajeshwar Uncle. What is it that the family does not have? But they are so far away from happiness. In fact a lot more unhappiness seems to be in store for them. Gyaneshwar is so frustrated that I worry for him."

The mention of Gyaneshwar's name took Rahul back to the conversation he had with his mother the previous night. He asked Shahnaz, "What is your opinion of Gyaneshwar? I've been toying with the idea of suggesting him for Sita."

She thought for a while and said, "As far as I'm concerned, I find him to be quite eligible and good in every respect. But in the context of marriage, I suppose the chemistry is of utmost importance and the boy and the girl must take a decision in these matters."

Rahul commented, "At least one thing is settled, and that is that you're not interested in Gyaneshwar!"

Shahnaz laughed and said, "Certainly not!"

Rahul cross-examined her, "Then whom are you interested in?"

She replied firmly, "Nobody." She continued, "In fact, I am not interested in marriage at all for the time being. I want to have a meaningful life. I seek to serve my soul more than anything else and I think I have found a way to do that. Selfless service to the community and shedding off all the frills of life is what I am looking for."

He clapped and said, "I'm already impressed by your ideas. I'm reminded of someone who said that money meant nothing in life, but unless this statement came from someone sitting over a pile it was not acceptable."

They both laughed and Shahnaz said, "You could be right, because the environment in which a person is brought up has a direct bearing on his or her psyche."

Continuing in the same mood, Rahul observed, "I see a lot of likeness between you and Samir Uncle and I do hope that you do not end up like him. He has really had it bad. A person who had known him earlier would not be able to recognise him in his new *avatar* of a recluse. My God, what an amazing personality he was!"

Shahnaz said, "I'm not aware of his past but I'm a great admirer of his. Living with one's conviction, by itself, is a great contribution to the society. Such people help the society in sustaining its values. You must tell me about his past. From what you said just now, it seems to have been very eventful."

"I also hold him in high esteem but I do think that instead of resigning to a secluded existence he should have taken a more positive approach to life," said Rahul.

Shahnaz could not understand why Rahul seemed to have certain reservations about Samir uncle. She said, "I don't understand all that you say about him but I would certainly like to hear about his past, since you say it was amazing."

Rahul was silent for a moment and then began to recount Samir's story. Samir Saxena hailed from the hilly terrain of Kumaon and had a very deprived childhood. But he was gifted with enormous grit and determination from the very beginning. Rahul told Shahnaz that there were several legends about him doing the rounds in his native village.

One such story was that once, during the British Raj, he was going to the town with his father when the awe-inspiring convoy of the District Magistrate passed by. The Magistrate himself was on horse-back, and was being escorted by several armed horsemen and attendants on foot. At the tail end of the procession there was a horse driven carriage, perhaps carrying the food and other items.

Young Samir was impressed by the regalia of the convoy but he was far from being intimidated by it. "What does one have to do to become a District Magistrate?" he asked his father. His father replied, "One has to always come first in his class and win all the debating trophies, besides being good at sports. And one has to pass an examination for appointment to the post of District Magistrate."

The little boy's fingers gripped his father's hand firmly as he announced, "I will become a District Magistrate one day."

Rahul told Shahnaz that after this incident Samir never looked back. He was always on top of his class and excelled in extracurricular activities. Notwithstanding the impediments that came in his way, he got into the Indian Administrative Service. His integrity and efficiency earned him a reputation as an outstanding officer. He could speak as charmingly as he could wield his pen. He was also a very keen sportsman. He was the life of any party and could enthral the audience for hours with his anecdotes and songs. He was charming and inspired immense love and respect in everyone. He was alleged to have had many affairs but what he was seeking was love and perhaps that was the one thing he could never find in the umpteen relationships he had. As a result, he had remained single. But then suddenly, something happened and to the dismay of all those who knew him, he resigned from his service and withdrew into oblivion. Rumours had it that he did eventually find his love but somehow could not marry her and that was what brought him to his present state.

Shahnaz, who had been listening to Rahul carefully, asked, "I understand he was very close to your parents. Did he not take them into his confidence?"

Rahul replied, "He may have, but I really don't know because nobody has told me about it and I never tried to find out either. All I know is that he came out of his hiding after about a year and ever since then he has been living a very aloof existence. Not meeting anybody, just confined to himself and his writing, sometimes sitting at the piano and playing the melodies of yesteryear."

Shahnaz told Rahul that she had read four of his books – *Love After Life, Father Without Identity, The Void and The Guilt Of Love.* She said that the books were very interesting but they all seemed to revolve around a common theme. She added that if one were to draw an inference from the books he had written, one might conclude that his present situation was the result of having been jilted in love.

Rahul said, "Quite possible, but a person of his calibre should have approached the problem differently. After all, love is not the be-all and end-all of life.

Shahnaz had tears in her eyes. She said, "Rahul, you're not being fair to him. In fact I cannot make out where he went wrong. From what you tell me, it seems that he pursued his goal successfully, led a full life and made a niche for himself in society. What else could one do? And he is still contributing to the society by sharing his thoughts through his books. The rumour about his being jilted in love may be correct, but that raises him even higher in my esteem. It shows commitment and sensitivity and I have great regard for such values."

Rahul was not in agreement with Shahnaz. He also held Samir in high esteem but was of the view that emotions and sentiments should not be allowed to get the better of a person. He said, "Sensitivity and the finer values of life are very great assets but once they get on top of you, you end up being a loser. And I'm afraid Samir uncle has been just that. His pain is understandable but there is a big 'but' about it."

The train slowed down, passing through the inhabited areas of Delhi and soon it steamed into the New Delhi railway station. The conversation took a pause and Rahul suggested to Shahnaz that she must not take anything that he had said about Samir uncle seriously. He admitted that there was a lot of sense in what she had to say. He also mentioned that the first thing he intended to do in Delhi was to call on him to find out how he was doing. She said that she would like to accompany him when he went, to which he readily agreed. Her liveried chauffer was waiting right in front of their compartment and a porter was in attendance by the time the train came to a full halt. It was understood without mentioning that Shahnaz's car would drop Rahul at his residence and then take her home.

❖❖

Shahnaz got a most affectionate welcome at home. Her pet, Kai, was ecstatic with joy. His barks showed no sign of subsiding. The moment she came out of the car she cuddled him and did not appear to have any intention of releasing him. Meanwhile, Zaroo ran towards her with her arms open and the family retainers lined up with broad smiles to express their happiness at the arrival of the darling of the family. Shahnaz, with great difficulty, got herself out of the tangle of the dog and ran to embrace her mother, giving a fleeting glance with a warm smile to the retainers. Zaroo said, "You have tanned a bit but you look good. And this muslin dress you are wearing is very becoming."

Shahnaz asked after the health of the attendants. They were unanimous in their reply that the house was not the same without her. Zaroo informed her that Rustom had an important meeting to attend but would be coming home immediately after that. They went inside the house. Zaroo told her to freshen up and join her on the lawn where they would wait for her father. Shahnaz took her own time to wash and change and when she went to the lawn she found that Rustom had already arrived. Seeing her, he got up and hugged her. He said , "Your mother told me that you had tanned but I find you more radiant than ever. You seem to have enjoyed your stay at Rahul's home, but we were miserable without you."

Zaroo remarked, "Shahnaz, you have worn my saree which the maid put in your wardrobe. You may take it if you like but I wanted you to wear the *gharara* suit that *Begum Saheba* has sent for you. Do you know, the *suit* has been designed by a special tailor?"

Rustom was being the doting father. He said, "My Shanoo looks the ultimate in whatever she wears but *Begum Saheba's* proposal is not acceptable to me, unless of course Shahnaz is interested in it herself. She has the pick of the world."

Shahnaz looked a bit startled. She asked, "What are you talking about? What is the proposal? And why is it not acceptable to Dad?"

Zaroo replied brusquely, "Nothing very important! *Begum Saheba* wants your hand in marriage for her son, and your father insists that there is no way that he can part with you. That is why he does not even want to mention it to you."

Shahnaz replied, "Dad is right, marriage is the last thing on my mind for now. At the moment I'm obsessed with the idea of working with Gayatri Devi on her community development projects in Rasulabad."

Rustom was obviously not very pleased with this proposal and yet, trying to conceal his feelings, he said, "I'm glad that you've found something after your heart. Tell us all that you felt and saw at Rasulabad."

Shahnaz recounted the details of her visit – the community centers run by Gayatri Devi and her unique personality; the selfless service she was rendering to the society; the respect that she commanded among her people and the efficiency with which she ran her organisation.

Rustom was all admiration but was surprised that Rahul was not quite satisfied with his lot. He enquired, "Where does Rahul fit in? He has immense merit but his objectives do not seem clear to me. I wonder if he will be able to put his merit to good use."

Shahnaz maintained a discreet silence but Zaroo could not help saying that Rahul was a darling and that he seemed to be trying to make a niche for himself in the top echelons of the society, by dint of his own merit. She added that she was sure he would realise his goal one day.

At the mention of Rahul's name, Shahnaz recalled that he had promised to take her to Samir uncle. She asked, "Is there any news about Samir uncle? I understand that of late he hasn't been keeping good health. I wasn't aware that he'd been posted at Rasulabad and that he had been very close to Rahul's family."

Rustom was not aware of the exact situation but he did know that all was not well at Samir's end. He confessed that he was guilty of not keeping track of Samir's health but added that he would make up for it during the weekend, when he would have some time to spare.

The next day Shahnaz slept till late in the morning. She had got into her bed after a long time and its comfort enveloped her like a long lost friend. She was roused by a call from Rahul. The telephone bell was indeed irritating but Rahul's cheery voice across the wire seemed to compensate. She saw the clock hanging on the wall and whispered into the telephone, "Hi, Rahul. I'm still in bed and it's past nine – time when I should be in the fields working on some project or the other." She laughed and continued, "How things change with the environment! I've already got back to my old routine."

He told her that he was going to see Samir uncle and if she too wanted to come, he would pick her up after an hour.

❖❖

Samir Saxena lived in a huge bungalow built over an area of three acres. It looked deserted and unkempt but it did give the impression of having seen better days. Seeing Rahul's car in the portico, an old servant who seemed to know him very well approached him and asked, "When did you come back from Rasulabad? I was hoping that you would come soon. *Saheb* is not well at all and he has been asking for you and Gayatri ji. I wanted to call you up but *Saheb* said that you were scheduled to come shortly anyway."

Rahul replied, "*Ram-Ram, Satai Kaka*. You should have contacted me, it's not advisable to delay in such matters."

Then pointing towards Shahnaz he said, "You know Shahnaz, don't you?"

Satai replied, "I've known Shahnaz bitiya since the time of her birth. Let us go to *Saheb*, he will be very happy to see you both."

On the way to Samir's room, Rahul told Shahnaz that Satai was also from Rasulabad and had been attending on Samir uncle ever since his posting there. He added that Satai's ancestors were retainers of Rahul's family and were treated like their own kith and kin. Satai ushered them into Samir Saxena's room and said, "*Saheb*, see who has come. Only this morning you told me you were missing him. "

Samir was lying in a large bed with a writing table laden with scrap of papers and reading materials by its side. The room had several book shelves filled with books occupying different corners. There was a sofa set with a coffee table, over-burdened by the weight of newspapers and magazines. The room was sparsely furnished but it was well-ventilated and neat. He seemed a little surprised to see Shahnaz, but nevertheless welcomed them both warmly. He got up to welcome the two visitors, hugged Rahul and gave Shahnaz a peck on the cheek. Moving towards the sofa he said, "Rahul, you have a long life. I was just thinking of you. And how is your mother?" And to Shahnaz he said, "Your visit is a bonanza. Least expected but indeed very refreshing."

She said that she had gone to Rasulabad and she had heard such good things about him there that she decided to come and see him.

Samir, despite his failing health, was in full possession of his famous wit. He said, “So I had to muster support from Rasulabad to earn a visit from you. I, by myself, am not good enough for it.”

Shahnaz too was not one to give in. She replied, “Here I know you as a great gentleman and an intellectual but there I came to know that you are a cult figure.”

They all laughed and moved to the sofa which had an old carpet under it. Samir asked Satai to organise some *nimboo-pani*. He instructed him to make it well because that was the first visit of Shahnaz to their house. Satai made himself scarce and Rahul said, “Uncle, you look pretty good. What is all this talk of your not being well?”

He said, “Don’t you know that at my age it is advisable to sham illness and attract attention? It’s just a part of the system. I’m alright, except that I declare myself ill when I get an urge to see someone dear to me. And what a great day today is? You’ve come and brought with you the *mademoiselle*.” Looking at Shahnaz, he said, “You must be all praise for Gayatri and her work. I hope you met Sita, and the two of you hit it off well!”

Shahnaz replied, “The community development work at Rasulabad is very inspiring. I’m toying with the idea of joining Sita as her apprentice. It would be great working with her. She is so capable and charming!”

Rahul told Samir in detail about all that was happening at Rasulabad and that development work at the centers was progressing well as per schedule. He added that they were all anxious about his health, especially because he had to bear everything single-handedly. He added that his mother was keen that Sita married and he was wondering whether Gyaneshwar would be a suitable match for her. He was aware that Samir had a special fondness for Sita.

Rahul's remark seemed to strike Samir like a bolt of lightning. He exclaimed, "What? I thought Sita's marriage to you was a foregone conclusion! Does Sita even know Gyaneshwar?" He glanced at Shahnaz quizzically.

Shahnaz had some idea what Rahul had in mind for Sita and Gyaneshwar but did not know that the thought had concretised enough to be discussed openly. She did think that Gyaneshwar and Sita would make a good couple. They were both idealists and both had similar education and exposure to public life. Although Gyaneshwar's father did not have a very clean image, he himself enjoyed a very good reputation. The two together would be great assets for Gayatri Devi and her work. Suddenly the thought that the proposed alliance might mar her chances of joining Gayatri Devi in her work at Rasulabad dawned upon Shahnaz and she felt a bit anxious.

Rahul told Samir, "Sita knows Gyaneshwar but I don't know if the thought of marrying him has ever occurred to her. Once I talk to Gyaneshwar, I'll talk to her about the proposal. Don't worry, Uncle, I'll make sure everything works out."

Samir was quiet for a while. In the meantime Satai walked in with some fruits and *nimboo-pani*, put them on the table and walked away. Samir said, "I'm sure you have Sita's interest upper most in your mind but don't do anything in a hurry. As far as I'm concerned the entire scenario seems to have undergone a sea change. But I'm sure Gayatri Devi and you are the best to decide. All I have to say is that Sita's consent in the matter is imperative. She is a darling and I've always looked upon her as a daughter."

Rahul asked him, "Has anything ever happened in our family without your concurrence? In this matter also nothing will be done without your explicit approval."

Samir remarked, "Gyaneshwar is a good boy. I like him but I was more partial to the earlier arrangement – the two of you made a perfect match." He got up to go to his bed, saying that he had a backache and wanted to lie down. Rahul remarked, "Playing sports keeps one healthy but can take its toll on the knees and the back. In your case Uncle, it has done both."

But Samir would have nothing said against sports. He said, "The pleasure that one derives from sports is worth any setback one might have to face at a later stage. And talking of setbacks, here comes the doctor." Satai had entered holding the bag of the doctor following him.

Seeing the doctor Samir said, "Come, come my friend. Your aura emits cheer, but it is also a reminder that all is not in the clear!"

The doctor was an old friend of Samir. He replied in the same mode, "Satai told me that you weren't quite well, but I find myself in the midst of a party. And how nice that it is so!"

Samir said, "I'm enjoying myself. Diabetes, blood pressure and heart problems have a direct bearing on the well being of a person and his station in life. And by God's grace I have had a very long innings of prosperity and success. The best part of all this is that I attract a lot of attention." They all laughed at his good humour.

"Ill-health is not the prerogative of the wealthy," remarked Rahul. "Haji ji has his own collection of rare ailments to boast of."

Sameer seemed to remember Haji ji. Going down memory lane he said in a distant voice, "Haji, I remember him. A very loyal ally, how is he?"

Shahnaz told Samir that Haji was also getting on in age but was still there and his brick business was thriving. She added that his children were also doing well. The doctor, done with his check-up, informed them that Samir was improving but suggested some more tests to decide the line of treatment. He asked for leave and said that he would make necessary arrangements to have the tests conducted. Rahul and Shahnaz too got up to take leave. Samir bade them goodbye and reminded Rahul to keep him abreast of developments regarding Gyaneshwar and Sita.

❖❖

Gyaneshwar was a fine young man. He was rooted in his culture but had enough exposure of the western world not to be bogged down with regressive Indian beliefs. Rahul had asked him for a time to meet him at his house but Gyaneshwar suggested that the club would be a more appropriate place to meet. So they met at the club over lunch. They found a quiet corner in the lounge, and both being teetotallers, ordered fruit juice. Once they settled down, Rahul started, "I returned from Rasulabad only the day before yesterday. There an idea struck me and I thought that I must discuss it with you at the earliest opportunity."

"Shoot," Gyaneshwar replied with a smile. "Flattered that you picked me to brainstorm with."

Rahul came to the point straight away, "Now that you're through with your education and have decided to settle down in India, you might be toying with the idea of getting married." After a pause he continued, "Have you already decided in favour of someone, or is the subject still open?"

Gyaneshwar was startled. He had not expected this subject to come up for discussion in his meeting with Rahul. He had always thought that Rahul did not believe in arranged marriages. He said, "Come on. This is a bolt from the blue. All I can say is that there is no Madonna in my life as yet. But you seem to have some plans for me. Go ahead."

Rahul wondered if he had opened the subject too abruptly. After a pause he said, "Well, it's common knowledge that you, being the only son of your parents, have very little choice insofar as your career is concerned. Your family needs you to manage its huge business and also its political legacy. And your not having anyone in mind for marriage makes my job easier."

Gyaneshwar had still not recovered from his shock. He said with a smile, "Well, real life is very different from what it appears to be. I'm not quite in agreement with my father's politics. I also have reservations about taking over his business but the underlying factor is that I love my parents immensely. They've always given me unstinted love and care after their own fashion. Notwithstanding my father's ways of handling his personal matters, the exposure he has provided me with has been greatly responsible for making me what I am today. My parents spared no pains to help me imbibe the right values in life. I think that while I may not like his business and politics, what I get by virtue of my birth I should accept without any inhibition, because inheritance is not a sin and the inheritor does not have to worry about the manner in which the wealth has been created. My father lives with his conscience and like me, he too has a right to make his own choice insofar as his style of functioning is concerned. So, as far as my financial position is concerned I'm on a sound footing, but my career is still quite undecided. I would much rather devote my time to making this world a better place, than to sit back on my haunches and add to the family wealth through business and politics. I find myself on the horns of a dilemma."

Rahul's face lit up. He thought he had struck the right chord with Gyaneshwar. He said, "What I have in mind might be the answer to your dilemma. You know Sita? She helps Ma in her community development projects. She is a highly accomplished and committed person. You have a lot in common with her and the two of you could carry on with the community development programs that seem to be so dear to you. But I realise that marriages are best decided by the boy and the girl after weighing all the pros and cons of the situation. I'm just making a suggestion and it is for the two of you to decide. Sita is not even aware of this. I'll inform her only after I know your mind."

Gyaneshwar maintained silence for a while, sipped the juice from his glass and then said, "Rahul, I hold you in high esteem and I really don't know what to say. But all that you have said baffles me because what I have heard from you is in complete contradiction to what I understand." He paused and continued, "Please forgive me, for I was under the impression that your mother brought Sita up and she was keen on getting her married to you. You too have a huge estate to manage and Sita is already entrenched in the business."

Now it was Rahul's turn to be baffled. He collected himself and spoke in a low voice, "Some of your observations are correct but not all. I've never looked upon Sita as anything but a close friend. Ma might have had some ideas about marrying me to her but believe me, it was a secret confined only to Ma. Sita assists her in her work. The huge estate as you call it, belongs to a trust which is a liability that Ma carries on her broad shoulders. What is left of the family estate just about suffices for Ma to take care of her personal needs. I'm doing ok at the bar but, living with one's principles, one can hardly make it big. My upbringing and the halo around the name of my family have put shackles around me. If I continue like this for long, I'm afraid at the end of the day I will have only my vanity to show for my efforts, because success seems to lie beyond me."

Rahul's explanation could hardly satisfy Gyaneshwar's anxiety. All that Rahul had said was in absolute contradiction to his own understanding of the subject. Although it was rumoured in certain quarters that the Modys were keen to marry Shahnaz to Rahul, the number of those ready to scotch the possibility on the grounds of it not being pragmatic was also sizeable. Rahul's talk gave him the impression that maybe he had veered around to the idea of marrying Shahnaz, and that was the reason he wanted Sita out of his way. What he could not fathom was the cause of Rahul's frustration with his life and career. He thought that he, like Vinay Khosla, was a man with very high values and a High Court judgeship was round the corner for him. That Rahul's life held an element of frustrated ambition was a revelation to him.

He decided to speak his mind without any reservations. "Rahul, pardon the impertinence, but may I ask if the rumour that you and Shahnaz are likely to tie the nuptial knot soon correct? Also, is it not true that you are doing well at the bar, having inherited the entire legal practice of Vinay uncle after he became a judge? Some believe that your becoming a High Court judge is a foregone conclusion."

Rahul kept his cool. He was on a delicate mission and tact was of the essence. Moreover, he believed that if there was a misunderstanding, it ought to be cleared. He said, "Of course we must be absolutely forthright with one another. The rumour, as you rightly call it, is entirely unfounded. Shahnaz and I are just good friends, nothing more, and nothing less. And your impression that I've made the proposal of Sita's marriage so that I can get Sita out of my way and marry Shahnaz is, to say the least, preposterous. I've made the proposal to you honestly with my conscience as clear as can be." He paused and continued, "Vinay was of very great help to me as a teacher and a patron but the nature of his practice was not such that it could be passed on from one person to another. Vinay had a very clean practice at the bar and his relationship with his clients was only professional, without any commitment of continuity. I'm doing alright in my profession but here, as in any other walk of life, merit has taken a backseat and many alternative routes to success have cropped up. There are no leading lawyers now; every court has a leading lawyer. I'm doing quite well, and as things stand today, I might very well be offered a Judgeship, but what happens after that? Another Vinay Khosla emerges – very honest, very upright and very poor. Unpopular for being unhelpful, with no one to espouse his cause, and frustrated because the fools are stealing a march over him in the journey to the Supreme Court. No sir, that's not what I call success."

Gyaneshwar was still not in-sync with all that Rahul had said. He did believe that Rahul was an honest man. He was also willing to accept what he had to say about his relationship with Sita, but he could not fathom the reason for Rahul's disappointment with his achievements. By his own admission he was doing well at the bar and in good time there was a possibility of his making it to the bench; then where was the place for disenchantment from life?

He told Rahul, "I must apologise for what I conjectured about your relationship with Sita. What I said was on the basis of hearsay, but as far as your career is concerned, by your own admission you are on the right track and you should be really happy. With your calibre and background, I have no doubt that you will reach the top of your profession and then become a judge."

Rahul spoke sarcastically, "Not that I can stake my claim on any extraordinary merit but please rest assured that the days when merit was a criterion for reaching the top of any profession are gone. Today there is a topper in every court and the topper changes each time the roster of the Bench changes."

Gyaneshwar was quite aware of the situation in the Indian courts. He said jocularly, "In that case, practicing law from the Bench may be more advisable than from the Bar."

Rahul smiled at the remark and continued, "Do give a thought to what I proposed to you about Sita. I shall talk to her only after knowing your mind. There may not be a ready 'yes' from her side because she is too committed to the work she has undertaken. The silver lining is that you also seem inclined to do what she is doing and the show can go on with the happy consent of both sides."

"The show at Rasulabad or the show at Delhi?" inquired Gyaneshwar, still facetious.

Rahul replied, "Both." They both got up to leave. Rahul told Gyaneshwar that he had to visit Samir who had been keeping indifferent health. Gyaneshwar requested him to convey his regards to Samir uncle and tell him that he too would visit him in a day or two.

❖❖

When Rahul reached the house of Samir Saxena, he was sitting in the verandah overlooking the large patches of grass that once used to be well-manicured lush green lawns. His face looked pinched and haggard but his eyes retained their old lustre. He received Rahul with a broad smile and pointing at the chair nearest to him asked him to sit down.

Rahul realised that Samir was in some kind of discomfort so in order to boost his morale he said, "The doctor told me that you had an uncomfortable night, but you look good. Uncle, you know many ways of attracting attention. Then why harass the poor doctor?"

Samir was not the one to give in. He said, "Let the doctor sweat for his money. I cannot allow him to fleece me without working for it. Let me assure you that not only do I look well, I also feel well. I'm in no hurry to go." They both laughed. Samir's serious mindedness did not come in the way of his ability to extract laughter from any situation, even his own failing health.

When the laughter subsided, Samir held Rahul's hand and said, "I'm glad to find you alone. I I couldn't speak my mind yesterday as Shahnaz was there. I must tell you that I was rather intrigued to hear that the proposal of your marriage with Sita is off. I was under the impression that it was all sealed, signed and delivered. What happened? Is Shahnaz the reason?" Suddenly he was looking unsettled and uncomfortable.

Rahul kept quiet. He was surprised that so many others knew of his mother's plans to get him married to Sita while he was totally oblivious of it. He wondered if people who seemed to be sure about Gayatri Devi's plans would even believe him if he told them the truth. And he found it most surprising that Gyaneshwar's conclusion that Shahnaz was the villain of the piece was the same as that of Samir Saxena.

Rahul released his hand from Samir's clasp, collected himself and said, "Uncle, as far as I am concerned I have always looked upon Sita as a close friend, the one I could confide in and whose support I could count on. But I have never thought of her as a beloved. Ma did surprise me by revealing her plans to me during my last visit to Rasulabad but when I apprised her of the reality, reasonable person that she is, she appreciated the situation and relented. And Shahnaz! What about her? She is just a friend." He stopped for a while and then started again. "Honestly Uncle, I don't intend marrying now. I'm way behind my target and I have a long way to go."

Samir had been listening to Rahul intently. He said, "I can understand your feelings about Sita and my conjecture about Shahnaz was obviously wrong, but what passes my comprehension is your statement that you are not prepared for marriage because, as you put it, you have a long way to go. What is the long way that you're talking about? Am I wrong in understanding that you have already made a niche for yourself at the Bar and that the leftover of the erstwhile Rasulabad estate is enough to fill the gap between what you have and what you aspire to have? Or is it that you are waiting to attain the age of retirement and then marry so that you can devote enough time to your wife, just to ensure that she does not feel neglected?"

Rahul could not help laughing. He said, "Uncle, you and your sense of humour are inseparable, but let me tell you that the so called Rasulabad estate is in debt and resources are fast dwindling. Whatever little income is generated from the properties does not suffice even for meeting Ma's personal requirements, however meagre they may happen to be. And the social work also takes its toll from time to time. At this rate, very soon, there may not be enough resources to maintain the *Haveli* in its present form."

Samir once again became serious. He did not have any idea about the finances of Gayatri Devi. He, like everybody else, thought that she was a very wealthy lady. Her austere life seemed to be in line with her philosophy and because of the austerity that she practiced, there did not seem to be any want in her life. He spoke haltingly, "That is indeed news, but assuming that all you say is correct, how long do you think you can wait to get married? There is a time for everything. A girl in your life may bring good luck to enable you to achieve your desires. Look at me, I missed the bus and I'm still waiting." And he laughed again, then was seized by a bout of severe coughing which subsided only after Rahul got up and caressed his back for a while. There was silence for some time and then he asked Rahul, "How did your meeting with Rajeshwar's son go? How did he react to your proposal about Sita? I do think that they have met before but how well they know each other, I do not know."

Rahul replied, "Yes, I met him and had a frank talk with him. He too was very frank and had the same apprehensions as you did regarding Sita and Shahnaz. But when I apprised him of the reality, he understood the situation. He is open to the idea but such things naturally take time. He said that he knew Sita quite well and I told him that I had broached the matter with him without Sita's knowledge, and would speak with her only after knowing his mind. We parted without any commitment. Let him think it over for some time, and if I find that he is open to the idea, I will speak with Ma and Sita. The final decision would naturally rest with Sita and Gyaneshwar."

Samir enquired, "You seem to be making good progress. But Rajeshwar might be sceptical about the parentage of Sita – about her being an orphan."

Rahul replied, "That is not an issue at all. Rajeshwar ji has no qualms about it. He knows that Sita has been brought up by Ma and would only be too happy to have her in the family."

Samir became visibly relaxed. He said, "That was one aspect that was bothering me. You know the politicos are very concerned about the public reaction to their image and our society has yet to learn to be objective and broad minded. I must say that you've handled the matter very deftly and all will be well. Please do let me know about Sita's reaction to the proposal after you have discussed it with her. I'm not too sure if she will agree because from all I know, her commitment to Gayatri and her work is impregnable."

Rahul got up to take his leave. He told him to take care of his health and assured him that he was always at his beck and call. Samir beckoned him to stay back and continued, "I think I'm in a position to offer you some advice. Let me tell you that marriage has a direct relation with love, and there should not be any confusion about it having any bearing on one's financial situation. Nothing gets precedence over love. The kind of money you apparently have in mind comes only when it is destined. Chasing money only makes a person base and tempts him to get into trouble. The endeavour for making money by honest means must continue, but it may not be possible to synchronise the date of arrival of wealth in your life with the date of arrival of your bride. A person with your qualities of head and heart has to realise his ambitions sooner than later without having to overly worry for no one has been able to control the tide of time."

Rahul was indeed touched by Samir Saxena's genuine solicitude. How wonderful that in spite of his failing health he was so intensely concerned about the well-being of others. But he did have reservations about his observation that wealth could be created by honest means also. All he had experienced was that honesty lead to poverty and that it was not really natural to human character.

He got up saying, "I agree with most of the things you've said, Uncle. The day I find my love, I will marry her but before that you'll have to be fighting fit and teach me to create wealth in an honest manner. My forefathers amassed enormous wealth but I doubt if all that they did to do that could be construed as honest." And he left, promising to return on the following day. At the time of leaving he asked Satai, who was standing in a corner, to keep a constant vigil on Samir and call him the moment a need arose.

Rahul went home and informed Gayatri Devi over the phone about his talk with Gyaneshwar. He suggested that she sound out Sita about the proposal and gauge her reaction. He said he would talk further about the matter with Gyaneshwar after knowing her mind on the subject. He also told her that Sita and Gyaneshwar had already met and were quite familiar with each other. About Samir, he told her that the report of the doctors about his health was not very encouraging but that he was his usual, hearty self. Gayatri Devi was not expecting any good news about Samir, but this was the first time that the reality of Sita going away dawned upon her. At the end of the telephone call, Gayatri Devi found herself irritated with Rahul. Helplessness leads to irritation and an irritated mind looks out for a scapegoat to put the blame on. In this case she, in her mind, put the blame for the possibility of Sita leaving her on Rahul. She put the telephone down with a request that Rahul not spare any time and resources to ensure that the best medical facilities were provided for Samir.

❖❖

When Rahul got a message that Vinay Khosla wanted to see him in his chamber, he was surprised at the apparent formality of the request. He had been visiting him very frequently at his residence and they were like family. It was common knowledge that Vinay Khosla was his mentor. When Rahul entered Justice Vinay Khosla's chamber, he was sitting all alone with a grim face. Rahul asked him, "Sir, what is this honour in aid of? I hope all is well."

Khosla replied, "If all was well I would not have summoned you to my chamber. I have something important to discuss with you. How was your visit to Rasulabad and how are your wonderful mother and Sita?"

Rahul told him that they were doing as well as ever. He also told him that he wanted to come over to his house and seek his advice about a proposal he had conceived for Sita's marriage.

Vinay Khosla's reaction to this news was exactly the same as that of Gyaneshwar and Samir Saxena. He asked, "Is Shahnaz the cause of a change of plan?"

Rahul laughed and said, "I'm surprised at such universal unanimity of impression. All my well-wishers seem to be thinking on the same lines. I don't know where this impression has germinated from, but let me make it clear to you that I don't do anything important without discussing it with you first, and since there has been no discussion between the two of us on the subject, there has been no such development in my life. I have never harboured any romantic inclinations toward Sita or Shahnaz."

Vinay said, "My impression about Sita was just a logical conclusion, duly confirmed by your mother, and I mentioned Shahnaz's name because of late you have often been seen in her company."

Rahul told Vinay that he was aware of the confusion that his mother had unknowingly created regarding Sita. He said that he wanted to make sure that no further misunderstanding was created with regard to his friendship with Shahnaz and clarified again that she was just a friend.

Vinay thought he should not waste any more time and broached the subject for which he had called Rahul. He said, "I've called you for something very important. I've come to know that some of the *members* of the Bar, who have been my friends in the past, have been trying to take advantage of my being on the Bench. I want you to discreetly find out if there is any truth in the rumours." After a pause he said, "I know that the entire judicial system has collapsed, the lawyers are having a field day and the judges are contributing in their own way to perpetuate the rot. But what I was told the other day concerns me directly and I thought that there could not be a better person than you to find out the facts." He halted and added further, "I would like to caution you too, to take extra care to ensure that your name is not sullied in the profession, because your forefathers have built a name for the family after centuries of dedicated work and toil. Your mother is still at it and I must confess, I admire her for this."

Rahul was very free and informal with Vinay. Vinay's elevation to the Bench had made no difference in the personal equation between the two. He kept quiet for a moment and then, after readjusting his position in the chair he said, "Most lawyers are sitting idle in the bar room and their indulgence in idle gossip is understandable. But your reaction to the gossip may not be fair. In our High Court, judges often hear cases argued by their relatives and by lawyers who were their former colleagues before their elevation to the Bench. Moreover, it's well known that a lawyer cannot derive any favour from the court unless the judge wants to extend it, and it is also widely accepted that no one can extract an unfair order from your court, regardless of who appears before you. Sir, I think you're getting unnecessarily worked up about a non-issue."

Vinay Khosla was unmoved even though he was listening intently. Rahul sensed that he was not cutting any ice. He chuckled and continued, "With your long experience at the Bar as well as at the Bench, you're well aware that it's very difficult to succeed in the profession and at the same time ensure that tongues do not wag. I think your reputation is good enough to protect you against any mudslinging." Vinay remained quiet and Rahul felt encouraged to continue. He said, "I'm also keen to build a good reputation for myself in line with that of my family. But to say that reputations are built on the foundation of honesty and integrity may not be quite correct. Yes, hard work has always been an integral part of success. My family is respected because my ancestors were very rich. Then once they became wealthy, other things followed – power, credibility and respectability."

Vinay could not help admiring the manner in which Rahul was tackling the subject. With a back handed compliment to him he was also trying to justify that all was fair in the pursuit of success. He wondered whether he was preparing a defence for himself, as his appearances in his court had increased noticeably.

Vinay spoke in his lawyer's baritone, "Rahul, a democratic society is different from a feudal society. In a democratic society the area of visibility is very high and if tongues wag they can't be ignored. They have to be answered. All orders of a court may not always be right and in the event of an order not being right, the integrity of the judge may fall under the scanner. I have cautioned you also because I consider you to be a very bright lawyer with considerable abilities to contribute to nation-building. I want you to channelize your energies in the right direction. I'm sure you understand what I mean."

Rahul couldn't understand what was at the back of Vinay's mind. He even thought that Vinay was being impolite. On the one hand he said he was going to entrust him with a certain personal investigation, and on the other he was hinting that Rahul too needed to mend his ways. He said, "I appreciate your anxiety about putting matters right but I do get the impression that you've found my conduct to be wanting."

"I haven't come across anything inappropriate in your behaviour," Vinay said, "except that of late you've started appearing in my court a couple of times daily." He continued, "There's no bar on doing well at the Bar, especially for a person like you, who has been endowed with all the traits for success. But one would do well to be continuously conscious of keeping ones reputation intact. Your integrity is the last thing I can suspect but certain very disquieting facts have come to my notice, and I find myself in a quandary. I've decided that as a good gesture to my old friends in the profession, and in the interest of continuing my friendship with them I must take certain measures. You being the closest to me, I thought you should be the first to be alerted."

Vinay was obviously relieved to be able to speak of things he had been struggling to bring up. He further added, "Greed is inherent in human nature and every person has his price, but fixing one's price at a level that interested parties are willing to pay makes a beast out of a human being. Many disconcerting incidents have been reported to me, but today I'll confide in you about one friend whose name I leave for you to guess. He had been my colleague at the Bar and our friendship remained unchanged even after my elevation. Sometimes I discuss law points with him generally to clear my own mind, and I understand that during our personal interactions he tries to gauge my mind about certain matters pending my decisions in the court. On the basis of that, he communicates to the interested litigants the outcome of the case, and claims the credit if the outcome is in the litigants' favour. I also understand that one day, while a litigant was parked in the car outside my house, he came in and 'inadvertently' left his briefcase behind, which was collected by him the following day thus giving the litigant the impression that a briefcase full of currency notes was given to me by him on behalf of the litigant. My order in the matter was as expected or, shall I say, as predicted by him because he had discussed the legal side of the matter with me in detail and was fully familiar with my opinion on the subject."

Vinay seemed both hurt and upset at the conduct of some of his friends. He remarked contemplatively that he had heard that some lawyers practiced from outside the courts, because in that case, there was no ceiling on their remunerations and also there was always a possibility to switch sides should a need for it arise. Rahul realised that, considering the delicacy of the situation, he had to tread with utmost caution. He could not readily identify the person Vinay was talking about but he did not find the incident unusual. Leaving something behind and collecting it the following day from a friend's house was not uncommon. He told Vinay that he had no idea about such things happening, but he promised to do his best to find out the truth and get back to him.

Vinay warned Rahul that knowledge of such events was likely to upset his wife and therefore the matter should not be discussed with her. He enquired from Rahul about the health of Samir Saxena and told him that Samir had sent him a message that he wanted to see him. He suggested that Rahul should fix up a time for him to go visit Samir. Rahul promised to do the needful and left.

He reached home quite disturbed. He could not appreciate the role of investigator that Vinay had assigned to him. He was also sceptical about the advice he had offered to him about his own conduct. He wondered if Vinay had anything specific against him but then rejected the idea. "If he had anything specific against me he would not have entrusted me with the assignment."

While he was pondering over his meeting with Vinay, he received a call from Samir Saxena's residence. Satai was at the other end. He said, "Rahul *baba*, I've wanted to get in touch with you for some time but you were not at home. *Saheb* has your cell number but he told me not to bother you while you were away."

Rahul said, "I'll give you the number of my cell phone when I come to your place but what is it that you wanted me so urgently for? I hope all is well at your end."

Satai said, "Everything is alright now but last night *Saheb* was very uncomfortable and restless. I called the doctor, who was here till *Saheb* could retire to sleep. He is still asleep but last night he was asking for you and Vinay *Saheb*."

Rahul requested Satai to let him know when Samir woke up and telephoned the doctor to find out what had happened.

The doctor said, "You have a long life. I was going to dial your number just this minute. The problem is that the old man has not accepted that he's old and that his heart is less than robust. He does not take the medicines regularly and Satai is too weak to prevail upon him to take due care. Today his blood pressure went down to fifty over seventy. With the malfunctioning of the heart it could be fatal. Thank God that I got the message in time and reached him before it was too late. I'm on my way to his house again but I strongly feel that he should be hospitalised without any delay. Of course, he has been resisting this tooth and nail. Only you can persuade him to go to the hospital and that is what I wanted to speak to you about."

Rahul said, "I'm surprised that I wasn't informed about the development immediately. I'm also heading to his house. In the meantime please make all arrangements to hospitalise him because if that is imperative, it should not be delayed."

❖❖

When Rahul reached Samir Saxena's house, the doctor was sitting in the inner patio and Satai was standing beside him with a grim face. The doctor told Rahul that Samir was quite stable and was still asleep. He also told him that he had booked a room for him in the Apollo Hospital and that he could be moved there any time. While the doctor was apprising Rahul of the condition the call bell from Samir Saxena's room rang. Satai went inside and put on the lights. The doctor, along with Rahul, also entered the room. Samir was surprised to see the doctor as well as Rahul at that time of the day. He thought it was morning and that he had slept through the night. He said in his usual manner, "Having the doctor visit you in the morning is not a very good sign. I hope I'm alright."

Rahul replied in the same vein, "With this doctor around how can you be anything else but alright? It is six in the evening and we have come to have tea with you."

Samir realised that there was something amiss. If it was six in the evening, why had he just woken up from sleep? Then he realised that he was feeling weak and a bit uneasy but before he could say anything further the doctor went to him and felt his pulse. He asked him to take deep breaths and examined him with the stethoscope. He also measured his blood pressure and pronounced that the worst was over. Samir repeated what the doctor had pronounced and said, "Let us celebrate over a cup of tea." He asked Satai, who was standing nearby, to organise some tea for everyone.

Tea was served but the doctor insisted that Samir should have it in bed and, surprisingly, he agreed to do so. While sipping tea, Rahul said, "Uncle, you were slightly indisposed this morning but luckily the doctor could be contacted immediately and he has brought the situation under control. If there was any delay in contacting the doctor and bringing him here things could have gone out of hand."

Samir, trying to brush it off, said, "Ok, now that the situation is under control, let us enjoy the cup of tea."

Rahul didn't want to communicate the correct situation to him for fear of upsetting him, knowing little that he was fully aware of the exact situation and was putting up a brave front because he did not want others to get anxious on his behalf.

Rahul said, "Uncle, the doctor is of the view that although your ailment is common in nature, you do need continuous medical attention and therefore we have decided to move you to the hospital for a while. The doctor may not be on call all the time and a situation where the doctor is needed and is not available must be avoided."

Samir asked, "And what happens if the situation gets out of control? Can the inevitable be deferred? Yes, by moving me out of my home and hearth you will certainly make me uncomfortable but I'm sure that is not what you want." He smiled and continued, "You are at liberty to move this house to the hospital or move the hospital to this house but for God's sake, do not move me from here. I'm very happy being here and any dislocation will disturb my peace."

Rahul appreciated Samir's sentiments which he had expressed

earlier as well. He said, "Since you insist on staying at home, we will not move you to a hospital but you will have to promise to take the medicines as per the doctor's advice, as and when given to you by Satai."

Samir looked sternly at Satai and asked, "Who has given you the impression that I don't follow the doctor's orders? Satai will tell you that I follow the doctor's advice to the last letter." Satai with a pliant smile nodded.

When the doctor left and Samir was alone with Rahul he asked him, "Have you been able to find out Sita's reaction to your idea of her marrying Gyaneshwar? She may agree to marry him but her relocation from Rasulabad may be the stumbling block. She would resist parting from her work and your mother."

It suddenly struck Rahul that Samir was taking an unusual interest in Sita's marriage, but instead of finding out the reason for it he decided to make use of the opportunity to involve him more deeply in the proceedings. He said, "Uncle, I've already spoken to Ma about it. She must be on the job, but I also envisage the same problems that you do, in Sita making up her mind." He suggested, "Why do you not speak to Ma over the phone? She has been very anxious about you and she'll be very happy to hear from you directly. You could speak to her about Sita also."

Samir received the suggestion with alacrity and asked Rahul to connect him to his mother. Gayatri Devi was very happy to receive a call from Samir. She said, "I'm very happy to hear from you. I will not waste my time telling you to take care of yourself because I know that wouldn't make any difference to you. But I do think I have a right to know the exact condition of your health."

Samir never lost his touch of humour. He said, "I'm glad to note that your capacity for affectionate tongue-lashing is still intact. I've been missing it all these days. Having tasted it now, though in a very small measure, I've already started feeling better."

She softened her tone and said, "Alright, if that is your medicine you will get it in abundance every morning from me, but tell me exactly how you feel?"

He replied, "Gayatri, you know I've always had a sensitive heart which keeps playing truant from time to time. I have no control over it. When it misbehaves, the doctors put me in bed for some time till I'm alright. Otherwise I have no problem. But tell me, how has the plan of Rahul's marriage with Sita undergone a change?"

She was familiar with his peculiar way of communicating very serious matters in a humorous way. She said, "Your information about the change in my plans for Rahul's marriage is correct. Rahul is not interested in marriage for the time being." .

Samir was quite informal with her. He asked, "And what are Sita's views on marriage?"

Gayatri Devi had drawn a blank from Sita when she had made the proposal to her to marry Gyaneshwar, but the reason was not that she was against marriage. She was against leaving her work and going away from Rasulabad. She said, "She is ambivalent about marriage but she would certainly consider it if she finds a suitable boy here. But Samir, tell me about your health. Do you feel weak and restless, maybe nauseous at times?"

He replied, "I feel alright generally. When I am less than alright the doctors, under Rahul's orders, put me in bed and allow me out only after I'm back to my usual self. But tell me, how on earth can Sita find a suitable boy for herself there? Rahul told me about his talk with Gyaneshwar in this connection and I do think that Gyaneshwar is a very fine boy."

Gayatri Devi told him that the desirability of Gyaneshwar was not in dispute, the problem was Sita's insistence on not leaving Rasulabad. She further mentioned that she too was not happy at the thought of Sita leaving her, but since all girls had to leave their homes to go and live with the husband, she had reconciled to the idea with a heavy heart. Tears trickled down Samir's eyes when he told her that he appreciated the delicacy of the situation and he was confident she would handle the matter in the best possible manner. He suggested that she visit him in Delhi at her convenience as he had some urgent matters to discuss with her. She told him that she would certainly visit him the following week and once again reinforced her request that he should take care of his health.

As she put down the receiver, her mind went back to the days when her husband was alive and Samir Saxena was posted at Rasulabad as a young officer. They were great friends. She recalled that Sam was a *bon vivant*, who wore his heart on his sleeve. He was a real charmer with the ladies, though he never married. She thought that the lack of marriage should have caused some bitterness in him, but mercifully he did not allow negative emotions any place in his life.

Samir wiped off his tears and, feeling a bit embarrassed, told Rahul that talking to his mother after such a long time brought back old memories. Rahul had never seen him in a position of weakness and he attributed his tears to his failing health. He assured him that his nostalgia was understandable.

When Rahul got up to leave, Samir asked him to visit him sometime with Vinay Khosla as he had something very important to discuss with them. He said that he wanted to write his last will and needed some legal assistance. Rahul left saying that he would visit him every day and that he would bring Vinay also as soon as possible. He added that he would assist in writing his last will.

Next morning Rahul saw Vinay in his chamber and after apprising him of Samir's health, mentioned that he wanted to see them both. He suggested that they visit him during the weekend. Vinay told Rahul that he was going out of station that evening and would be back only after a week. He pointed out to him that if it was only the will, Rahul could handle it without any assistance but added that he would certainly like to see Samir on his return.

Samir seemed to be well rested and much better than when Rahul had seen him last. When told that Vinay could not visit as he had to go out of station, he accepted it without any regret. He said, "Just as well! Before writing the will I want to let you into a secret of my life and it can be best done alone."

Rahul knew that Samir's life was like an open book except the alleged torrid love affair in which he had been jilted. He guessed that perhaps he wanted to share knowledge about that part of his life with him, but he could not connect Samir's lost love to his will. Moreover, he was not aware of any sizeable estate that he was likely to leave behind. He was under the impression that he lived on his pension and the house he lived in would go to some charity or the other on his demise. In fact, he thought that there was hardly any scope for discussion or work on his will. He kept quiet.

In a pensive mood, Samir closed his eyes and started, "The will is just an excuse. When I did not ever care for what I possessed in this world, why should I bother about what happens to my belongings after I am dead and gone? And I don't have much in any case. I have had a very good life and in turn I've tried to give back as much to life as I got from it. Normally I should have been very content but it has not been so. I have been living with a guilty conscience and I can't find a better person than you to confess my guilt." Tears welled into his eyes.

Rahul had never seen Samir in this condition. He was conscious of the fact that an excess of emotion was not the best thing for a heart patient, but since Samir had started he thought it best to allow him to unburden himself. He kept quiet and Samir continued, "I've been watching her from a distance but I could not come out in the open because she was very happy and was shaping out well. I didn't want to upset the apple cart for fear of causing unnecessary upheaval in the beautiful world that had been carved out around her. I thought that the idea of her marriage with you was God-sent, something that would have put an end to my anxiety for all times. But that was not to be!"

Rahul felt lost. He was unable to make out the meaning of all that Samir was saying. He said, "Uncle, what you are saying is Greek to me but I'd certainly like to do whatever I can to soothe your nerves. Ma did mention to me that in your younger days you fell in love with someone who jilted you, and ever since then you've been living with just her memory. Is that what is pricking your conscience?"

With his voice barely audible and tears coursing down his face, Samir said, "I have never intended to be unfair to anyone in my life but I could not defy destiny."

Rahul was getting more and more puzzled. He asked, "Is the lady still alive, and what's her connection to me?"

Samir said, "The tale goes back to my Rasulabad days. I was a bachelor and my house used to be run by the staff. The epidemic of cholera took its toll on my cook and I was left high and dry. There was no dearth of cooks but I wanted someone par excellence. Your mother suggested that I employ Haji's sister who, besides being a very good cook, also had a fair idea of western and Chinese cuisine. She told me that Farah was very well versed in Urdu, and later on I found out that she was a poet and had a basic knowledge of English, good enough to carry on a simple conversation in small sentences. Your mother also told me that Farah was not the typical cook and that she could make an excellent house keeper."

Rahul suddenly found himself at the edge of his chair, listening with rapt attention. In fact he was getting impatient to hear the end of the tale. He thought of the gossip he had come across in Rasulabad about Samir Saxena's transfer under a cloud.

Samir continued, "I was apprehensive about the idea of a lady cook in a bachelor household but the idea of a housekeeper of the description that your mother gave seemed tempting. I told her to send Farah and Haji ji to see me. When they came, Farah was wearing a *burqa*. She spoke from behind her mask but sounded very articulate and courteous. The arrangement however could not mature because Haji was not keen on her taking up a full time job. He said that he wanted an engagement for her for a few hours in a day, because she was hell bent on not marrying. She considered marriage to be nothing short of slavery for the wife. To my question as to why he did not consider educating her, he said that she had passed the matriculation examination and that in their community girls were barred from college education. I told Haji that I was looking for a full time help and they left."

Rahul asked, "So she did not take up the job? I was also wondering why Haji ji's sister should have been looking for a domestic job. After all he was always well off."

But Samir was not finished. "I decided to make do with my old staff and the orderlies but the household was in disarray. One day, when I was narrating my tale of woe to your mother, she suggested that I employ Farah for four hours a day and see if she was able to put things in order." He smiled and continued, "I agreed to take her in on the condition that she shed off her *burqa* that was a part of her ensemble. Your mother told me that she would send her to me the following day and she arrived as per the arrangement. This time she was not with Haji ji and the *burqa* was also missing. I set eyes on her for the first time and until my orderly told me who she was I could not recognise her. She looked like an epitome of goodness and grace. She told me that your mother had already explained to her the nature of her work, and that I had to only tell her what I wanted done. I told her to take care of the household and told my orderly to show her the house and take her to her room. I further told her to take things easy and take her own time to familiarise herself with the ways of the household. She spoke very little but there was something in her personality that inspired confidence. She started working and soon took over the entire household. I hardly had any direct communication with her but I got everything I wanted – nicely washed and pressed clothes, polished shoes, the right socks and ties, the food of my choice, and all this without any fuss. The arrangement of her working for four hours a day was only for the record. She never allowed any work to suffer and remained in the house till her work was performed to her own exacting standards. I found her amazing."

Rahul was in a daze. "Incredible," he remarked.

Samir continued, "'Incredible' is the right word for her. When I had an attack of jaundice the doctors suggested that I would be best looked after in a hospital. But she put her foot down. She said that there was a fully established household at my beck and call. I was deeply touched by her statement that if the master, during his illness, could not be looked after at home, then there was no point in his spending so much money on the staff. She came to me and most importunately requested that I should not move out to the hospital. I succumbed to her request and I must say, I was looked after by her better at home than I could have been at any hospital. Your mother, who was in constant touch with me during my illness, told me that even she could not have done a better job of nursing me. The routine of her going back to her home after the day's work had to be abandoned. Everybody had a word of appreciation for her but some tongues started wagging. After all, why so much devotion to a stranger?"

Samir told Rahul that after he recovered from his illness, he offered her a monetary reward in appreciation of her services but she declined to accept it saying that he, being her employer, had the option of using her time in any manner he wanted. There was no extra reward due, she had declared, to a servant who did her job well. She said that her biggest reward was that I had recovered fully from my illness and that her services were appreciated."

Rahul remarked, "I'm not surprised."

Samir said, "But I was. I couldn't understand how someone could be so devoted. The only answer I could get from within was that she was a very sincere and committed person. Your mother was in full agreement with me, but she had her reservations about Farah spending the night in my house. She suggested that once I had recovered my health the old arrangement should be put in order. She warned that with Farah being so dedicated, her hours of proximity to me could cause undue attachments. And by doing so it was she who unconsciously sowed the seed of my love for Farah. I started wondering why Farah could not be my life partner?"

Rahul could not help asking, "Was she beautiful?"

A gentle smile spread over Samir's weakened face. He replied, "How could a person with such competence, sincerity and devotion not be beautiful? Yes, she was very beautiful and the best part was that she wasn't even aware of it."

Rahul asked, "If you were so enamoured of her, why did you not marry her? I understand you were very eligible and Farah could not have been oblivious of that fact."

Samir hesitated for a while and said, "She was perhaps aware that she had a special place in my life, but on my part I didn't have the courage to express my love to her." He said that gradually Farah stopped going home after the day's work, and started spending all her time at his place.

Rahul was surprised to hear this, because he thought that this change in Farah's schedule must have caused raised eyebrows. But Samir explained to him that she had been spending nights in his house before as well, and it was well known that she was the house keeper of the Saxena establishment. Also, he said, in those days the society was so class-conscious that any kind of intimacy between the master and the maid was inconceivable. Samir told Rahul that one day he asked Farah whether she would like to live with him permanently. She had replied that as far as she was concerned, she had decided to serve him all his life unless he had reservations about it. Samir said that, encouraged by her statement, he mustered courage and asked her, "Do you know what that means?"

She replied in a tone that said that she understood all the implications. She said, "Let us talk only of what is possible. I'm at your service for life, nothing less and nothing more." Then, reciting the following couplet she slowly withdrew,

'A wave lives but for a moment
On the bosom of the ocean deep
And whispers its secrets for a while
For the ocean to forever keep.'

That was the first time Samir had got an inkling that Farah had an interest in poetry. Later he discovered that she herself was a poet of substance. The incident did not bring about any change in Farah's attitude except that she reverted to her old routine of going back to her home for the night. Farah's ambivalence to the idea that Samir had sown in her mind impressed him all the more, because it would have most likely turned the head of any other girl in her place.

Samir continued, "One day it was raining cats and dogs and I developed a high temperature. She decided to stay back for the night to nurse me. The fever turned into typhoid and Farah had to alter her daily routine again. She and I became even closer to each other during my illness and one day, while I was in the process of recovering, our closeness turned into intimacy. I reiterated my desire to marry her but she turned it down on the grounds that it wasn't practical. The defeatist in me prevailed upon me to agree to her suggestion, because I too was aware of the possible aftermath of such an incident. I said to myself that I would marry her if the need for marriage arose. The idea was perhaps to avoid immediate turbulence."

Rahul was getting restive. He knew very well that there was no marriage in the life of Samir Saxena, so he asked, "What finally became of her and your intimacy with her?"

He said, "I appreciate your impatience. The long and short of it is that Sita was born and Farah passed away while delivering her."

Rahul looked as if he had been struck by lightning. He asked, "Which Sita are you referring to and where is this Sita?"

Samir calmly replied, "She is the one you call your childhood buddy."

There was pin drop silence for a while. Rahul could not believe his ears. A storm of thoughts, recollections, and emotions prevented speech. Samir continued, telling him that when Farah became pregnant, he again proposed to her but she turned him down saying that they would take a decision once the child was born. But when the child was born she had gone too far away to get married.

He told Rahul that she was keen that the child should not be born at Rasulabad and therefore she secretly left Rasulabad and shifted to this house in Delhi, where she breathed her last. He said that sometimes he wondered whether she deliberately planned her end, to avoid the ignominy of giving birth to a child outside marriage. He told Rahul how he had felt depressed and guilty and thought that his world had come to an end. He would have ended his life, but could not do so because he now had the responsibility of bringing up a daughter. Rahul continued to struggle with emotions he had never experienced before.

Samir continued, 'I took Sita to Rasulabad with the help of one Dr. M.A. Wood, an English lady who specialised in maternity services. I was aware of the daily routine of Diwan Mithai Lal. So I put Sita, wrapped in a bundle of clothes, on the steps of the temple and watched the entire episode from a distance. I kept a close surveillance on the subsequent developments and, in my own way, put in my two cents into her upbringing, mainly because of my proximity to your parents."

Rahul asked, "Why didn't you own up Sita as your daughter?"

Samir replied, "That's a good question. I didn't own her up because I found her well ensconced in the Rasulabad setup and I wasn't sure if disturbing her was right. Moreover, I had very little to offer in comparison to what she had in Rasulabad."

Rahul asked him if he still wanted the status quo to continue. Samir said that the reason for spilling the beans to him was to make a clean breast of everything. He said he was aware that he had very little time left in this world, and that Sita was mature enough to appreciate the situation and deal with the emotional upheaval that was likely to follow such news. He felt that the time had come to tell everyone. He said that before writing the will he wanted to apprise Rahul of the true situation for obvious reasons.

Rahul realised that in this situation Samir needed his company for the evening, but he also wanted to break the news to his mother immediately. Considering Samir's state of health it was imperative that Sita should be told the truth at the earliest. He suggested that Samir speak to Gayatri Devi over the phone and after telling her the truth, speak to Sita directly. Samir hesitated for a while and then said, "Alright, connect me to Gayatri."

Rahul got her on the line and handed over the phone to Samir. Gayatri Devi was very happy to hear Samir's voice, because she was under the impression that he was bedridden and not in a position to communicate. He assured her that he was improving and handed over the phone to Rahul, saying that her son had something very important to tell her. Rahul took the phone to the adjoining room and spoke to his mother for almost half an hour. Considering the delicacy of the situation, Gayatri Devi told Rahul that it was not advisable for Samir to break the news to Sita directly. She offered to speak to her in her own way, in due course.

When Rahul came back to Samir's room, he told him that he was sorry he could not muster enough courage to speak with his mother and asked him if he had spoken to Sita directly on the subject. Samir had a sense of relief when Rahul told him that his mother dissuaded him from speaking to Sita and told him that it was advisable that she herself disclose the secret to her. The dinner was quiet. Rahul left after dinner with the parting remark that all would be well and that Samir had an added responsibility now to take care of his health. Samir laughed and said, "Ok, ok. And please follow up the proposal with Gyaneshwar. Now you know why I am so involved in this."

Sita's Turmoil

When Rahul had spoken with Gayatri Devi, the *Haveli* had been almost empty. Sita had gone to see her mother and the servants were inside the kitchen. Gayatri Devi was stunned to hear this news. What surprised her most was that Samir, in spite of being close to her, did not consider it fit to apprise her of such a major event. She went to her prayer room and closeted herself to decide her course of action. She had to break the news to Sita very delicately for obvious reasons. Going down memory lane, certain incidents did come to her mind when Samir had shown an unusual interest in the upbringing of Sita, but back then it did not occur as misplaced because Samir was known to be a kind man who wanted to do good to all. She was not even sure if it was advisable to let the secret out to Haji ji and his family. Knowing Sita's honest nature, she had no doubt that she would not like to shroud any part of her life in secrecy. She was also worried about the reaction of Diwan Mithai Lal and his wife. After all, they were Sita's legal parents and they might not be happy at the prospect of someone else staking his claim on her after all these years. She decided that the first step was to tell Sita.

Having decided on a course of action, she retired to her room and instructed the servants to send Sita to her when she came. Sita did not come to the *Haveli* for dinner that evening. Gayatri Devi went through the motions of dinner with half an apple and a glass of milk. She wanted to sleep lightly to prepare for the visitation of her husband's spirit that she felt sure would come to guide her in her hour of need.

Sita came to the *Haveli* in the morning. She used to meet Gayatri Devi at the breakfast table, but having come to know from the servants that Gayatri Devi had retired early and had a very frugal dinner, she went straight to the prayer room where she found her in deep meditation. She waited until she opened her eyes. To Sita's query if all was well, Gayatri Devi gave her an affectionate smile and holding her by her waist said, "How can anything go wrong with you by my side?"

They went to the corner patio where she had told the servants to lay the breakfast. Sitting across from her, Sita asked, "I understand that you retired early last evening and had very little dinner."

Gayatri Devi replied, "I'm in perfect health. Rahul spoke with me last evening over the phone and I could not remain unexcited after what he told me."

Sita did not think it necessary to ask what Rahul had said, because she knew that Gayatri Devi would tell her all about the conversation on her own. But being well aware of Rahul's equation with his mother, she did conjecture that he must have said something that was at variance with her values.

Sipping tea Gayatri Devi asked Sita, "I want your help to understand a social problem. Tell me, is there anything you miss in life?"

Sita was not prepared for this question. She thought that Gayatri Devi wanted to broach the subject of her marriage with Gyaneshwar again. She said, "Ma, haven't you made sure that there is nothing wanting in my life? I'm very happy in my present situation. I've already made it clear to you that for the moment there's no one in my mind for marriage and also even if I get married, I wouldn't like to snap my ties with the work I have been doing with you."

Gayatri Devi realised that indirect questions might not bring the right answers from Sita. She asked her directly, "Don't you ever think about your biological parents and do you not miss them?"

This was a bolt from the blue. The thought of having any parents other than Savitri Rani and Dewan Mithai Lal had seldom crossed Sita's mind. She was aware that they were not her real parents but they gave her so much love and care that she could not imagine anything better. Moreover, the patronage of Gayatri Devi, laced with enormous love and affection, had served as icing on the cake. She thought for a while and said, "Ma, it wouldn't be honest if I say that I've never thought of my natural parents, but I cannot say that I've ever missed them. At the same time, I don't know of anyone who is the recipient of more love and care than I have been. Suffice it to say that I would consider myself lucky if I'm able give to my child as much as my parents have given me. And your own contribution to my life has also been that of a mother and more. I have ended up having two mothers, both equally affectionate and caring. How can I ask for more?"

Gayatri Devi had already decided to talk straight. She asked, "How would you react if you were told that your parents were alive and that they wanted to meet you and own you up?"

Sita felt numb. Tears rolled down her eyes and she said, "Please tell me if at last my natural parents have surfaced and if they have got in touch with you, maybe through Rahul."

Gayatri Devi said in her calmest voice, "Why are you getting upset? The person concerned is someone else. Since I have been entrusted with the responsibility of breaking the news to her, I thought of finding out through a little role play with you, what her reaction might be."

Sita did not quite accept her story. She thought that if it was someone else, Gayatri Devi would have certainly taken her into confidence. In the past she had divulged to her even the well guarded secrets of her family in order to get her opinion. Why then, Sita thought, would she talk to her in riddles unless the subject was likely to cause her emotional turbulence?

Sita said, "Ma, my upbringing has been perfect and enough courage has been instilled into me to withstand any kind of mental trauma. Please tell me the truth. That will make you feel lighter and also put me at ease. After all, the facts have to come out sooner or later and the sooner they do the better."

Gayatri Devi could not hold back anymore. She put her arms tightly around Sita and said in a low voice, "Your natural parents are Samir and Farah. Samir, as you know, has been keeping very indifferent health and it may be a good idea for you go to Delhi and spend some time with him."

Sita heard her with complete control over herself. Her face was calm and serene. Tears welled up in her eyes, but that was all. She asked in a hushed voice, "Are you referring to Samir uncle? And who is Farah? And Ma, don't you think that accepting or rejecting someone as one's parents is not like switching a light on or off?"

Gayatri Devi nodded and said, "Yes, Samir is your father and Farah was our Haji ji's sister. I do appreciate your predicament, but the fact has to be faced. On my part I will go along with whatever you choose."

Sita maintained her calm and asked, "Have you known about it all these years?"

Gayatri Devi told Sita that she did not have any idea about the matter till she got a call from Rahul the previous day. She added that Samir had called Rahul and revealed the secret to him. Samir did not want to disturb the present arrangement but he was very keen to accept Sita as his natural child. Sita closed her eyes and continued to be calm. The thought of her natural parents did haunt her from time to time but she had largely reconciled to the idea that they did not exist. Now her main anxiety was to provide a healing touch to Savitri Rani and Diwan Mithai Lal, who might feel completely broken on receiving this news. She decided to face the situation honestly and squarely. After a while she opened her eyes and said, "I know Samir uncle. He is a fine gentleman. I've always admired him. I do want to know more about Farah and possibly meet her."

Gayatri Devi pulled her closer and pouring all her affection into her voice told her that she was proud of her for the equanimity with which she was handling all this. She decided to tell her about her mother. "Your mother was a lady with extraordinary abilities and talents. Her physical personality was captivating but the main trait of her character was her uncompromising commitment to any cause that she undertook. She unfailingly rose to the occasion, depending on the need of the time, and always delivered. She did not have much exposure to life but her confidence was amazing. You have a lot of your mother in you. In the past I did see Farah in you several times, but back then I attributed it to coincidence. Now I know better."

Sita could not contain herself any more. She became inconsolable. She clung to Gayatri Devi, crying that she wanted to meet her mother. But Gayatri Devi had decided to break the news of her mother's death to her gradually. She said, "You certainly will but no one knows where she really is at the moment. Samir has been earnestly trying to locate her and the moment he succeeds in his mission, the first thing he will do is to unite the two of you."

While Gayatri Devi was still in the process of strategising she received a call from Shahnaz. Shahnaz did not seem to know about the recent developments. She told Gayatri Devi that ever since she reached Delhi she had been thinking of her and the more she thought, the more convinced she was that she wanted to join her at Rasulabad. She said that she had spoken to her parents and they did not have any objection, especially because they had full faith in Gayatri Devi.

Gayatri Devi told her that while she would welcome her with open arms, she was planning a trip to Delhi to see Samir Saxena who had been ill for some time. She suggested that Shahnaz might consider accompanying her back to Rasulabad. Shahnaz was excited at the thought of her visit to Delhi. She told her to inform her about her program so that she could receive her at the railway station. She also suggested that she should bring Sita along and stay with the Modys at Delhi.

Gayatri Devi assured Shahnaz that she would inform her and would bring Sita along, but she was not sure if she could stay with the Modys. She told her that she would leave it to Rahul to decide where she should stay. She put the telephone down and looking at Sita said, "We must go to Delhi to see Samir, but before that I think I should have a talk with Savitri and Diwan *Saheb*. I don't know how they'll react to the news."

Sita responded, "The news is indeed important but as far as I'm concerned, I don't see it making any change to my life. You and my parents are the constants in my life. That cannot change for anything in this world. Samir uncle is known to me and he's totally acceptable as he is, but I do want to know the reason for his deserting Farah and me. Ma, I want to meet Farah without any delay. I can feel nothing but love and consideration for her. Poor thing, God alone knows what she must have gone through. And if she is still alive..."

Gayatri Devi seized the opportunity and nodded her head in agreement. She said, "I appreciate your sentiments, and agree that she may not even be alive."

Sita looked alarmed. She was not prepared for this. She asked, "Ma, don't withhold anything from me now. Tell me, is she alive or not?"

Gayatri Devi, told her that Farah had breathed her last while delivering her. She added that barring Samir no one else was aware of the incident. Sita lost control once again and started sobbing. She said, "Ma, let's go to Delhi as soon as possible. We will divulge the news to *Amma* and *Babuji* later on. Since I am absolutely clear that there should be no change in the present equation, it should not make any difference to them after the initial shock."

Train tickets were booked for Delhi for the following day. Diwan *Saheb* and Savitri Rani were told that Samir Saxena was critically ill and therefore they had to take this sudden decision. Gayatri Devi spoke with

Rahul over the phone and apprised him of the latest position. She made it a point to request him to inform Shahnaz about her arrival in Delhi. She also suggested that the news about Sita's newfound relationship with Samir be kept under wraps.

❖❖

Rahul and Shahnaz, both looking uncharacteristically anxious and unhappy, were at the railway station. Gayatri Devi understood Rahul's anxiety but could not make out the reason for the unhappiness on Shahnaz's face. She hugged her and said, "You look tired! What's the matter?" Then she looked at Rahul who was in the process of bending down to touch her feet and said, "You too seem to have kept awake all night."

Rahul said, "Let's go to the car and then we shall talk."

Shahnaz and Rahul both had brought their cars but it was decided that the four would go to Rahul's house in one car and the drivers would follow them in the other car. While driving, Rahul said, "Ma, Samir uncle had a bit of a problem this morning and had to be hospitalised."

She was alarmed. She asked, "What is the problem? Let us first go and see him in the hospital."

He told her that it was not possible to go to the hospital because that was the time when the doctors visited the patients and no visitors were allowed inside. Sita said that even though it was not possible to see him it would be worthwhile going there to ascertain the exact condition of his health. Rahul realised it was no longer possible to avoid telling the truth that Samir uncle was in the Intensive Care Unit and that no visitors were allowed. He said, "No news trickles out of the ICU except that the condition is stable or otherwise. Shahnaz and I were there and he has been sedated. His parameters are said to be stable but there is no harm in checking again."

He steered the car towards the hospital. Inside the car there was pin drop silence. Gayatri Devi was sitting in the front seat but she could see Sita on the verge of tears through the mirror. She looked back and said that all cases in the ICU were not necessarily critical. Sometimes doctors put the important patients in the ICU just to exercise extra caution. Sita maintained her silence which Shahnaz noticed and found unusual.

Rahul parked the car in the main portico, leaving his driver to take it to the general parking area of the hospital. The large reception hall was crowded and noisy. The atmosphere in the food court did not suggest that inside the hospital people were struggling between life and death. The telephone booths were all busy with anxious visitors standing in queues, awaiting their chance to reach their friends or relatives inside the hospital. Rahul led the group inside the hall and to the lift, to go to the second floor where Dr. Dinesh Mani and his team had their offices. Dr. Mani knew Gayatri Devi. He welcomed her with folded hands and pulled out a chair for her. He asked the others to make themselves comfortable in the other chairs placed around the table. He did not have to guess the purpose of their visit. He was familiar with the close relationship that existed between Gayatri Devi's family and Samir Saxena. Greeting Dr. Mani, Gayatri Devi said, "I'm most relieved to see that Samir is in your care. How is he now?"

Dr. Mani replied, "Well, I can't say he's out of the woods but it could be worse. Thank God Satai took the decision to bring him here in an ambulance and inform Rahul. It was a massive attack of coronary thrombosis and very seldom do people come out of such attacks. He is in the ICU under sedation and should not be disturbed. Any kind of excitement must be scrupulously avoided. He needs a lot of care and rest."

Gayatri Devi said, "All I can say is that God is very kind. Now that we are here we shall keep in touch with you and visit Samir only after getting your clearance."

They bid good bye to Dr. Mani and left. Sita had maintained a stoic silence so far. Too many things had happened too soon. Gayatri Devi and Rahul sympathised with her predicament but Shahnaz found her melancholic attitude strange. Gayatri Devi suggested that Shahnaz go back to her home while they drove to Rahul's place but Shahnaz insisted on going with them.

Rahul's house was comfortable but not ostentatious. Gayatri Devi had a permanent room earmarked for her and the smaller room adjacent to it had been done up for Sita. On reaching Rahul's place, they all settled down in the patio and a servant entered with a tray of tea and snacks. But no one was in a mood to eat or drink. Samir's health was the focus of everyone's thoughts. The problem was that nobody could do anything to help. Even the doctors could do precious little. Leaving things in the hands of the Almighty was all one could draw consolation from.

Shahnaz was keen to discuss her plans to shift to Rasulabad. She was totally unaware of the developments that had taken place in Sita's life. She told her, "I wonder if you'd like to go out for a little shopping. Aunty might like to lie down while the budding lawyer hurries up to the courts. Or we could all go home and spend some time with Mom and Dad."

Gayatri Devi was conscious that the sequence of events had been too hectic and tumultuous for Sita to absorb in such a short time. She thought that a change of scene might help in soothing her nerves. Agreeing with Shahnaz's proposal, she told Sita that a bit of fresh air would do her good. She also told Shahnaz that she was very keen to meet her parents but that she would defer her visit. Shahnaz told her that her parents were very keen to talk to her about her moving to Rasulabad. Sita felt a strong urge to confide in Shahnaz. She requested her to wait and went to her room. She returned as quickly as she had left and said, "Let's go."

They got into the car and Shahnaz told her chauffeur to take them to the India International Center. Looking at Sita, she said, "I suggested that I take you out for a selfish motive. As you know, I'm very keen to work with Aunty and you at Rasulabad and I want your guidance. I realise that I will be entering a totally alien territory, but something within tells me that at last I've found what's best for me. You've had as much exposure, if not more, of the outside world as I have and yet you fit like a pair of gloves into Rasulabad. That's why I attach immense importance to your views on the subject."

Sita kept quiet. Her mind was somewhere else and she was not very keen on imparting advice at the moment. It struck Shahnaz that she had made the proposal too abruptly for Sita to react and she joined her in her silence. It also crossed her mind that perhaps Sita did not want any intrusion into her domain and therefore preferred to avoid talking on the subject. But she brushed aside the idea because she was convinced of her honesty and selflessness.

Sita broke the silence. She said, "What a coincidence, for even I came with you for a selfish motive. You want to talk to me about a problem which does not really exist as far as I am concerned, and I want to let you into a secret that has shaken my life. Ma holds you in a lot of affection and esteem and I'm sure that she'd be delighted to know that you sincerely want to work with her." Having said this from the sincerity of her heart, it did strike Sita that Shahnaz's appearance on the scene would certainly reduce her own authority in the organisation. But she decided that her immediate problem had to be addressed in preference to any other.

They arrived at the India International Center. The lush greenery there made the intellectual aura of the place complete. They sat in a corner of the coffee shop. A bearer approached them. Shahnaz ordered two cups of coffee and asked Sita what she wanted to eat . Luckily, there were not many people in the coffee shop and they could be by themselves. Shahnaz seemed happy to hear what Sita had to say but she told her that whenever she broached the subject with Aunty she did not get a clear response. She thought it was quite likely that Aunty suspected that she might not be cut out for the job. Changing the topic, Shahnaz said with a naughty smile, "Forget about my problem, which as you say is non-existent, tell me who has brought such an upheaval in your life. Does he match up with you in all your accomplishments?"

Sita remained serious. She said, "Upheaval is an understatement." After a pause, she asked, "For how long have you known Samir uncle?"

Shahnaz replied, "Ever since I can remember, why?"

Sita asked, "Do you know anything about his wife?"

Shahnaz responded, "Wife? He never had one. And if he had one you would have certainly known about her. You've been closer to him than I, but I must say that your question arouses a whole lot of curiosity."

Sita said, her voice soft, "He had a wife and I want to know all about her. It's very important because I am his daughter."

Shahnaz felt as if a ton of bricks had fallen upon her. Sita was obviously in earnest. "This is a bolt from the blue, Sita," said Shahnaz. "Please stop talking in riddles and tell me the whole truth."

Sita narrated the entire story as told to her by Gayatri Devi. She said that she was anxious to know all about her mother and how she met her end, but her anxiety was more for Samir uncle who apparently had suffered enormously in silence and was now perhaps on his last legs. She said that she wanted Shahnaz's help on how to bring some cheer in his life.

Shahnaz had still not recovered from the shock but she knew she had to react fast. She said, "No one can tell you more about your mother than Samir uncle, so you have to wait till he recovers. And you can play a role in his speedy recovery. Your appearance on the scene won't agitate him, because he's been fully aware of your existence all this time. In fact, by being by his side you will provide solace to him and act as a spur to his recovery. I think it prudent for you to stay back and look after him till he gets back on his feet."

Sita was not surprised at Shahnaz's suggestion. After all, Shahnaz would like to have an independent playing field in Rasulabad. At the end of the day all that Gayatri Devi wanted was a trusted and faithful ally and Shahnaz filled that bill adequately. It suddenly dawned upon her that the impression that Gayatri Devi was more than a mother to her was nothing more than her mind's fancy. She recalled how smoothly the idea of her marriage to Rahul had been dropped only because Rahul had expressed his reservations about it. It also occurred to her that Rahul might be interested in marrying Shahnaz, and if that was so, then things would fall perfectly in place. She said, "I don't want to bring about any change in my equation with my adopted parents. Any change will tear them apart. It's true that you may be able to fill my place insofar as Ma is concerned, but my parents will be left high and dry. At the same time, I also cannot neglect my real father who needs me now."

Shahnaz saw the sense in what Sita was saying. She had a high regard for her. She was surprised that she did not hold anything against her father for having been missing during her childhood. She told her, "My being at Rasulabad may be a boon for you. I may be able to reduce the pressure of your work there to enable you to spend more time with Samir uncle."

What Sita had secretly suspected only a little while ago now came out in the open. She could clearly see what Shahnaz had planned for herself. Ever since she had set her eyes on Shahnaz she had a lurking suspicion that there was something brewing between her and Rahul, and now everything seemed to be falling into place.

Aloud she said, "I'm sure that you'd be a great asset to Ma, and I would naturally be happy to work with you. But I would like to strike a note of caution regarding your intentions to settle down at Rasulabad. The idea may appear romantic but it is not a bed of roses. It is poles apart from the life you're used to and therefore, unless you have a thorough feel of the situation, you should not plunge into it."

Shahnaz told Sita that she had weighed the pros and cons of her decision with all the wisdom at her command and was clear in her mind that what she had planned was the best thing for her. Sita got up to leave, saying, "There is nothing better than knowing your mind. Let's go. We have to visit Samir uncle in the evening."

❖❖

Gayatri Devi, along with Rahul, Sita and Shahnaz reached the hospital and made straight for Dr. Mani's chamber. He told them that Samir was feeling much better but the nurse had reported that she had heard him talking in his sleep. He told them that he would permit only one person to meet Samir at a time so that no excitement be caused to him. Gayatri Devi suggested that she go and see Samir alone; the others could follow her subsequently. Sita gave her an anxious look but did not say anything. Assuring Sita that she would be the next to go, she got up to go to the ICU when she saw Gyaneshwar ascending the stairs leading to the elevators. He touched her feet and told her that he had arrived earlier and visited Samir. He added that he had appeared to be absolutely alright. In fact, he looked his normal self. Gayatri Devi said, "I'm glad to see you. Will you be around till I come back? I have something to talk to you about."

Gyaneshwar had some papers in his hand. He said, "I'll wait, for I also have to talk to you and Rahul."

When Gayatri Devi entered the ICU, Samir Saxena was lying in bed, immersed in deep thought. He was delighted to see her and made a gesture to rise but the nurse held him back. She held his hands, gave him a peck on his cheek and said, "Naughty boy! How can you go and fall sick?"

Samir's face lit up mischievously. He said, "Who's ill? This was just a ploy to get you here. Do you know how long you've taken to come?" Tears rolled down his cheeks, and Gayatri Devi did not know what to say. They sat in silence, smiling at each other. The thought of Farah and Sita dominated their thoughts. Finally, Samir asked, "Has Sita come?"

She nodded. After a while, when Samir seemed steadier, she said, "All I have to say to you is that you've indeed been brave in putting up with so much in silence. Even on the health front you seem to be doing much better than I had expected, but I insist that you take me into confidence about your exact condition."

By now Samir had recovered his composure and his wit. He said, "They say you should always keep God and the doctor happy because if you get on the wrong side of God, He sends you to the doctor and if the doctor is not happy with you, he sends you to God. I have erred in the eyes of the Almighty, but the doctor and I seem to be hitting it off quite well." They both laughed and Samir continued, "I'm very relieved to have you here. My health has been misbehaving for quite some time. But believe me, my suffering has been inconsequential. Doctors do frighten me about my blood pressure and heart ailment, but I don't experience any pain."

He paused and then started again, "I must say that you have done a great job with Sita. You've brought her up with such caring and love that expressing my gratitude to you may be out of place. Suffice it to say that I'm indeed proud of you." Tears rolled down his cheeks again. Gayatri Devi, cajoling him to calm down, drew herself nearer the bed and held his hand. Samir said, "I know that my end is near and I've made out a draft of my will. I have given it to Gyaneshwar to finalise after vetting by you."

Gayatri Devi smiled and said, "Don't you know, it is the good that die young. As far as you're concerned, you have to live for many more years. Now I shall leave and send in Sita, but one of these days I'd like to hear from you the great love story of Farah and Samir."

He replied, "Oh, it was great while it lasted and when it ended, it left behind enough for me to live on for a lifetime. At the time of delivering Sita, Farah breathed her last with the same serenity and contentment in her eyes that she always had. That is the long and short of it, but you're the only one I can talk to about Farah. I must do that some day." Gayatri Devi then left quietly to make room for Sita.

Sita's meeting with her long lost father was characteristic of their respective personalities. They were quiet but their eyes revealed everything. His eyes were as clear as his heart and conscience and they expressed enormous happiness at their meeting. Sita too looked happy but she seemed anxious about something, perhaps her mother. It did not take long for her to appreciate why her father could not own up to her earlier, but she was certainly keen to know all about her mother and her life. There was no place for tears in their meeting. No tears for Samir, because he was committed to present the deepest part of himself in their first meeting as father and daughter. No tears for Sita, because she felt that she had already wept enough for a lifetimeShe quietly went and sat by her father as if nothing had happened. Caressing his feet softly she said, "Ma has told me all that you wanted to be conveyed. I'm very proud of you. I've known you all along as Samir Uncle and I've always admired you. I know you must have taken the best care of my mother and if she is not here today, it must be because it just could not be. But one day, when you are back on your feet, I want to hear from you all about her. She must have been special to receive your love and more than anything else, to continue to stay in your heart for so long – even after she is no more" She could not maintain her composure anymore and two teardrops trickled down her eyes.

Samir said, "The end of your mother at the time of your birth would have marked the end of my life too, but I had to live for your sake. Believe me, you have not been out of my sight even for a moment ever since you were born. God has been kind and your life has shaped out exactly as I wanted." He continued, "I understand you know Gyaneshwar quite well. What do you think of him? He admires you and has asked for your hand in marriage."

Sita found the mention of this proposal out of the place, but realising that Samir was running out of time, replied feebly, "Uncle, you've carved out my life for me. You have even provided me with parents and security. Ma is a paragon of goodness. *Amma* and *Babuji* are angels and now you have found somebody as good as Gyaneshwar to marry me. Please, I beseech you not to burden yourself with so much. You need to be cared for. You have done enough."

There was a prolonged silence, broken only by the steady beep of the medical equipment around Samir's bed. He realised that he had spoken about Gyaneshwar abruptly and prematurely. It was possible that Sita might construe it as an affront to her independence. She may already have someone in mind, or she may want time to find love by herself. By not answering his question about Gyaneshwar directly, was she perhaps hinting at something? He realised that a new equation would have to evolve between them before they could talk openly to each other. He was not sure if he had the time to build that, and he had so much to say and to do!

As for Sita, everything was happening so fast that she was not fully able to absorb the changes. Gayatri Devi was a very fine person, but Sita was aware that in her priorities, she figured a few notches below Rahul. Like everybody else, she too had always thought that her marriage with Rahul was a foregone conclusion. She was clever enough never to reveal her emotions, but somewhere inside her she did nurse a soft spot for him. The entire edifice had fallen like a house of cards only because the foundation was weak, she thought. She had not known any parents other than *Amma* and *Babuji,* but now that she had found her real father, she could feel the difference between real parents and adopted ones. She now realised that in spite of the best treatment she had received from everyone, she had always felt she needed to keep proving herself in order to belong to the inner circle of the Rasulabad household. All said and done, she did feel that the changed situation had given her an added sense of confidence and independence.

Samir had always kept a close watch on Sita and he was very clear in his mind that she had been provided with everything in plenty. But still he felt guilty for not providing her with a home comprising her real parents. He was conscious that in spite of everything, Sita was aware that she was an adopted child and that always made a difference. Ever since she walked into the room, Farah was constantly in his thoughts and, engulfed by sadness, he found himself visualising the difference her presence would have made to their meeting. Suddenly, it dawned upon him that he had caused enormous suffering to Sita and that saddened him all the more. He felt that she perhaps held him responsible for the loss of her mother.

Samir opened the conversation again. He said, "Life with your mother was bliss. She had a multifaceted personality which few could match, but each time I proposed marriage she avoided the issue by saying that there was no hurry. She was sceptical about its aftermath and therefore took it upon herself to protect me from the likely consequences. You know Haji ji? She was his sister and that was the reason for her desire to keep things under wraps. As far as I was concerned, my mind was made up and I was ready to face the consequences. During her confinement, I was posted at Rasulabad and she came to live here in Delhi, where you were born. But she did not live to see you."

Samir's voice became feeble and he stopped, overcome with emotion and weakness. Sita, with tears in her eyes, drew closer to her father and clung to him. They remained in that position for a while till Sita realised, not with shock but with calm realization, that what she had heard from him had been his last words. Sita wiped her tears, covered Samir's body up to the chest with the white sheet and went out to call the doctor.

Samir's end was expected but his large circle of friends were shocked to hear about the love in his life. Some said that was the missing link of his life and that after this revelation many things fell into place. The fact that he could guard his privacy so perfectly and deftly further heightened his esteem in the minds of his friends and admirers. They were unanimous in their view that the fathomless depths of this outstanding man had not been fully appreciated in his lifetime.

❖❖

Diwan Mithai Lal and Savitri were shocked to hear about the sad demise of Samir. Their apprehension about the possible change with regard to Sita was even greater. They knew she was very mature and was deeply committed to them but one could never say anything with certainty about human nature. They were always conscious about the constantly lurking uneasiness in her mind regarding the fact they were employees of the household, even though she herself was loved and treated as family. Their most immediate concern was to be by her side to provide her solace and to set her obviously troubled mind at rest. They left for Delhi immediately to be present for the funeral. Throughout the journey they talked about Sita's childhood, how adorable and intelligent she was, how well she fitted in with the different echelons of society and how she was accepted with open arms wherever she went.

Going through the sequence of events, Diwan Mithai Lal said to his wife, "Sita's journey in the short span of her life has been quite bumpy. In spite of everything, her childhood had the scar of being an adopted child. The jibes she had to face only subsided when her marriage to Rahul became a possibility. Once that myth was demolished the smirks staged a comeback. When everyone had reconciled to the changed situation, her father appeared from nowhere and then just as swiftly disappeared into the unknown."

She, nodding in agreement said, "Sita is very strong. She has a very balanced mind and her thoughts are well grounded. She knows how to face new situations and build new equations independent of the past. You'll see, she will come out with flying colours even this time. After all, nothing has changed except that her biological parents have been identified. And they aren't even living. This must have upset her enormously but she's capable of handling this with wisdom and fortitude."

Mithai Lal said, "I agree with you entirely but you don't seem to read between the lines. You must realise that Samir *Saheb* has left behind a sizeable property and someone has to look after it. I'm aware that in spite of everything, Sita does feel a bit curbed at Rasulabad and if she decides to shake off her shackles and stay in Delhi, the equation with us might have to undergo a change. In that case even Gayatri Devi may have to look for someone to replace her."

"Not as far as I'm concerned," said Savitri Rani. "A girl eventually goes to her husband's home in any case and if she decides to settle down in Delhi, I will think that she has got married and gone. We shall get her married to someone worthy of her in Delhi itself. Her leaving our home to go to her own is a foregone conclusion and that should not make any difference in our equation."

❖❖

Gayatri Devi had assumed charge as the head of the family and a large number of Samir's friends and admirers had gathered to bid farewell to the departed soul. Sita took charge of managing the affairs at the cremation ceremony, tickling the curiosity of all present. She joined the others in carrying logs of wood to the pyre and to the dismay of many, she herself lit the fire. Besides the fact that Sita's relationship with Samir was not known, girls, as prescribed in the Hindu rituals, did not even come near the pyre, let alone touch or light it. The other thing that surprised everybody was the absence of Rahul and the very noticeable presence of Gyaneshwar during the last rites. Sita was a picture of dignity throughout but tears welled up in her eyes as she stood with folded hands at the cremation ground, thanking the large gathering who had collected to mourn the death of her father. Many were moved to comfort her for Samir's death without even knowing that she was his daughter.

After the cremation ceremony, Gayatri Devi, Sita, Diwan Mithai Lal, Savitri Rani, Satai, Vinay Khosla and Gyaneshwar converged in the large drawing room where Samir used to meet his formal guests. Rahul was absent and Gyaneshwar had assumed importance. After becoming a High Court judge, Vinay had cut himself from the social circles and his presence at this very private family gathering seemed out of place. Gyaneshwar had prevailed upon Gayatri Devi to personally request Justice Vinay Khosla to join them as he had been privy to certain decisions taken by Samir during his life time. He made himself available for the meeting but seemed very distracted. Obviously Samir's death was weighing on his mind.

The atmosphere was sombre and everyone was sitting quietly when Gayatri Devi broke the silence. She said, "Samir has made a will in consultation with Vinay and Gyaneshwar. I would like Gyaneshwar to read it out and also announce it in the papers tomorrow so that on the day of *Chautha* everyone may know about the relationship between Sita and Samir."

She looked at Justice Khosla and whispered into his ears, "I'm shattered that Rahul has been called by the Directorate of Enforcement for some kind of questioning. Although I'm sure that it's a case of mistaken identity, the matter has to be nipped in the bud before the press starts devouring it." He whispered back that he too had heard about it and cautioned against jumping to premature conclusions. He added that he was aware of the existence of a will and turning to Gyaneshwar, asked him to read it out aloud.

Gyaneshwar started reading from the sheaf of papers in his hand.

"I, Samir Chandra Saxena, son of late Kabir Chandra Saxena, aged seventy years and a resident of Sunder Nagar, New Delhi have lived a full and happy life. I am known to be a self made man but that is an unadulterated lie. The support and help I got from various people at different stages of my life is beyond imagination and therefore calling myself self-made would be tantamount to ignoring their contribution in my life. Above all, I must place on record the enormous help and support I received from my family – particularly from my parents. They hardly had any means, barring the two acres of land and the house in which we lived, but my father felt committed to educating me owing to the freak incident of my coming across the convoy of a District Magistrate during my childhood."

"Only a few boys from my village went to school, and those who did so, did not normally go beyond the eighth standard because their families needed them to augment their incomes. Only a few passed the matriculation examination and then took up some odd job or the other to support their respective families. My parents, despite their very meagre resources, never told me to discontinue my studies. My father used to say that he was committed to supporting my education till such time as I continued to excel in debating and sports in my school, because he was sure that those who were good at studies and extracurricular activities made it to the post of District Magistrate."

"By the time I passed my intermediate examination, the last ornament of my mother had been sold. The small holding of land that my father possessed had already been pawned to the money lender of the village and my father had taken up a petty job in a sugar factory situated in the nearby village. We ate very frugal food but something special was made by my mother for me every day and books and school uniforms were never in short supply. The thought of the hardships that my parents had to face to enable me to fulfil my dreams is incomprehensible in an age of individualism. It never occurred to me that my parents were old and that they had very little time at their disposal. They died in penury, leaving behind a fund of blessings that stood by me all my life."

"The scholarships that came my way took care of my college and hostel expenses and sports like tennis provided me with exposure to the higher echelons of society. By the Grace of God I got into the Indian Administrative Service. I received love and recognition from all quarters but the thought that my parents were not there to see me remained a constant source of sorrow in my heart."

"I was singularly lucky in my postings. I could always indulge my passion for sports and was blessed with the most wonderful friends. I had no family of my own but the number of families that adopted me in all earnestness was countless. Of all the places I remember, Rasulabad holds the most special place in my heart. I went there as the Additional Collector but the people there hailed me as the Chairman of the District Board. They looked upon me as one of them and not as a government officer on a posting. There I found an elder brother in Rai Ravi Prakash Bahadur. He and his wife, Gayatri Devi, have played a very important role in my life without realising what a great boon they have been for me."

"While at Rasulabad I came across the love of my life. It was like a fairy tale. She was not beautiful in the conventional manner. She had not received formal education. She had been born and brought up in a common segment of the town. Until one came into close contact with her, it was not possible to find anything out of the ordinary in her. But once one came to know her well, she stood out in every walk of life. She was tall, slim and a shade short of being fair. There was magic in her voice and her knowledge of Urdu poetry was unbelievable. She could recite Ghalib, Meer and Faiz with great aplomb. Her blue eyes were extremely expressive and her personality had the glow of a shooting star. She had the gift of a razor sharp mind which she used to match up to those who had had the benefit of a better education. She had the art of articulating her mind in such a manner that the other person felt compelled to accept her viewpoint. She was a paragon of love and kindness. She had a penchant for details and attained perfection in whatever she did."

"To start with, she joined me as my house keeper. I seldom met her but in a very short time, by sheer observation and common sense, she understood all that I wanted — the food I relished, the clothes and shoes I preferred to wear at different times and occasions, the way I wanted my parties organised, my idea of furnishing and upholstering – all of this she seemed to know. Soon she took control of everything that concerned me. She once mentioned to me that during her childhood she had gone to the same school as Anna, the daughter of Col. Furgus, who was posted as Superintendent of Police at Rasulabad. The Police officer's daughter had taken to her instantly. They became great friends and while the officer was posted at Rasulabad she used to frequent her friend's family very often. The family accepted her as one of them and she got an opportunity to learn from them many things that she would not have known otherwise. Even after Col. Furgus was transferred out of Rasulabad, the two girls kept in touch with each other and Farah went and spent long vacations with Anna at the places where Col. Furgus was posted. Even after Anna left India for England, the two girls corresponded with each other but with the passing of time they gradually lost touch. Farah still remembered them very fondly. She used to say that God had provided her with that exposure to enable her to discharge her responsibilities at a later time, efficiently."

"An illness I contracted brought out the best in her. Her abundant compassion, her absolute commitment and her selfless approach to life, all came to the fore. I realised that unless I got married to her, I would not be able to retain her with me for the rest of my life, and that life without her was not worth living."

"But she always shunned the idea of marriage. Whenever I broached the topic, she evaded it on one pretext or the other. Besides hailing from a conservative Muslim family, she was also conscious of the vast difference between the social standing of her family and mine. She did not want to hurt the sentiments of her family and community and was of the view that her marriage to me would sully my reputation and mar my flourishing career. I offered no argument in return. She had so much confidence in my love for her that she considered marriage to be inconsequential. On my part I was very clear that if and when I got married, it would be to her and her alone and therefore I allowed time to take its own course."

"She kept the secret of her pregnancy from me for a long time. It was only when I noticed certain changes in her that she revealed to me that very soon the stork would be visiting her. What was most surprising was that she did not seem to be worried on that count at all. She, as usual, brushed aside my suggestion to get married by saying that *Allah* would take care of everything. My conscience was clear. I was not for aborting the pregnancy and even more than me, she was vehemently against it. She firmly believed that we had not sinned and that God would show us the way out of our predicament."

"One day she asked me if I could send her somewhere away from Rasulabad on the pretext that she had gone to learn English and western cooking. She said that her family was very happy at her assignment in my household but they were aware of her limitations in western cooking. She added that they would accept this reason because they knew that she would be well looked after by me in all circumstances. I asked her, 'If they are so assured about my concern for you then why do you think they would come in the way of our marriage? Why don't you tell them that I want to marry you?' I also pointed out to her that after the birth of the child, the cat would be out of the bag in any case and we would be left with no choice but to get married."

"She said that normally eyebrows would have been raised and tongues wagged at a single girl working for a bachelor, but because of the difference in our respective stations in life the thought of there being any relationship would never occur to anyone. She pointed out that the proposal of marriage would be outrageous and scandalous. She said that people would attribute lechery to me and bad character to her, which she was not willing to accept at any cost. She said, 'Once I deliver the child, I will leave her in the care of a nurse and come back. After some time you may adopt her as your child and bring her to my care and we shall live happily ever after with your adopted child'."

"I was not happy with the idea because at no cost did I want to give my child the ignominy of illegitimacy, but since nothing else was acceptable to Farah and I had to yield. I sent her away to stay at the very house where I live now and where I will probably breathe my last. Satai, who is now a member of my family, was quite young when Farah came to Delhi but he was as competent and loyal at that time as he is today. He looked after Farah very well and never asked me anything about her."

"Sita was born, a healthy and beautiful baby, in the Holy Family Hospital near New Friends' Colony, but Farah did not live to see her child. It was almost as if, after paying back her debt to the world in the form of her replica, she decided to depart. The expression in her eyes and the smile on her face were mysteriously saying, 'Did I not tell you marriage was unnecessary?' I was stunned beyond words. For the first time in my life I realised what it meant to be heartbroken. As a tribute to Farah, I decided to dedicate my life to our daughter."

"I did not want the little one to grow up in a motherless home and could not think of anyone better than my friends Rai Ravi Prakash

Bahadur and Gayatri Devi to take care of my child. By the grace of God I managed to succeed in my mission of bringing her under their care. Equally important was the fact that Diwan Mithai Lal and his wife, Savitri Devi, are nothing short of angels. I wonder if anyone else could have given my child the love, affection and care that they have. They came into Sita's life as a blessing from God and I cannot be grateful enough."

"Gayatri discharged her role of a godmother in a manner that no one else could have done. Without her Sita could not have attained the level of accomplishment in various walks of life that she has done. The genes of her mother and the exposure that was provided to her by Gayatri have made her blossom along the lines of her natural personality. My most precious possession is the trunk lying under my bed. It contains Farah's personal belongings – her clothes, her jewellery, her diary, and a copy book containing some poems written by her. Sita will be able to assess her mother's personality by examining her last worldly possessions."

"I have been periodically investing in stocks ever since I joined service and I never found it necessary to encash them. I understand that over the years the value of the stocks held by me has multiplied manifold. I deposited my provident fund against a Fixed Deposit Receipt number 009870000 with the State Bank of India, Parliament Street, New Delhi and I have a savings bank account number SB 78777 with the same bank. Besides the house in a one acre plot in Sunder Nagar, New Delhi, I have two residential plots measuring a thousand square-meters each in Noida. Custody of these accounts, ownership of my property, the silver and curios, along with the cars, furniture, carpets and all that is there in my Sunder Nagar bungalow should go to my daughter Sita. I want that she should continue to look upon Diwan Mithai Lal and his wife Savitri as her parents. If she so desires she may donate one of the plots in Noida to the Holy Family Hospital in memory of her mother."

"Satai, who has been an epitome of loyalty and sincere service, should be given rupees ten lakhs and a place to stay in the Sunder Nagar house. If this house is sold, or if for some reason Sita does not consider it possible to accommodate Satai in the house, then she should provide him with a suitable accommodation of his choice."

"This is my last will and there is no other will in addition to this. This will has been drafted by Gyaneshwar Singh under my advice, to be produced as and when necessary after my demise."

The silence that followed the reading of the will was broken first by Justice Vinay Khosla. He looked at Gayatri Devi and said, "I must take your leave. There is nothing more to be done about the will for now." The entire gathering got up to leave but before Justice Khosla got into his car, Gayatri Devi took him aside and spoke with him.

❖❖

An ocean of human beings converged on Samir's bungalow for the *Chautha* ceremony. By now most people had come to know that Samir had been survived by a daughter. A life size photograph of Samir adorned the center of the stage that had been covered with flowers. A group of singers sat on one side of the stage, singing religious songs, and the large gathering of Samir's friends and admirers sat in numerous rows facing the stage. Gayatri Devi was still at the helm of affairs. She appeared distracted and people attributed it to her grief at the death of Samir Saxena. But by now many had also heard of the other news, and they surmised that the main cause for her anguish was the problem that Rahul had created for himself. After an hour of singing, a short ritual was performed to mark the end of the ceremony. Following this the *members* of the bereaved family stood and thanked everyone for coming. Gayatri Devi, Diwan Mithai Lal, Savitri, Gyaneshwar and Sita represented the bereaved family. Rahul's absence and Gyaneshwar's presence struck everyone as odd. The refreshments that were served after the ceremony were sparse and only people very close to the family joined in.

Nawab Saheb commented to Rustom, his voice conspiratorially low, "I didn't know that Gyaneshwar was so close to Samir, or is it that he is close to Sita?"

Rustom replied, "I don't know about that, but where is Rahul? I haven't seen him for any of the ceremonies."

Rajeshwar, who did not quite like the idea of his son standing with the bereaved family, overheard the conversation and butted in. He said, "Gayatri Devi is very keen on getting Gyaneshwar and Sita married. I suppose that by making him stand with the bereaved family she is trying to win him and us over. She's a very clever lady, but now it seems she has met her nemesis."

Nawab Saheb and Rustom both found Rajeshwar's observation very inappropriate. They held Gayatri Devi in high esteem and the news that she could have a nemesis was disturbing. Rustom asked, "Why, what has happened ? She seems to be perfectly alright to me."

Rajeshwar looked at the two of them and said, "If you don't know then you better find out for yourselves. I don't want to be branded as a rumour-monger."

Rustom said, "Your reputation would remain intact regardless of whether you reveal the secret to us or not but please, for heaven's sake tell us what you know. Gayatri is a very noble person and does not deserve to suffer."

Rajeshwar said cryptically, "What glitters is not always gold. Her son has been summoned by the Directorate of Enforcement and may have been locked up by now."

Nawab Saheb and Rustom gave each other a bewildered look. They could not believe their ears. Rahul was a paragon of upright conduct. What on earth could he have to do with the Directorate of Enforcement? This seemed to be a case of mistaken identity. They both remarked simultaneously, "Are you sure that your information is correct? Rahul places dignity and honour above everything else in life. There must be some misunderstanding."

Rajeshwar was unrelenting. He said, "In public life one has to make sure that one is not found making inaccurate statements," and walked away.

Nawab Saheb and Rustom walked towards Vinay Khosla who was standing in a corner with Gayatri Devi and sipping tea. They seemed to be immersed in some serious discussion and were talking in whispers. Seeing them approaching her, Gayatri Devi disengaged herself and said, "Come and join us. I'm glad that you've been able to come. Sita will draw a lot of solace from Nikhat and Shahnaz's presence."

They realised that they had innocuously intruded into a private conversation. But they could not hold themselves back. Rustom said, "The suddenness of the events has left everybody dumbfounded. But what we have heard about Rahul from Rajeshwar is indeed shocking, if it is true at all."

Vinay pondered over the implicit question for a while and spoke serenely, "Well, there is some problem and it's being investigated. I hope Rahul is able to get over the problem, otherwise it could be serious."

Rustom, who was known to be very fond of Rahul said, "I'm sure that some misunderstanding has cropped up somewhere and will be cleared in no time." Gayatri Devi kept quiet and moved towards Sita to join her in bidding goodbye to the guests who were leaving.

Gyaneshwar dropped Diwan Mithai Lal, Savitri and Sita at Rahul's house and left only after being satisfied that Sita did not require his presence for the time being. Sita was intrigued at the intensity of interest he was taking in her affairs. She was aware that Samir Saxena had entrusted the job of working out his will to him and Rahul had even proposed that they get married, but she did not consider these two reasons sufficient for him to take charge of the situation. She had expected

Rahul to stand by her side and do all that was being done by Gyaneshwar. But where was Rahul? In the midst of all the frenetic activity of the last few days, she had almost missed Rahul's absence.

Sita had always had a peculiar relationship with Rahul. She had never admitted to herself that she was in love with him, but for a long time had lived under the impression that she would be married to him. The news that Rahul was not conducive to the idea did hurt her but she took it in her stride. The hurt was still there, but only like the memory of an old wound. It did occur to her in passing that if Samir Saxena had made the proposal of her marriage with Rahul, it might not have been turned down.

Gyaneshwar's obvious devotion to her was gratifying but Rahul was the polestar in her life. She had hung on to every word he spoke, adored every careless gesture, and accepted every shade of his complex personality for as long as she could remember. How would she find the strength to cope with the sudden change in equations?

While Sita was going down memory lane, Gayatri Devi arrived, very contemplative but serene. Diwan Mithai Lal and Savitri got up and Sita led her to the comfortable chair in which she usually sat. She embraced Sita and said, "I appreciate the turmoil in your mind and heart but I have confidence in your courage and understanding. Every upheaval has an automatic ability to settle down."

Sita, keeping her cool, asked her, "Where is Rahul? I haven't seen him the last few days."

Gayatri Devi signalled for Sita to occupy the chair next to her. She started talking, her gaze distant. She said, "Time has passed like a whirlwind in the last fortnight. Rahul has got into serious trouble and if even part of what I've heard is true then I'll be left with no choice but to disown him." She shook her head sadly and kept quiet.

Sita could not believe her ears. All along she had assumed that Samir Saxena's death and the news of his relationship with her was what was making everyone morose. But this news about Rahul was a bolt from the blue. She asked, "I'm sure that whatever you've heard is not true. But where is he, and what have you heard about him that has upset you so much?"

She replied, a note of defeat in her voice, "The Directorate of Enforcement has taken him in for questioning. Do you recall Ranjit? He is the Chairman and Managing Director of Ranjit International, one of the largest corporations of the country. He had engaged Rahul as the counsel for his company. Ranjit has made a complaint to the Bar council that Rahul is defiant of the ethics of the legal profession and has been passing on sensitive information to parties litigating with his company, resulting in their losing the cases and incurring enormous losses. Some lawyers have complained that he takes advantage of his familiarity with the judges, without the judges getting the wiser of it. It is also alleged that his ill gotten money has been invested in buying properties in Cannes, Paris, London and New York."

Sita knew that a mere brushing aside of the issue as baseless would not provide any solace to Gayatri Devi. The matter was so serious that she had to say something to soothe her nerves. She said, "Is Ranjit the same person who used to live with Neha? They used to look for some pretext or the other to fight with each other."

Gayatri Devi nodded her head and Sita continued, "Neha is devoid of any sense of dignity. She used to make passes at Rahul and when he would snub her she would proclaim that she was only teasing him. He always disliked her and she could have played the vamp in this whole matter. I'm sure that Rahul is innocent."

Gayatri Devi was not convinced. She said, "Even if he does come out of it unscathed, tongues will wag and I can't have that. I've always lived with my honour intact and I will tolerate no scar on it at the fag end of my life."

Rahul's Trial by Fire

A letter from the Bar Association of the High Court was awaiting Rahul when he had returned home after visiting Samir Saxena for the last time. He was most surprised to go through the contents of the letter. His thoughts immediately went to Ranjit and Neha. He had handled a case for Ranjit's company and Ranjit had not been satisfied with the court's verdict. Neha, who had been nursing a grievance at being snubbed, must have convinced him that Rahul had mishandled the case with an ulterior motive. Rahul was aware that she had been bad mouthing him but although Ranjit and Neha were live-in partners he had assumed that Ranjit's relationship with him was independent of Neha. The thought of a few colleagues at the Bar, who were envious of him also crossed his mind, but he could not have imagined that things would come to such a pass.

The letter said that some members of the Bar had brought to the notice of the Association that Rahul had been indulging in unethical practices, and that unless he explained his conduct satisfactorily, the Association proposed to proceed against him under section thirty-five of the Advocates Act of nineteen-sixty one. The charges had been couched in general terms but it was mentioned that should there be a need, the Association was in a position to substantiate its allegations with specific cases. It was also alleged that certain instances of him trying to influence the witnesses of the opposing side had been brought to their notice. But those matters would be handled by the honourable courts and he had been warned that proceedings for contempt may be in the offing against him. It was further alleged that he was in the habit of giving his clients the impression that due to his proximity to certain judges he was in a position to tilt the balance of the judgments in their favour. Rahul had been asked to meet the President of the Bar Association after fixing up an appointment, and in the meantime respond in writing within fifteen days of the date of the letter.

Taking into account the mood of the family, he did not consider it prudent to add fuel to the fire. After reading the letter he had kept it in his pocket and made no more of it. On the day Samir Saxena breathed his last, Rahul received a call from his friend who was the Joint Director of Enforcement saying that certain complaints against him had been received and that it was advisable that Rahul saw him immediately. The friend did not elaborate further over the phone.

Rahul was most surprised at the sudden turn of events. He wondered how everyone seemed to have turned hostile towards him at the same time. He wanted to avoid sharing the latest developments with Gayatri Devi. He knew that she would not believe anything that was being alleged against him, but he also knew that the allegations would disturb her all the same. At the same time, he realised that as and when she came to know that she had been kept in the dark about such important information, she would be very upset.

He told his mother that he would not be able to attend the funeral because he had to attend to some important work which could not wait. Gayatri Devi raised her eyebrows and said, "How can you be so insensitive? What could be more important than the funeral of Samir uncle, Sita's father?"

Rahul told her that some adversaries had made a false complaint against him to the Directorate of Enforcement and that Ravi Sharma had rung him up to suggest that he should see him immediately. He added that although there was no substance in the allegations, the fact was that if an enquiry was ordered, a lot of mudslinging would take place regardless of the outcome. Therefore, it was very important that necessary action be taken without wasting any time. Gayatri Devi was convinced that the allegations would not have a leg to stand upon and therefore was not worried. She was however concerned about the family's reputation and so permitted Rahul to leave. She did however request him to attend to the work swiftly and return to the funeral as soon as he could.

❖❖

Ravi was waiting for Rahul in the office. Ravi and Rahul were old buddies and their interactions were marked by an easy informality. But this time Ravi's face was grave. They shook hands cursorily and Ravi came to the point straight away. Handing over a few sheets of paper to Rahul, he said, "This complaint has come from the Income Tax Department, saying that you have apartments in Cannes, Paris, London and New York. They also suspect that you have accounts in foreign countries. Unless you can prove that the allegations are false, I may have to detain you for questioning. Since I want to help you, I've taken permission to handle the case myself, but I can help you only if you are absolutely in the clear."

While Ravi was talking, Rahul was scanning the sheets of paper handed over to him. He went through the three pages quickly. The crux of the complaint had already been communicated by Ravi. He looked up and asked Ravi, "What do you want? All this is humbug. I've already clarified the matter to the Income Tax Department, and I thought that they were satisfied. Do you know that today is the funeral of Samir uncle and I had to leave that and come here to answer these irrelevant questions?"

Ravi became sombre. He said, "I wanted to attend Mr. Saxena's funeral too. He was a very highly respected officer, but in your interest I decided to attend to this case before doing anything else. The matter is not at all innocuous, it's very serious. The addresses and the photographs of the properties, along with the name of the owner are all in the file. The evidence is foolproof and it all points to you. I have a search warrant for your houses and establishments and also an order to detain you for questioning."

Rahul sank in his chair and looked lost. Ravi looked perplexed and did not know what to do. He got up to get a glass of water and brought it to Rahul. Rahul controlled himself, and sipping from the glass he said, "The allegations are indeed false, but a search warrant for our Rasulabad establishment would be tantamount to a death warrant for my mother. I'm here to answer all your queries but no searches please. Spare my mother."

Ravi said, "Your mother is like my mother too, and I know how righteous and self-respecting she is. But the truth must come out. There is no evidence about your bank accounts in foreign countries but the properties are all registered in your name and your passport shows that you have been visiting these countries frequently."

Rahul looked more in control of himself now. He said, "The conclusion that you've drawn about there being no bank account is absolutely correct and I have nothing to add to what you've already said yourself. About the properties you are talking about, all I can say is that I wish I had them. For the record, I categorically deny that I have any property in my name outside of India."

Ravi straightened in his chair and said, "I've not drawn any conclusions about your foreign bank accounts. All I said was that there was no evidence at the moment to substantiate the allegation that you have bank accounts in foreign countries. As far as the properties are concerned, your name, your address in India and your passport number are all there to prove that the allegations are authentic. Since you categorically deny the charges, I'm afraid that I'll have to detain you for further questioning."

Rahul contacted Gayatri Devi over the phone and told her of the allegations. He assured her that they were absolutely false but said that he might have to go out of the country immediately to collect some evidence and establish his innocence. He said that if timely action was not taken, the adversaries might succeed in their mission. He disconnected the phone with a parting note that he might not come home for a few days. Gayatri Devi was so taken up by the fast changing circumstances that all she could register was that the allegations against Rahul were fictitious and that he had to go out of town to sort out certain matters. She had full confidence in his integrity and ability so and she decided to avoid pondering over the matter any more. But when she met Justice Khosla after the *Chautha* ceremony, she thought of talking to him about Rahul's problems and seeking his advice. Justice Khosla was not aware of the matter related to the Directorate of Enforcement but he did know about the complaint that the Bar Association had received about Rahul's professional misconduct. Without committing himself in any manner, he told her that he was aware of the matter and that it had to be handled delicately but swiftly. Gayatri Devi was sure that Rahul could not have done anything wrong, but could there be smoke without a fire?

Rahul was produced in the court, where he decided to defend himself. The charges against him were read out and he addressed the court in a very composed manner, as if he was arguing on behalf of a client. He said, "Lordships, I plead not guilty to all of the charges made against me. It has already been established that I do not hold any account in any bank of foreign origin. The Directorate of Enforcement does not have any evidence for it and their case is based only on hearsay. I have nothing further to add to what the Department has already admitted. With regard to the charge of owning properties overseas, all I can say is that it is just an idea of a fertile but perverted mind. Anybody can purchase property in my name and sign the papers as Rai Rahul Prakash Bahadur of Rasulabad, but the authenticity of the signature is of essence and a closer scrutiny of the matter would establish that the signatures on the papers are not mine. I can say this with absolute confidence because I have never signed any paper related to the purchase of property overseas. A reference to my passport has been made in the charge sheet. In this connection I would like to bring to the notice of this honourable court that my passport got lost three years ago and a Police complaint vide an FIR had been lodged in the Police station. I do not have the number of the FIR with me just now but I should be able to furnish it to you in a day or two. In any case, it can be verified from the Police station. As far as my visits to these countries are concerned, I admit that I have been visiting them but I have been visiting these countries since I was three years old. I have lived overseas for a considerable part of my life. Will the neighbours verify that I have been visiting the properties that I am alleged to have bought? This honourable court will naturally give its verdict only after checking the records, but assuming that what I have stated is correct and also that the addresses of the properties as well as the name of its owner are also correct, is it not possible that someone has purchased the properties in question by forging my signature and giving my address and my passport number? If that is so then an obvious question emerges, why was the property purchased in my name and address? The answer is as simple as the question – because the buyer got hold of my lost passport with my genuine signature and address, and there could not be any better proof of identification than a passport, for buying property in a foreign land. I put it to you that my lost passport was optimally used with the view to sell the properties later on at a profit. Lordships, I deny that the signatures on the relevant papers are mine. They have been forged and the passport whose reference has been made in the FIR is the one which I had lost. The passport that had been issued to me subsequent to the loss of my earlier passport bears a different number."

Rahul paused, the skilled and timed pause of a natural orator. Then he continued, "I'm a practicing lawyer and hail from one of the most prominent families of my state. My mother, Shrimati Gayatri Devi, is an honourable Member of the State Legislative Assembly. My father, Rai Ravi Prakash Bahadur was a legal luminary and had the good fortune of practicing in this honourable court for a number of years prior to his death. If I am kept in custodial lockup, the matter will unnecessarily come into the public domain. A first hand enquiry by the department will reveal that what I have stated about my signatures and the loss of my passport is correct."

After another pause he continued, "I pray that the honourable court may be pleased to grant me bail for the time that it might require to ascertain that the statements I have made are correct."

The two judges talked with each other in whispers and then the senior judge spoke, "Your submission, that there is no evidence with the Enforcement Directorate to substantiate that you hold foreign accounts, does not prove that you do not have foreign accounts. The matter is under investigation and a conclusion can be drawn only after the enquiry is completed. Your submission, that if your signature does not tally with the ones on the relevant papers connected to the properties in question, then you cannot be looked upon as the owner of the properties is valid, but the question who is the beneficiary of the properties acquired in your name remains unanswered."

Rahul humbly suggested that that question had already been answered. "The properties have been bought by someone with unaccounted money and since he had somehow got hold of my passport he superimposed his photograph over mine and used it as his own."

The judge said, "Everything hinges around the authenticity of your signature on the papers." The judge looked at the counsel for the Directorate and asked, "How much time do you want to verify the signature?"

The counsel conferred with Ravi and said, "A month!"

The judge asked, "Are you through with the questioning of Rai Rahul Prakash Bahadur? Has he been cooperating with you in the discharge of your duties?"

Ravi and the counsel both got up together and spoke simultaneously, "Yes Lordships, we don't want him for any further interrogation for the time being and we do not oppose his plea for bail."

The judge dictated the order, which was accepted by Rahul and the opposing counsel with a grateful bow. The crux of the order was that since the genuineness of the signature was of essence in the matter, the Enforcement Directorate must verify it and report its findings to the court by the third of January – the date fixed for the next hearing in the matter. Taking into account the social standing of the accused and also in view of his full cooperation, the court was pleased to grant him bail on payment of rupees one lakh, in addition to a surety for a similar amount. The judge asked Rahul to present himself in the court on the third of January and with a stroke of the gavel the next case was called.

❖❖

After finishing the matter in the court, Rahul headed straight for his house but the news from the court proceedings had preceded him there. That he had spent two nights in a Police lockup was still a secret, but Gayatri Devi and Sita knew that he had been summoned for questioning and subsequently produced in the court. Gyaneshwar had been in touch with them and he had all the inside information through his father. They all believed that Rahul had been unduly implicated in the case. They had no doubt that he was innocent and that he would come out of the situation vindicated. Gayatri Devi told Sita that her heart could not accept that he was guilty, but her mind was pulling in a different direction. Sita said that there seemed to be a concerted effort to malign Rahul, because she had also come to know that there was an enquiry ordered by the law commission against Rahul's professional conduct. Gayatri Devi said that things would become clear once they met Rahul.

Rahul entered the house looking dishevelled but composed. Sita walked up to him and gave him a hug. Gayatri Devi got up and embracing him said, "My dear boy, what all you have gone through in the last two days? You don't have to tell me that you have been wrongly implicated in the matter, but do tell me if it's just an accident or if someone is trying to settle a score with you?"

Rahul too felt as emotional and sentimental as his mother and Sita. He felt guilty that he had caused them so much anxiety and anguish. He said, "I'm at a loss myself in trying to make out how all this has happened, but I am sure that ultimately the truth will prevail."

Sita wanted to leave the mother and son alone for a while and left the room on the pretext of organising some refreshments for Rahul. After she left, Gayatri Devi said to Rahul, "I hope all this will be over soon. As you know, in my life nothing gets precedence over honour, not even the love for my only son."

Rahul put his arm around his mother and said, "There is no truth in the allegations, Ma. But naturally, I need some time to tide over the problems."

Having said what she did, Gayatri Devi realised that she could have avoided expressing her inner feelings for the time being, because more than anything else what Rahul needed was support and sympathy. She said, "I'm sure it will pass off as a bad dream and you'll be able to answer all the charges to the full satisfaction of the authorities. I think that what you need most at the moment is something to eat and some rest."

A servant brought in a tray containing tea, fruits, sandwiches and *samosaas* and placed it on the table. After the servant left, Gayatri Devi poured tea and gave it to Rahul. Sipping the tea, he said that he had missed good tea all these days. Caressing his back, she remarked that the house was not the same without him and that he had brought back a lot of cheer with him. He said, "Tell me honestly, did you feel scared and did you miss me?"

Gayatri Devi said that the news was like a volcano erupting inside her and therefore she hardly had any time to miss him. She added that she was greatly relieved to see him. Rahul put his arms around her again and repeated that all would be well.

She said, "It had better be, otherwise I will die! Is there a problem with the Bar Association too?"

Rahul was not surprised that his mother was aware of the development with the Bar Association, as nothing escaped her attention. He said, "Yes, there's trouble on that front as well. There is nothing to worry about, but it does seem that someone is making a concerted effort to malign me."

She said, "I pray that you come out of this problem unscathed but more than that, I want to be sure that you're not even distantly connected with the allegations hurled at you. I'm of the belief that integrity is the greatest asset of a person."

Rahul said, "Let's face it. All one can do is to refute the charges one by one, hopefully to the complete satisfaction of all concerned."

He finished his tea in silence and left for his room, saying that he did not want to be disturbed for dinner as he was tired and would like to retire early. In his room he sat down to reply to the letter he had received from the Bar Association.

"I am in receipt of your letter", he wrote. The charges against me, as enumerated in your letter, are so ludicrous that after going through them I thought that someone had played a joke on me. My family and

I have been associated with the legal profession from its inception and my predecessors distinguished themselves both as judges and as lawyers. I too, in my humble way, have always tried to emulate my ancestors and my late father Rai Ravi Prakash Bahadur."

"The role of the human element cannot be ruled out from any legal proceeding and judgment. A judgment delivered by one court is sometimes trashed by a higher court, not necessarily because the initial judge was corrupt. The views and opinions of individuals differ and this results in divergent observations and judgments. The mischief mongers attribute motives to differences of opinion and weave their own yarns to malign those people whose success they can't bear."

"With all the humility at my command may I, with your indulgence, revive your memory about my considerable success at the Bar and its normal fall out? Do my colleagues at the Bar, who have been struggling for their existence, not have the motive to at least malign my reputation, to derive vicarious pleasure?"

"The allegation, that I have been able to influence the judgments delivered by the judges, is nothing short of casting aspersions on the ability of judges. The judges have the ability to arrive at the truth of a case, the tactics of lawyers notwithstanding. A counsel claiming favours from the court on the basis of his personal equation is guilty of contempt of court. In fact, professional ethics demand that the entire truth be presented before the courts, to enable them to reach the right conclusion, but that does not happen in real life. Both parties contesting a lawsuit try to conceal their weaknesses from the court, and it is the responsibility of the court to arrive at the truth. No lawyer who wants to make a mark in the profession can afford to reveal complete truths to the court at the cost of his client. And the records provide enough evidence of my doing not too badly at the Bar."

"I categorically deny all the allegations made againist at me in your letter and am willing to confront anyone who comes forward to prove otherwise. I do expect, that as a professional courtesy to me, the matter will be treated as top secret, as the leakage of information will mark the end of my career. More than that, it will mar my family's reputation, and that is neither just nor acceptable."

Matters of the Heart

Sita found herself emotionally and mentally drained as never before. So much had happened in such a short time, and Rahul's problems had only compounded the confusion. She knew that Gayatri Devi needed her the most but she was also conscious that she had to do something for her bewildered parents. She was aware of the emotional setback to them. And then there was Gyaneshwar, who seemed to have almost taken it for granted that they were going to marry each other. That night she found she could not sleep and woke up with a heavy head. When she went to Gayatri Devi's room, she found her sitting with Rahul. Both were looking very grim. There was complete silence.

Hesitantly, Sita broke the silence. She said that Gayatri Devi needed some respite from all that had been happening around her and it would be better if she returned to Rasulabad and rested. She suggested that since Rahul had to be in Delhi to sort out his immediate problems, she would accompany her.

While she was talking, Sita saw an anxious looking Diwan Mithai Lal and Savitri entering the room. They both bowed with folded hands before Gayatri Devi. Sita got up, put her arms around Savitri Rani and showed her to a seat.

Gayatri Devi, looking at Sita, said, "It's not only Rahul who has a lot to attend to here. Even you have your hands full and can't leave just now. I'll be alright with Savitri and Diwan *Saheb* who have offered to go with me." She looked at Diwan Mithai Lal, who did not seem sure that Sita could be left alone to handle her new responsibilities.

But he was also aware that Gayatri Devi needed company at a time like this. Looking at Sita, he said, "I've spoken with Gyaneshwar ji. He seems to be well versed with the affairs of Samir sahib. He's assured me that he will offer all assistance to you in tiding over the problems. Moreover, Rahul ji will be here to guide you in your work. You'll have no problem."

Gayatri Devi, Diwan Mithai Lal and Savitri Rani reached Rasulabad the next morning. Gayatri Devi was very depressed. This was the first time in her life that she was feeling what could only be called humiliation. The honour of her family had been threatened, and she was certain that if Rahul did not come out of his dilemma unscathed, she would end her life.

What she had not revealed to anyone was that the previous night, as per her old practice, she had meditated on her late husband and prayed to him for guidance. As usual, he had appeared in her dream. She heard him say, "My lord, I seek no mercy for my son. I'm aware that the facts of the case are well known to you and I pray that you pronounce judgment on the merits of the case. If you find him guilty, please give him his just deserts, but if he is not, please spare him any ignominy. If my son is implicated in a matter of this nature, my wife will have no choice left but to end her life." In the dream, Rai Ravi PrakashBahadur was dressed in his lawyer's robes and was addressing the court. But when he bowed she saw, with surprise, that the person sitting in the Chair was none other than Rahul. The dream had continued and Rai Ravi Prakash Bahadur had told her to leave Delhi immediately, as a very great calamity had befallen their family. He warned her that if she did not hold her ground, the entire edifice of the family would fall apart. On his part, he assured her that he would ensure that full justice was meted out to Rahul. He had left her saying that he was always besides her like the rock of Gibraltar and that a very lovely girl would join her soon and provide her lasting solace.

❖❖

After Samir Saxena's prayer meeting, Rustom, Zaroo and Shahnaz did not go back to their residence but went to their farm house in Mehrauli. Too much had happened in too short a time. Rustom's desire to get Shahnaz married to Rahul was not based on a whim or an impulse; he genuinely felt that Rahul was a very outstanding person. He was so enamoured of Rahul's personality that he was willing to overlook the allegations recently hurled at him. Whether the allegations were true or not, Rustom was sure that Rahul would come out in the clear before long. On his part, he was willing to go to any extent to bail Rahul out. He said to himself, "Let the corruption in society be put to good use for once by getting a good man out of trouble."

Chairs had been laid under a tree. A bearer brought tea and refreshments. He poured the tea, well aware of the quantum of sugar and milk the three desired individually.

Zaroo said sipping her tea, "Samir was as remarkable in his life as he was in his death. He managed to redeem his love through Sita, without her knowing about it. What devotion and commitment!"

Rustom replied, "He had his own way of doing things but whatever he did had a class of its own. Rahul has a lot in common with Samir – ability, understanding, commitment and compassion! I'm sure there's nothing at the bottom of the scandal that he has been roped into, but only time will be able to heal the wound that it has caused to Gayatri."

Shahnaz, equally concerned about Gayatri Devi said, "It's such a pity that Sita's hands are full at a time when aunty needs her most. She is so emotionally torn that she needs personal attendance. Sita may not be able to go with her for some time and that may make things worse."

Looking at her parents she continued, "Don't you think I should go with aunty to Rasulabad? I want to join her work there anyway, and she is open to the idea."

However, the proposal was not acceptable to either Rustom or Zaroo, though for different reasons. Zaroo wanted Shahnaz to marry Azhar, who was presently visiting his parents. *Nawab Saheb* and *Begum Saheba* were both eager for this alliance as well. The only fly in the ointment was Shahnaz and as a solution to the problem, Zaroo wanted Shahnaz and Azhar to meet as much as possible. Her first preference had been Rahul but the changed circumstances had changed her mind as well. Rustom, on the other hand, had complete faith in Rahul and was clear that he was the most eligible boy for Shahnaz. Shahnaz had never given her consent for Rahul but she seemed to be quite friendly with him. Regarding her proposal of accompanying Gayatri Devi, Rustom was of the view that the situation, presently, was too disturbed for an outsider to make an entry.

Zaroo said, "I don't think Gayatri will leave in a hurry. Gayatri can't leave until her son's matter is sorted out, and you cannot leave in any case because *Begum Saheba* is planning to take six families to their farm for a week or so. She was very insistent that Rustom, you and I go with them. Rustom and I have been there before but I'm told the weather there at this time is gorgeous, and I am quite looking forward to it. You must come with us."

Shahnaz was not naive. She understood quite well why her mother was keen on her going to the farm. She decided to close the issue once and for all and said, "I'm sure that Iqbal too will be going with us."

Iqbal was one of the hangers-on in *Nawab Saheb's* family. His father was a petty government official and the family was not too well off. Iqbal and Azhar had been playmates since their childhood. However, no one in the extended friend's circle took any notice of him. All that was known was that he was Azhar's crony. He accompanied Azhar everywhere and had taken a few trips abroad while Azhar was there. It was believed that Azhar took care of most of his needs and had financed his foreign trips as well. *Nawab Saheb's* family had accepted him as their own, but Iqbal's family was not too happy about the friendship, as whatever little he earned was spent on the upkeep of his friendship with Azhar.

Zaroo said, "He may go with the party, but what difference will that make?"

Shahnaz decided to spill the beans. She said, "Mom, I'm not oblivious of your designs and I have no doubt that you've been weaving dreams in your mind about Azhar and me. But aside from the fact that Azhar and I share no chemistry, do you know that Iqbal is a constant mill around Azhar's neck?"

Zaroo was getting annoyed now. She said, "They're childhood friends and maybe they will remain like that all their lives – that's real friendship. Where do you get real friends these days? Azhar is lucky to have one and we should feel happy for him, rather than criticising him for fraternising with a person with lesser privileges."

Rustom, who had been listening to the conversation with rapt attention, butted in. He said, "Shahnaz is perhaps not able to convey what she really wants to say. Maybe what she is unable to tell you clearly is that she suspects Azhar is gay. I don't know how right or wrong she is, but Azhar's closeness with Iqbal does seem curious. I've noticed eyebrows being raised on this issue. Once, I overheard Rajeshwar whispering something of this kind into Rahul's ears and Rahul's reaction was just a faint smile."

Buoyed, Shahnaz said, "It is common knowledge in the friends circle, and Iqbal is not the only one in Azhar's life – there are some others as well. In America, he is alleged to have joined a gay fraternity, but I'm not sure." She looked pointedly at her mother and said, "I can't object to someone opting for a certain lifestyle, but please leave me alone."

Rustom, noticing that the conversation was turning into an

argument, made an endeavour to change the topic. Looking at Shahnaz, he said that he had no objection to her going to Rasulabad with Gayatri Devi. But he thought it was advisable for Shahnaz to have a frank talk with her to know her thoughts on the matter. Zaroo could not help concluding that Rustom's advice was part of his old game plan to bring Shahnaz and Rahul closer. She could not pardon him for it, considering that Rahul had made himself so vulnerable.

Shahnaz said that she had spoken with Gayatri Devi about joining her and her response had been positive. Rustom looking at his wife said, "In all such matters Shahnaz should decide. We are there for her always, but we shouldn't come in the way of what she thinks she should do. I don't think Gayatri will be leaving in a hurry but as and when she goes, I think she would welcome Shahnaz's company. Sita, at least for some time, will not be able to devote time to her work. In fact, she may not be able to work there as she used to, any more. The changed circumstances might make Gayatri's life at Rasulabad lonely and Shahnaz's presence may turn out to be a breath of fresh air."

Zaroo conceded and said, "You two are surely wiser than me and perhaps I'm backing the wrong horse. I have no objection to your going to Rasulabad. After all, at the end of the day, all I want is to see you happy." And so it was decided that Shahnaz should go to work with Gayatri Devi.

❖❖

Next morning, when Shahnaz rang up Rahul's residence, Gyaneshwar picked up the phone to tell her that Gayatri Devi had left for Rasulabad and that Sita had stayed back to attend to the work connected with her late father's estate. It was still strange for Shahnaz to consider Sita the daughter of Samir Saxena. It was strange to imagine that the simple girl who worked with Gayatri Devi in the villages was now busy handling a large inheritance in the prime locations of Delhi. But this also meant that Shahnaz would now be needed at Rasulabad more than ever. She asked for Sita who instantly came on the line. Sita told her that Gayatri Devi was quite distraught and she had taken the entire episode about Rahul as an affront to her honour. Shahnaz told her that she had also wanted to go to Rasulabad but was not aware that aunty would leave so early in the morning. Sita said that she too had wanted to go with her but could not, as she had to tie up the loose ends left behind by her late father. She did concede that Gayatri Devi needed someone around her and endorsed Shahnaz's plan to go to Rasulabad. Shahnaz told her that she would talk with aunty and finalise her program. She told her that she would keep her posted about the plans and then hung up. As she replayed the call in her mind she realised that there had been a hint of excitement in Sita's voice when she had talked about her father.

When Sita put the telephone down, Gyaneshwar walked up to her and told her that they had to go to Samir's chartered accountant to discuss the tax and investment plans. He also said that he had arranged a meeting with the architects in the evening to work out the renovation of the bungalow.

Sita was grateful to Gyaneshwar for all the assistance he was rendering her, but she wanted to take her own time to reflect on the new situation. She said, "Don't you think that all this can wait till Rahul gets out of trouble? At the moment he needs all the help he can get. And he needs you most, with all your wisdom and influence. Once he is rid of his problems, the three of us can plan out things together."

Gyaneshwar was quite fond of Rahul, but he did not like the mention of his name in the present context. He did not think that a committee was needed to manage the estate left behind by Samir, but he thought it best to agree with her. He said, "Rahul's problems with the Directorate of Enforcement will be over soon. Dad told me that they've not been able to find any evidence against him. The properties that have been acquired in Rahul's name overseas will be confiscated, but that makes no difference to Rahul as they don't belong to him in any case. They had been purchased by some trickster using his stolen passport."

She said, "There's some complaint from the Bar Association too, and if he does not come out clean they may cancel his license to practice."

Gyaneshwar was well versed with Rahul's troubles. He said, "My father is of the view that such complaints are difficult to prove and even if they suspend his license, there is a provision for appeal. Proceedings under contempt of court may be initiated for trying to disrupt the process of the court, which is another charge against Rahul. But in contempt proceedings, the conduct of the court comes under greater scrutiny than that of the lawyer and courts avoid initiating such proceedings. I don't think any tangible harm is likely to come to Rahul, but he'll certainly find it difficult to protect his reputation. Rumours travel like wildfire and the entire population of India thrives on rumour mongering."

Sita agreed. "That's the problem. The family accords the highest priority to honour. God forbid, but I know for sure that *Ma* will not be able to live with her honour compromised."

Gyaneshwar said, "I appreciate your sentiments but there is precious little you can do about the family honour."

Sita kept quiet for a while then said, "Rahul's problems have disturbed me greatly. He is an outstanding person and he is going through hell. He has been my childhood idol, philosopher, friend and guide. I could never do anything without him, and today when he needs help I find that I can do nothing for him."

She sat lost in thought. Old memories started coming back one by one. Rahul — the darling of all and the apple of his parents' eyes. His father had great dreams for him. He provided him with the best education and training in every respect and Rahul always exceeded his expectations. He had always lived with his convictions. Sita recalled an all-India inter-university debate that Rahul had participated in and won. The subject of the debate had been 'Life with conviction is more rewarding than life rolling in wealth.'

Sita remembered the day of the debate. Rahul always walked to the podium like a winner and spoke with such force and authority that one could hardly believe that he was participating in a simple, university debate. He had no trouble in convincing the audience that living with one's own convictions was the only way to experience lasting happiness, and that wealth created a desire for more wealth which only caused anxiety and discontentment. The applause after his speech had left no one in doubt as to who would win the debate.

Tears rolled down her eyes as she thought of the times when had she lived under the impression that they were destined to marry each other. She realised that even now there was a wrench left in a corner of her heart. The idea had been dropped so easily only because of the low status of her surrogate parents. This, she was now convinced of. Deep inside, she felt insulted and rejected.

She broke her silence. She told Gyaneshwar, "You've already done so much that I can't thank you enough. Rahul will have to help himself. No outsider can get him out of his predicament because no one is aware of the true facts. From what you told me just now, it seems that he has to fight on several fronts and unless one is aware of the real issues one can only draw conjectures."

He said, "I've always held Rahul in high esteem and I will do whatever I can for him." Then, changing the topic he said, "I've collected all the relevant papers from Samir uncle's solicitors and chartered accountants. I need to sit with you to iron out certain issues and you have to take a decision on what is to be done with the estate he has left behind. I suggest that we talk it over lunch tomorrow."

❖❖

Despite her appreciation for his help, Sita felt a burden upon her. It was obvious now that Gyaneshwar had presumed they would marry. But as far as she was concerned, she hardly knew him and he had suddenly occupied the center stage in her life. She was aware that Rahul and her late father were contemplating her marriage to Gyaneshwar. While she always knew that she wanted to get married at some point, she could not accept the idea of marriage being thrust upon her.

She told him, "I understand the urgency but I want to involve *Ma*, Rahul, *Amma* and *Babuji* in all the decisions around my father's estate." She had taken to referring to Samir as her father now and each time she did it, she felt good.

Gyaneshwar observed her gentle face and wise eyes. He could sense that she still had many reservations about him. On his part, he had fallen in love with her and was certain that she was the woman he wanted to marry. He said, "That is the right way of doing things but the loose ends have to be tied up as soon as possible. I have all the relevant documents in my possession and I'm keen on handing them over to you at the earliest. Do let me know when we can meet, and take care!" With that he got up to leave. Sita got up to see him off and accompanied him up to the main door.

❖❖

After he left, Sita found herself alone in the house. She realised that she was alone after a very long time. Her life had taken a very strange turn. Two people who did not really matter to her earlier had now entered her life, altering all her old equations substantially. The discovery of her father gave her an identity which she had not experienced before and she admitted to herself that it provided her with a lot of confidence and contentment. Diwan Mithai Lal and Savitri Rani had given her all the love and care that parents could give and she reciprocated their love in equal measure but the discovery of a real father did make a difference. Within a few days, Samir Saxena had come to occupy the most cherished place in her heart.

While Sita was in the midst of her reverie, Rahul entered the house and went straight to his room. She realised that he had returned only when she heard his voice talking to someone over the phone. She heard him say, "Well, I'm glad that you're happy at taking your revenge, but what is this revenge for? I've never harmed you consciously." The person at the other end said something in reply and Rahul said, "I can meet you any time. But give me an idea of what you want, so I can prepare accordingly."

Her curiosity piqued, Sita entered Rahul's room. On seeing her he put the phone on loud speaker and gestured for her to listen in. She heard a female voice saying, "You've been insulting me all these years only because you think you are Don Juan and I am an old hag. Perhaps you never realised that the females you've been chasing are much younger to you than you are to me."

Reddening, Rahul replied, "To the best of my knowledge, I've not been chasing any ladies. Perhaps I could spare more time and thought on the matter but I'm busy with all the hassles you have got me trapped in."

The female voice said, "I'm not saying that I've got you trapped. All I'm saying is that I look upon your sorry state of affairs as my revenge for your rude and snobbish behaviour towards me. But as a good friend, I'm asking you if I can be of some help. No one knows better than you what transpired with Ranjit, and he's hell bent upon teaching you a lesson. I can help."

Sita understood that the female talking to Rahul was far from sympathetic. She signalled for him to refrain from saying anything indiscreet, lest it got recorded on the other side. Rahul noticed Sita's signal and gestured for her to just listen. He said, "I've done nothing wrong and I'm sure that truth will prevail. Thank you for your offer of help, I do appreciate it."

The voice from the other side said, "So you've decided not to meet me even when you are in deep trouble and I am in a position to help. One day you will be sorry for it." And the telephone went dead.

Rahul asked Sita, "Do you know Neha?"

She shook her head.

He thought for a while and then said, "Neha is a socialite. She lives with a very successful business tycoon, Ranjit. I had no idea that she was livid with me for not paying her any attention despite her repeated overtures."

Sita asked, "And Ranjit is leading the campaign against you, is he not?"

He nodded.

She said, "Is it not likely that Neha is at the back of all the problems?"

Rahul replied, "She wants me to believe that. More than that, she wants to convince me that she can bail me out."

Sita replied, "At this juncture no help should be refused. We have to get out of this situation at any cost."

He smiled wryly and said, "I doubt whether she can be of any effective help, and even if she is in a position to help, I cannot pay her price."

Rahul asked her if she was up to a trip to the club. Sita welcomed it as she wanted a change of scene.

At the club, Rahul surprised her by sharing that he was toying with the idea of quitting his legal practice and burying the controversy. Shocked Sita exclaimed, "How can you think of something like that? Quitting will only confirm the allegations and *Ma* will never be able to accept that." She said that the only way to keep *Ma* at peace with herself was to come out of his predicament with flying colours.

"No matter what happens in the investigation I don't know if I will ever be able to get rid of the stigma," said Rahul.

Sita had never seen him so defeated. She could not relate to the man who sat in front of her. With eyes blazing she said, "Rahul, honour is not only to be lived in daily life, but fought for in the arena of the world. How can the son of Gayatri Devi speak in this way?"

He changed the topic. "There's a lot of sense in what you say. Do you know what else will provide solace to *Ma*?"

Sita said, "Yes, I know that she's very keen on your marriage. That is the first thing you should consider after you are through with these problems."

Rahul said, "It's not my marriage that is upper most in her mind for my marriage will take time. She's more worried about your marriage, especially now that so many changes have come about. So out with it, what is your opinion of Gyaneshwar? *Ma* and I have examined the match from all angles and we've come to the conclusion that he is worthy of you. I can make a formal proposal to him, provided that you approve. Even Samir uncle thought well of Gyaneshwar and had asked me to find out from you what you thought of him."

Sita thought for a while and replied, "Marriage is the last thing on my mind at the moment but yes, I do have to get married. Gyaneshwar is a fine person and since you all approve of him, it makes it easier for me to decide in his favour but I would like to play it by the ear for the time being as our family is going through such turmoil."

Rahul pointed out that there was no hurry for marriage and that she could take her own time to decide but he suggested that she meet Gyaneshwar frequently. He said that he was glad Gyaneshwar was rendering great assistance to her and in the process they were getting closer to each other. Sita did not say anything but it did occur to her that subsequent to her father's death, Gyaneshwar and she had in fact been spending a lot of time together and in the process they were indeed coming closer. She maintained a graceful silence. Rahul said, "I'll be free for dinner the day after tomorrow. Why don't you call Gyaneshwar? It would be nice."

Sita said, "What a coincidence? He suggested the same."

❖❖

Diwan Mithai Lal received Shahnaz at the railway station. He told her that Gayatri Devi had wanted to come herself but could not do so because subsequent to Samir *Saheb's* death there had been an unending stream of visitors at the *Haveli*. They went to the *Haveli*, where they found some local friends of the family awaiting Gayatri Devi's arrival. The news of Sita being the offspring of Samir and Farah had already travelled some distance. Haji ji was nowhere to be seen and it was rumoured that he had gone to his brother in Meerut.

After the initial pleasantries, Gayatri Devi caught hold of Shahnaz's hand and told her in an urgent tone, "You've come at a very opportune moment. I've never felt so lonely in this house as I have in the last few days. You have come like a breath of fresh air."

She said, "It has been my dream to come and be with you. Actually, I wanted to accompany you from Delhi itself but you came away without my knowledge."

Gayatri Devi introduced Shahnaz to all those who had come to meet her and told them that she had decided to join her in her work. Everyone nodded in appreciation and there was an implicit understanding among all that Shahnaz was Sita' replacement.

Ram Lal brought tea and homemade popcorn in a bowl and served everyone. After the visitors departed, Gayatri Devi told Shahnaz that she could take any room in the *Haveli* barring the ones earmarked for Sita and Rahul. Relieved at the departure of the visitors, Shahnaz said, "*Ma,* I'll be equally comfortable in any room. Tell me how you are and what is the latest news of Rahul? I tried to contact him before leaving but he wasn't available on the phone. Sita told me that slowly things were working out for the better."

She replied, "How can things be better? Our reputation has taken a beating and that cannot be undone. I'm keeping my fingers crossed, but more than anything else what is important is that I must be convinced of Rahul's innocence."

Shahnaz said, "As far as that is concerned, I have no doubt that he is absolutely innocent. I had half a mind to request Dad to get the latest facts from Vinay uncle but decided against it because I did not have your clearance."

Gayatri Devi noticed the confidence that Shahnaz had in Rahul's integrity and also the sensitivity with which she handled matters. She told her that she could trust her father for anything concerning her family but Vinay, being a sitting judge of the High Court, had his own compulsions, and it might not be fair to draw him into any controversy. Having said this, she remembered that while at Delhi, she had spoken with Vinay Khosla about Rahul's problems and he had not given Rahul a categorical clean chit. At the time she had brushed aside his observations as the cynicism of a righteous judge.

Shahnaz's arrival at Rasulabad revived Gayatri Devi's memory of the last dream she had had of her husband. She recalled that he had mentioned that a girl would come into her life and bring a lot of solace. Shahnaz's coming synchronised with the message in the dream and proved the prediction right but she was finding it an uphill task to interpret the meaning of that part of the dream, where her late husband was addressing Rahul the Judge. She missed Sita immensely, because on such occasions she could take her into confidence. She thought of speaking with her over the phone but, considering all the developments in Delhi, decided against it.

After some deliberation, she narrated the whole dream to

Shahnaz and asked her to give her interpretation.

Shahnaz said, "Aunty, I'm aware that spirits can be summoned but such practices should be adopted only when everything else fails, because the spirit that is summoned through this process goes through considerable hardship. You had very good reasons for doing what you did, your world was falling apart right in front of your eyes and there was very little you could do about it. To my mind, three messages have been given to you. One is that a girl will force herself upon you, and here I am. The second is that the family honour is in jeopardy and you have to protect it with all your might. These two messages are clear.But the third message has to be interpreted very carefully lest a wrong conclusion is drawn. Aunty, the strange part of the message is that the spirit did not plead innocence and also did not seek mercy. The spirit saw the judge in Rahul and therefore the message suggests that the authorities won't be able to find faults with Rahul. He will come out unscathed but if he is even slightly guilty, he will have to decide for himself the punishment that he should undergo."

Gayatri Devi was impressed with Shahnaz's interpretation of her dream. She said, "I fall back on the support of my late husband's spirit only when I am at my wit's end and find myself desperate. Your analysis is interesting and since the first prophecy has come out to be true, I see no reason for the others not to materialise. But in the unlikely event of Rahul being even distantly connected with any of the charges that have been alleged, I'll have nothing to do with him. I will do anything to protect the honour of my family."

They strolled around the *Haveli* for a while and finally converged on the library. Showing her the book-filled racks, Gayatri Devi told her that she would find books on almost any subject in the library. There was an old piano lying in one corner of the room which she could practice on, as and when she desired. Shahnaz told her not to worry about her comforts. In fact, there was so much to do that she did not expect there to be much free time. Gayatri Devi told her to live like a member of the family and to accompany her on all trips to the community development centres and other social engagements. She informed her that the finances of the centres were handled by Diwan Mithai Lal and she could deal with him directly just as Sita used to. She said that after Sita came back she would have more vibrant company. She also suggested that Shahnaz pay Savitri Rani a visit. Savitri was also going through much emotional upheaval and would be very happy to meet her. Though Sita spoke with her everyday over the phone, she did feel lonely without her physical presence in Rasulabad.

Shahnaz asked, "Where does Haji ji's family live? Why were the visitors saying that he has left town and gone to some of his relatives in Meerut? Should it not have been natural for him to go and meet Sita? She would like to meet the Hajis to know more about her mother." She stopped for a while and then asked, "Aunty, you must have known Sita's mother. Was she very beautiful? Could things have not been worked out between her and Samir Uncle?"

Gayatri Devi was not in a mood to explain the social structure of the town to Shahnaz. She simply said, "Yes, she was a very beautiful person in every respect."

❖❖

Gyaneshwar had accepted Sita's invitation for dinner. A simple, quiet meal at Rahul's place had been planned. It was Rahul's idea to express his gratitude to Gyaneshwar for all that he had been doing to help Sita. He also wanted to find out the gossip that was doing the rounds of the city's cocktail circuit regarding his problems. Gyaneshwar arrived on time to find that Rahul and Sita were waiting for him in the drawing room. Rahul had got up to receive him when he saw a bearded man wearing a *kurta-pajama* and a plain shawl with a turban following Gyaneshwar into the house. The face of the man seemed familiar but he could not place him straight away. Then it suddenly dawned upon him that the man was none other than Haji ji. Advancing towards him, Rahul said, "Haji ji, when did you come?"

Without even looking at him, Haji took out a revolver from his pocket and fired in the direction of Sita. Sita, who was in the process of getting up to welcome Gyaneshwar, fell down to the floor with a scream. Next Haji shot himself, and with the name of *Allah* on his lips collapsed to the ground. Sita remained prone on the ground. Gyaneshwar rushed towards her and picked her up. The bullet had missed her but she did not seem to have enough strength to stand on her feet. He gently helped her to her feet and then led her to the sofa. Rahul walked towards Haji ji's body, which was lying on the ground in a pool of blood. His revolver was lying on the floor. It was obvious that he was dead, but Rahul decided that the only ones to touch the body should be the Police or the doctors.

Sita was in a state of shock and had lost her speech. Rahul got a glass of water for her and sat by her side, holding her hands and telling her to be brave. Gyaneshwar, sitting on the other side, was consoling her as well. After a while, Sita collected herself and pointing towards Haji ji said, "He is my *Mama,* my maternal uncle. What happened to him?"

Rahul replied blankly, "I've known him from my childhood and he's been known to be very loyal to my family. I could not have imagined, in my wildest dreams, that he could be so rash and violent. We have to call the Police and the doctor. I shudder to imagine what could have happened today."

Rahul called the Police and reported the incident. The Police inspector told him not to disturb or touch any part of the body until the authorities arrived. Rahul called his family doctor, Dr. Pankaj Sayal, to see if Sita required any medical assistance.

Gyaneshwar was happy that he had talked to his family about Sita and they had approved of his desire to marry her, or he would have had to explain why he was there and had got involved in this. His father would have worried about the fallout to his political career and would have put the blame squarely on his immaturity and lack of vision. After all, he had not accepted the idea of his son marrying Sita without any reservations. He did not have anything against Sita, but he was of the view that Gyaneshwar could marry someone equally good and with much better credentials – status, wealth etc. Gyaneshwar did not have to work hard to cajole his father only because his mother was all for Gyaneshwar's choice. She was of the view that for a happy married life what was most important was that the boy and the girl loved and respected each other. Status and wealth, she thought, were passing phases of life. She always used to say that many colossal inheritances had been torn to smithereens and many one time paupers were known to have left behind huge inheritances for their succeeding generations.

Sita had resumed her usual calm demeanour but was not clear about what had really happened. This had been the first and only time that she had been faced with Haji as his niece. The Hajis had crossed her mind several times ever since she had come to know about her mother. With Samir Saxena's death, the Hajis were the last surviving blood ralatives she had been left with. And now this had happened.

Dr. Sayal and the Police arrived almost simultaneously. Haji was still lying in a pool of blood but it had yet to be medically verified that he was dead. Sita suggested that the doctor examine him first. The Police however asked everyone to keep away from the body. One of the officers took possession of the revolver and wrapped it with a piece of white cloth. Another took a few photographs of the site and asked Rahul, Gyaneshwar and Sita to accompany them to the hospital. While Rahul and Gyaneshwar wanted to allow Sita to stay back, she insisted that she would accompany them.

At the hospital it was ascertained that Haji had died instantly after shooting himself. His body was searched and a note was found, written in Urdu. It read, "I am not a Haji only by name. I am a true Muslim and have always abided by the rules of my faith. I am conscious that on the day of reckoning, I will have to answer for all my acts of omission and commission.

"Sita's mother, Farah, was my little sister who did the family proud. But we lost her one day, and we searched for her all over in vain. Her employer, late *Janaab* Samir Saxena, left no stone unturned to trace her. Anyone who knew her had complete faith in her integrity and character and therefore, the entire community came to the conclusion that she must have met with an accident and was dead. We bowed before the wish of *Allah*, the most benevolent."

"Ever since I have come to know that Sita is the illegitimate offspring of *Janaab* Samir Saxena and Farah, I have been haunted by the ghost of indignation. The honour of my family has been compromised and I am responsible for it. I had taken Farah to *Janaab* Saxena and therefore it is my responsibility to avenge the humiliation inflicted upon my family. I would have killed him if he was alive but since he is no more, I have decided to destroy Sita–the symbol of my family's humiliation."

"I know that it is a sin to kill someone and that is why I have decided to end my life. I have taken this decision independently and nobody should be blamed for it after I am no more."

The Inspector took the letter into his possession and kept it carefully in his file. The statements of Sita, Rahul and Gyaneshwar were taken and the three of them went back to Rahul's house. Rahul suggested that they go out somewhere for dinner but Sita was in no mood and Gyaneshwar wanted to go home and inform his father about all that had happened.

The Defeat of Gayatri Devi

Rajeshwar and his wife heard the entire story from Gyaneshwar and thanked God for sending their son back to them safe and sound. They felt that in a situation like that anything could have happened. His mother, looking at her husband said, "In any case, precautions should be taken to ensure that the incident is not repeated. It isn't unlikely that other *members* of the Haji family might try to kill her in the name of family honour."

Rajeshwar said, "That's no problem. I'll speak with the Commissioner of Police and make sure that she gets adequate Police protection." To the utter surprise of Gyaneshwar and his mother, he added, "But the question is whether we should still consider the proposal of our son's marriage with Sita. After all, she is an illegitimate child and that too from a Muslim mother."

Gyaneshwar said, "In the first place, there is no proposal. It is only my wish. I've not even mentioned it to her and secondly, I don't see any change in the circumstances."

Rajeshwar said, "Where is the question of her declining your proposal? I don't think her to be so devoid of sense. And the situation has changed drastically. It may not really matter to you, but I'm in public life. I'm answerable to my constituents and I can ill afford to take an unpopular decision. In a way it's good that you've yet to make a formal proposal to Sita. We will have to think about it."

Gyaneshwar was aghast at his father's observations. He said, "Dad, I see no change in the situation. You have been well aware that Sita is the daughter of late Samir Saxena and that she continues to be. I may not have proposed to her yet but that makes no difference because my mind is firmly made up." After a pause, he added, "In fact, this marital alliance will project you as a secular leader."

Rajeshwar's wife, feeling proud of her son handling the matter with such deftness, said to Gyaneshwar, "Your father has a knack for missing out the most important aspect of any issue. I'm surprised that you haven't formally proposed to her. You say you're in love with her. How many in this world experience love? I think you are blessed. Most marriages drag on without love creeping into them. You must propose to her and bring her home at the earliest."

Rajeshwar got the Police Commissioner on the line and after narrating the incident at Rahul's house, requested him for Police protection for Sita. The Commissioner told him that Rahul had already informed him about the matter and that he had taken the necessary action. But this irritated Rajeshwar all the more. He hung up and continued the conversation with his family. He said, "Love is just infatuation and it can't last forever, because circumstances are constantly changing. What matters in life is power and wealth, and that can buy love too." Since this subject had been discussed in the family time and again, no one was willing to stir up a hornet's nest so they preferred to keep quiet.

❖❖

After Gyaneshwar had left, Rahul spoke with his mother to inform her about all that had happened. Gayatri Devi was shocked and told him to speak with the Police Commissioner first and then call her back. When he called back, she asked him to give the phone to Sita. When

Sita came on the line she said, "I don't have to tell you that you're a very wise girl, but you must understand that what appears to be a bad time is actually only a test. If the time was really bad, the bullet would have hurt you; it could have even rendered you disabled. This is only a process of purification."

Sita broke down completely, unable to deal with setback after setback. She wailed, "Why did God make me so impure?"

Gayatri Devi consoled her. She said, "A diamond is not impure but it has to be rubbed to give it more lustre and shine. My sixth sense tells me that you are destined to do something big and the Almighty is putting you through the grind to prepare you for it."

All Sita's pent up emotions came to the surface. She could not control herself and said, "Ma, I was very happy as I was. I want to be in the midst of all of you at Rasulabad. I would like to take the next train and come to you."

This was an alarming suggestion, for with the presence of the Hajis in Rasulabad, it was risky for Sita to be here. Gayatri Devi said, "I do not want you to come here for while. You have a lot of work to attend to in Delhi. I'll come as soon as possible. In the mean time hold the fort and be a brave girl!"

Sita enquired about her parents and suggested that if possible the incident should not be revealed to them. She warned that there might be danger to their lives as well owing to their association with her. Gayatri Devi assured her that she would personally ensure the safety of her parents and would bring them along to Delhi.

❖❖

The next morning Sita had her breakfast alone as Rahul had to go out. The maid informed her that he had left word that he would be back for dinner. She got a call from Gyaneshwar saying that his parents wanted to visit her and that the three of them would be calling on her. Prior to his call, Sita had received telephone calls from Rustom and *Nawab Saheb*, both of whom wanted to come and see her.

The guests arrived a little before Rahul. Barring Rajeshwar and Gyaneshwar, everyone hugged Sita and thanked God that a major calamity had been averted. *Begum Saheba* and Nikhat suggested that Sita could move out to their home because Rahul was busy with his work and it was not wise to stay alone. Rustom and Zaroo offered to take her out to the farm for a change of air. Zaroo mentioned that she had spoken with Shahnaz and she had said that Rasulabad was not the same without her and that everyone, including Gayatri Devi was missing her.

Rajeshwar, who specialised in dropping bricks on such occasions, said, "The fact that her own relative is involved has made things so much worse. Imagine the emotional turmoil that she must be going through. I spoke with the Commissioner of Police to arrange for her security and he told me the whole story. Putting up with such a situation with such equanimity reflects on her strength of character."

Nawab Saheb and the others were feeling uneasy at Rajeshwar's comments. To change the topic Rustom said, "Where is Rahul? Has he gone to work?"

Sita kept quiet but Rajeshwar replied, "Rahul must have gone to Justice Vinay Khosla. I understand that he has agreed to mediate in the matter and iron out the charges or the misgivings, whatever you may call them." There was silence and then *Nawab Saheb* said abruptly, "Must you talk in riddles all the time? No one can make head or tail of your observations."

Rajeshwar replied, "I have to be discreet in my utterances because I am privy to many government secrets, and any irresponsible statement from me may cause havoc."

Nawab Saheb quipped, "What else have you been doing here except causing havoc?"

Rajeshwar was not amused. He said, "Rustom ji asked a question and I've given the answer. Should I not tell him what I know?"

Gyaneshwar looked at Sita and his mother sheepishly. His mother went to sit next to Sita and suggested that she accompany the Modys to their farm, where she would find some much needed rest. Sita understood that she wanted to invite her to her own place, but knew that it would be awkward given Rajeshwar's strange manner. She said, "There's so much to do in connection with my father's estate that I can't move out of here for a while. Anyway, the best place for me to rest is Rasulabad." If people found it strange that Sita was referring to Samir as her father, they did not mention it.

Amid the discussion Rahul arrived. Knowing well that everyone would have many questions for him, he proceeded to update them. He had had a very elaborate discussion with Justice Khosla about his problems and was in the process of making up his mind about the future plan of action. But before taking a final decision he wanted to talk it over with his mother. Not aware that he would find so many visitors at home, he had decided to discuss the matter with Sita first and then speak with his mother. She was the best person to guide him about his mother, because she knew her the best and it was very important that the matter be divulged to her in a manner that caused her the least harm.

Rahul walked up to Rustom and Zaroo and greeted them. They reciprocated with an embrace. *Nawab Saheb* proceeded towards Rahul with open arms and said, "God is great! Someone said that you had gone out on work and I inferred that we'll miss you today. How are you?" Rahul paid due courtesy to everyone and shook hands with Gyaneshwar, saying, "Good that you're here. Actually, you've been deputising for me. You're doing what I should have done to assist Sita."

Rajeshwar asked him, "How was your meeting with Justice Khosla? I think you should do whatever he advises."

Rahul said diplomatically, "Justice Khosla is a very sensitive and compassionate gentleman."

Rustom just smiled at Rahul's sense of discretion but *Nawab Saheb* could not stop himself and said, "Rajeshwar, I'm sure you know that a judge refrains from giving advice to people on legal matters; that too a man like Khosla!"

Rahul thought it was time he changed the topic. He said that Haji ji's body was being sent to Rasulabad for burial and a final report had been filed by the Police, declaring the incident to be an accidental suicide. Given the content of Haji's letter, the Police were anticipating a law and order situation at his burial. Sita heard everything in silence and a feeling of guilt enveloped her. She felt responsible for all that had happened, but there was nothing that she could do about it. Everybody knew about Haji's relationship with her and that he had attempted to take her life.

Everyone left one by one, praising her for her fortitude and assuring her that all would be well. Gyaneshwar stayed back.

❖❖

After everyone had gone Rahul poured himself a cup of tea and settled himself comfortably in a reclining chair. He looked at Sita and said, "Nothing has been proven against me. I've been clearly acquitted in the FEMA case by the Directorate of Enforcement, but in the matter of professional misconduct, the needle of suspicion has yet to change its direction. They are convinced that I've been influencing the witnesses and taking advantage of my proximity to the judges. The cases they've quoted are subjective and can be refuted, but it may not be worthwhile, because by the time the cases are over I won't be able to show my face at the Bar, let alone practice there."

Sita looked at him enquiringly because she was not yet sure if it was right to talk so frankly in front of Gyaneshwar. Rahul understood the cause for Sita's worry. He said, "I don't know how to break this news to *Ma*. You know exactly how she reacts to things and I want a dispassionate and intelligent man like Gyaneshwar to help me in working out a strategy to convey the news, because at no cost do I want to hurt her. It is important that the case is presented to her in a manner that, after hearing it, she does not have an iota of doubt that I am innocent. Gyaneshwar has been helping us in sorting out our other problems and I know that he can keep any secret under wraps."

Sita replied, "*Ma* will believe what is right and we all know that you have been framed. You should tell her what you're telling me, but I think that she would want you to vindicate yourself at any cost instead of giving up practice altogether. The only thing she won't compromise on is her honour. In any case, what is the latest? I understand you've visited Justice Khosla."

Rahul said, "Yes and he is of the view that the entire issue should be nipped in the bud, because the more it's prolonged, the more mudslinging there will be. In his opinion, my adversaries have succeeded in building up a case which may not eventually stand but will discredit me neverthless. He thinks that the best way to put an end to the episode is to quit practice and depend on fading human memory."

Gyaneshwar intervened. He said, "That's the problem. Gayatri Devi will not go by her gut feeling alone. She will certainly take into account the cases cited by the establishment. She has faith in you but she's a rational human being and won't believe that there can be smoke without a fire. I don't think that the solace of fading human memory will satisfy an upright woman like her."

Sita was in agreement with him. She said, "*Ma* will not accept this situation. She would like to know for herself that you've done nothing wrong and if she is satisfied about your innocence then she will take on the whole world to vindicate your position. Your theory of fading human memory will cut no ice with her because she has always lived with truth, as understood by herself as well as others."

❖❖

The telephone rang. It was Gayatri Devi. She did not know about the latest developments at Rahul's end. Hearing his voice she said, "I hope Sita is also there because I want to talk to both of you." After he told her that he was going to put the call on loud speaker she said, "I'm in a terrible dilemma. Haji ji's body came here for the burial and the District Magistrate suggested that I not go for the funeral, apprehensive that my presence might add to the tension in the atmosphere. But just now, two of Haji's relatives came to request me to come to his house, saying that the procession cannot start without me. Haji, as you know, had been very loyal to me and had served me well. But it's also true that there is a change in the situation and that there are definite signs of communal tension."

Sita asked her, "Have you informed the District Magistrate that his family is insistent that you join the ceremony?"

Gayatri Devi said, "I've had a long chat with him and he's still of the view that I should avoid going for the ceremony. He suggests that I can go and visit the family later, but I don't think he is right. If I don't go, the gulf between the two communities could widen and may even leave a permanent scar."

Sita said, "*Ma*, you must attend the ceremony, and the police should be able to make adequate arrangements to ensure that the law and order situation is kept under control. Your not attending the burial would send the wrong signal and I agree that it may make things worse."

Rahul said, "*Ma*, you're the symbol of communal harmony in Rasulabad. You've got to go."

Gayatri Devi said, "I hope things are working out well at your end. I tried to contact Vinay Khosla but he wasn't available. His secretary told me that he'll call me later."

Rahul knew that Vinay Khosla's advice to him would not be acceptable to his mother and therefore, in order to avoid the topic, he said, "*Ma*, I'll talk to you after you're through with the burial." And he put the phone down.

Gyaneshwar had noticed that neither Sita nor Rahul was inclined to keep family secrets from him anymore. Since Haji's attack, he had sensed even Sita warming up to him. He wanted to tell her that his father had come to know that the wrath of the Muslim community of Rasulabad was directed against her. Their leaders were of the view that she was the symbol of humiliation hurled upon them by a Hindu known as Samir Saxena. He said, "I must say, Gayatri Devi is a very wise person. She wanted to know Sita's mind on the matter but avoided telling her something of vital importance because she did not want to upset her. Through my father, I know that the Muslims there are ranged against her. Her visit may not be advisable for some time."

Sita's face fell. She said, "That's a bolt from the blue. I hadn't visualised this." There was pin drop silence.

Rahul said, "That is understandable but not much of a problem. She has to be in Delhi to adjust herself in her new environment."

Sita said, "I think *Ma* needs me the most at this time and I cannot shirk my responsibility just because somebody imagines that it is in the interest of communal harmony. Moreover, as far as the properties left behind by my father are concerned, I would like to build a maternity home as desired by him and donate the rest to the Cancer Institute of India. I don't want anything for myself. My life can go on as before."

Rahul said, "You're right. *Ma* needs you but your presence is required here even more. Mercifully, Shahnaz is at Rasulabad and that's some consolation."

Gyaneshwar said that the situation had become very serious and nothing should be done in haste. He asked if Shahnaz had decided to work with Gayatri Devi and stay there.

Rahul said, "Looks like that, but who knows? Could anybody have imagined all that has happened recently?"

When there was no reaction from anyone, he looked at Sita and said, "Your presence at Rasulabad would have been of great help to *Ma* but the forces of providence are perhaps working against this. At the moment you'll be a liability there rather than an asset. For the time being your contact with *Ma* will have to be confined to the telephone."

Gyaneshwar nodded and asked for leave. He said that he had collected all the papers of the late Samir Saxena's estate and asked Sita to look them over at her convenience.

She said, "The papers are safer with you than they are with me. Moreover, I've already told you what I wish to do with the property. I'm sure *Ma* and my parents will agree with my decision. We may start working in that direction."

Gyaneshwar found that things were moving too fast for his liking. He said, "I told you not to act in haste. Once you've made up your mind I will attend to everything. Why don't we meet after a couple of days? By that time, things will be clearer and it may be easier for you to decide."

❖❖

Rustom heard about the near-riot situation in Rasulabad and rang up Shahnaz. He wanted her to come back to Delhi immediately. He said that he had come to know from the authorities that the situation was alarming. Her mother was almost delirious with worry. Shahnaz flatly refused to come back. She said that, in the first place, their information about the situation was exaggerated and secondly, this was the time when she was needed the most.

Zaroo and Rustom felt proud of their daughter's commitment and maturity. They both decided to go to Rasulabad to see her. When Gayatri Devi heard of their plan to visit, she rang them up and declared that they would be staying at the *Haveli*. She added that she wanted to discuss certain important matters with them and that their visit would give her an opportunity to do that.

They arrived by car. The *Haveli* had been spruced up in their honour and a room adjacent to Shahnaz's room had been set up for them. Ram Lal was asked to personally look after them during their stay and he had arranged to produce special, non-vegetarian food for the occasion. Shahnaz was happy that so much was being made of her parents' visit.

Gayatri Devi was sitting with Diwan Mithai Lal and the superintendent of Police and Shahnaz in the verandah when Rustom's Bentley entered the compound. The car was parked in the portico and everybody got up to receive the guests. Rustom said, "Everything looks alright here. There is tranquillity in the atmosphere of this place."

Gayatri Devi said, "You take happiness and peace with you wherever you go. Your coming here has made the difference."

Rustom and Zaroo took turns to hug and kiss Shahnaz. They found her happy and well settled. Zaroo said to Shahnaz, "You look very happy. What has Gayatri done to you?" She said, "She spread the rumour that things were not good here in order to have you over. She knew how happy your visit would make me."

The three of them clung to one another, delighted at being together again. Then Gayatri Devi said, "There are others also waiting to receive you." She introduced them to the Superintendent of Police who had heard of Rustom. She told Rustom that there was peace and order in Rasulabad because of the Superintendent who replied, "I would not be able to do anything without the guidance and support of Madam."

He left after an exchange of pleasantries. Gayatri Devi asked the

Modys if they wanted to wash and stretch their legs before having a cup of tea. She suggested that they could all have their tea together but if they preferred to have it in their room, it could be served there. Zaroo replied that after a wash they would like to sit with her. Gayatri Devi told Shahnaz to take her parents to their room.

After settling in Rustom asked Shahnaz, "Now tell me honestly if you are happy with yourself and the new surroundings you have chosen."

She replied, "I could not have taken a better decision, but I must confess that I miss both of you enormously. I was seriously contemplating a visit to Delhi but aunty has been going through a harrowing experience and she's emotionally disturbed. The least I can do is to give her company and share a bit of her workload. If Sita was here, things would have been different. But I understand that she can't come here at present."

Rustom said, "Poor lady! If Sita's problem has depressed her so much then how is she taking all the problems faced by her son?"

Shahnaz told her parents that aunty was very apprehensive about the shape of things to come because, in spite of her best efforts, she had not been able to get in touch with Justice Khosla. Rahul's mother had full faith in his integrity but also suspected that he may have taken someone else's blame upon himself.

Rustom said, "I agree with her that the charges against him are figments of someone's imagination but I do think that Rahul is wise enough not to commit professional harakiri. One can't expect him to take somebody else's blame and ruin himself. I suspect that his adversaries have put shackles around him in such a manner that he finds himself totally helpless. I have discussed the matter with Vinay and some other members of the Bar and I can apprise her of the exact situation. I think Vinay hasn't been taking her calls deliberately. He has advised Rahul to consider giving up practice altogether."

Shahnaz was taken aback. She said, "How can an irrefutable case be built upon falsehood? They say cross examination is a tool that ferrets out the hidden truth. I'm sure Rahul will never compromise himself in a manner that his honour is affected. From whatever little I know of aunty, I'm sure that nothing short of that will be acceptable to her."

Rustom said, "Vinay tells me that he did try to warn Rahul about the impending dangers, and the nefarious characters in the profession. Apparently Rahul did not heed the counsel."

Shahnaz said, "His mind is razor sharp. If he didn't take the hint, it must be because his conscience was clear and he couldn't imagine that the reference was being made in his context. From what Vinay Khosla told you, it appears that even he isn't sure of Rahul's innocence. I think you must talk to aunty and apprise her of the correct position. The reputation of the family is at stake and the matter is to be handled with utmost deftness. Honour means everything to this family."

From outside the room, Ram Lal announced that *Mata ji* was waiting for the guests in the outside patio. Rustom and Zaroo joined Gayatri Devi. She was sitting with Mithai Lal and his wife Savitri Rani. They were introduced to Rustom and Zaroo as Sita's parents. They looked sober and affable but tension was writ large on their faces. They asked if Modys had met Sita recently and if she was alright. Savitri Rani said, "Sita is the apple of our eyes. I can't live without her." And tears welled up in her eyes.

Rustom told them that he had spoken with her before leaving Delhi and that she was busy settling Samir's estate. He was careful not to refer to Samir as Sita's father. Zaroo said that Sita was a wonderful girl and that any parent would be proud of her. To provide Savitri some consolation, she added that even she missed her Shahnaz immensely but since she was very happy here she had come to accept the situation. She suggested that they could visit Delhi more frequently.

Gayatri Devi said that she also missed Sita no end but she drew solace from the thought that daughters had to leave home one day. She considered it her responsibility to get Sita married suitably and was hopeful that her marriage with Gyaneshwar would become a reality one day. She was, in a way, happy at the circumstances leading to her stay at Delhi. She thought providence had given Sita and Gyaneshwar a chance to come closer.

Her observation that daughters had to leave home one day triggered a ray of hope in Rustom's mind. Nothing could make him happier than having Rahul as his son-in-law. He was confident that his problems would be sorted out before long and in any case firmly believed that small incidents did not change the basic worth of a person. He thought it fortunate that Shahnaz had a chance to be in Rasulabad, close to Gayatri Devi.

❖❖

Ram Lal had gone to town preparing delicacies for the evening tea and the Modys could see that special treatment was being meted out to them. The telephone rang. It was Sita. She asked for Gayatri Devi and when she heard her voice she said, "*Ma*, how've you been? I know that you're capable of handling horrendous situations with ease but for my own satisfaction I want to be with you. You've handled Haji ji's burial situation very deftly, I'm sure that you'll have the embargo on my visit lifted very soon. I'm desperate to be with you."

Gayatri Devi was touched . She said, "I'm all right, except that I don't know exactly what has been happening with Rahul. As far as you're concerned, I'm afraid that you'll have to stay away from Rasulabad till tempers cool further."

Sita said, "Rustom uncle spoke to me before leaving and he's fully conversant with the latest on Rahul. He told me that he'll explain everything to you. The long and short of it is that Rahul has been badly trapped for no fault of his." She repeated, "But *Ma*, do something so that I can be with you."

Looking at Rustom, Gayatri Devi said, "No, Rustom hasn't spoken to me about the matter as yet. In fact they've just arrived."

She put the phone down and asked him if he could go with her to another room because she wanted to discuss an important matter. Shahnaz suggested that the others could move out instead. Gayatri Devi rejected the idea for the reason that anyone from outside could approach the verandah and disrupt the conversation.

She requested Zaroo also to join them and the three moved to the adjoining room. Shahnaz wanted to be involved, but she was mature enough to realise that she was being kept out only so that Diwan Mithai Lal and Savitri did not feel isolated. On his part, Diwan Mithai Lal knew that he was trusted completely but that Gayatri Devi wanted to give Rustom the feeling of trust and security.

Inside gayatri Devi began, "I need hardly tell you that I've been spending very anxious moments, the like of which I have never experienced before. I'm a mother after all and Rahul is dearer to me than my own life. But it is not enough for me that Rahul is innocent. He must be cleared of all the charges by the authorities. I understand you're well conversant with the exact situation and I shall be grateful if you would share the details."

Zaroo was quiet but looked distraught. Rustom said, "I do appreciate your predicament. Vinay and Rahul must be too embarrassed, for their own reasons, to tell you everything. But before I narrate to you what happened, I wish to make it clear that I don't have an iota of doubt that Rahul is innocent. The only thing he is guilty of is not guarding his flanks against the onslaught of crooks. The long and short of the matter is that the Enforcement Directorate went through the entire process of investigation and no charge against Rahul could be substantiated. The charges framed by the Bar Association are supported by evidence that cannot be brushed aside, but its all circumstantial in nature. Vinay and I have had long dialogues on the matter and we're both of the view that if Rahul gives up his practice and takes up some other work, the entire episode can die a natural death. In any case, the Bar and judiciary have become so corrupt that only the unscrupulous can survive. Rahul has often told me that his profession offered very limited opportunities and that one could, at best, end up in glorified mediocrity. He has set his vision high and therefore this profession is not suitable for him. I don't know if it would be acceptable to him or not but I would be very happy if he joined me in business as a partner. Or he could set up something else of his choice."

Gayatri Devi said, "I get the feeling that you and Vinay both have a lurking suspicion about Rahul's integrity, otherwise why would you advise him to quit the profession altogether?"

Rustom softened his voice and said, "I certainly don't doubt Rahul's integrity. In fact, I rate Rahul's integrity as well as his abilities very high but I'm a businessman and I try to strike the best bargain in a given situation. The evidence against Rahul may not be strong enough to get him debarred or suspended, but it is also not so feeble as to get him a clean acquittal. Some kind of punishment is inevitable unless he quits the practice. That is the position in a nut shell."

Gayatri Devi kept her cool but looked disturbed. She spoke after a pause, "The situation seems to be more serious than I had imagined. Thank you for updating me. If you hadn't told me everything so clearly it would have been too late by the time I learnt the details. As it is, the matter seems to be getting out of control. I must speak with Rahul this minute."

Rahul's phone rang and he picked it up to hear his mother's voice. He hadn't planned on sharing all the details with her, but on finding that Rustom had revealed everything to her he relented and shared his side of the story. He said, "*Ma*, how is it that your wish is always granted by the Almighty? You wanted me to be in Rasulabad and by a quirk of fate I seem to be destined to spend the rest of my life there."

The joy that was present in Gayatri Devi's voice when she talked to her son was absent this time. She said, "Rustom has told me everything and I must say that I'm appalled at the idea of your quitting. People in the right don't quit; they fight and they win. I cannot stand by someone who is not in the right. After all, you wouldn't be quitting under normal circumstances and the reason for your quitting cannot be separated from the charges. By now, everyone is aware of the charges that have been levied against you. Regardless of court judgments, if you quit practice that will be a sign for people that you're guilty. It would be a stigma for life. You must stick it out and vindicate your honour. I will come to Delhi and discuss the matter with you. Till then, do not commit yourself to anything. Your stance should be that you're not guilty and that you will fight it out. You cannot destroy what your forefathers have taken generations to build, especially when you're not guilty."

She put the phone down and looked at Rustom. She said, "I appreciate your concern for Rahul. I know that you're of the view that he should leave practice but as far as I'm concerned, the honour of my family gets precedence over any other consideration. I want people to know that he has done nothing wrong and that nothing was found in the investigation."

Zaroo and Rustom both nodded in agreement as if they appreciated her point of view, but in his heart Rustom was of the view that this was not the time for a showdown with the establishment. He said, "No one has been able to control wagging tongues. What is of concern is that if some adverse action is placed on record, it will leave behind an indelible mark. It is that situation that I want to avoid."

Gayatri Devi was firm in her views. She said, "What you're suggesting is a practical solution to the problem, on the assumption that Rahul is guilty. I'm proceeding on the hypothesis that he is not guilty. In any case, I won't have anything to do with him if he's guilty. The idea is not to save him, but to bring out the truth and vindicate the family honour."

Rustom was not in agreement with her and decided that this was no time for diplomacy. He knew of several cases when innocent people had been declared guilty by manipulative manoeuvres. He was keen that Rahul should not fall prey to the evil designs of his adversaries. He said, "Rahul's track record will, for the future, bear irrefutable testimony to his character but he must be saved right now."

She said, "We have enough goodwill to have the grain separated from the chaff. What are friends like you for?"

He had to yield. He said, "Alright, I'm at your disposal. When do we go to Delhi?"

She said, "What a shame. We've been asking you to come here for such a long time and now that you're here, I'm suggesting that we go back to Delhi."

Zaroo, who had kept quiet all this while said, "We will come again at a more opportune moment and enjoy your hospitality. I think we must leave for Delhi without losing any more time."

Gayatri Devi smiled and said, "Well, I suppose twenty-four hours are good enough for you to get bored in Rasulabad. Now let's get back to the verandah and see what's happening."

The three of them went out to find that a discussion was going on regarding the ban on Sita's entry in Rasulabad. Savitri was saying that Haji ji's family had no objection to her presence there. She had heard that a few *Mullahs* who masqueraded as the leaders of the Muslim community had made it into an issue. She was of the view that once Gayatri Devi was through with Rahul's the problem she would solve problem without any difficulty.

Gayatri Devi told her not to worry. She said her immediate problem was that the Modys had come to Rasulabad for the first time and she was rushing them back to Delhi for her own selfish reasons. Diwan Mithai Lal asked her if she was also going to Delhi to which she replied in the affirmative. He moved closer to her and reminded her that she had invited a few people to meet the Modys and have dinner with them. He asked if that plan was still on, to which she replied, "The show must go on."

❖❖

The invitees were some of the old, elite residents of Rasulabad besides the District Magistrate, the Superintendent of Police and the District Judge. The cuisine had been carefully planned to suit every palate and the layout had an air of royalty and good taste. Everyone greeted the Modys with great cordiality and spoke very highly of Shahnaz. Rustom Mody did not need any introduction to the Rasulabad society. Almost every one either knew him or knew of him. The Modys were overwhelmed to see that Shahnaz had already carved a niche for herself. Rustom did notice that nobody was even mentioning Rahul's name, let alone making inquiries about him. Gayatri Devi was seen talking to the Superintendent of Police and Khan Bahadur *Saheb* in a corner.

Khan Bahadur was among the old aristocrats of Rasulabad and was held in high esteem. He was heard saying, "The issue of Sita's return here is very intricate. To say that the entire community is against her entering Rasulabad may be a gross exaggeration. The sensible people in the community do not hold her responsible for what has happened. In fact, what Haji did was an act of impulse. Poor thing, she could have lost her life! But the main problem is Haji's wife. She's of the view that Samir Saxena had compromised the honour of their family and the revenge for it lay in taking his life. But since he died, the revenge could only be extracted by extinguishing the last flame of Samir's life–Sita. In her she sees a constant reminder of the disgrace that had been hurled upon them. She thinks that her husband sacrificed his life for the cause of protecting his family honour and it is on her instigation, that some Maulvees have made this into an issue of a Muslim marrying a *qaafir* and the offspring of such a marriage being *haraam*. As you know, there are always some people in the community who thrive on raking up sensitive and provocative issues. Only because a couple of Muslims pronounce something in the name of the community it does not mean that it becomes a *fatwa*, and in any case the *fatwa* does not bind Sita."

There was a long pause after Khan Bahadur's speech. Then Gayatri Devi said, "I know what you're saying is right, but controversies should best be avoided. Haji's wife's feelings are understandable. She's frustrated and in her situation it's very difficult to maintain one's balance. Time will heal her wounds and then everything will fall back into place. In the meantime, nothing should be done to add insult to injury." She knew what she had said about Haji's wife would end up being communicated to her, and that might help in pouring oil over troubled waters.

Savitri Rani was watching Gayatri Devi talking to Khan Bahadur from a distance and it did not take long for her to guess that the topic of discussion was Sita. After Khan Bahadur moved on to another table, she walked up to her. She asked if there had been any new developments. Gayatri Devi told her that she wanted to talk with her and Mithai Lal but could not find time. She said that she was planning to leave for Delhi the following day and therefore suggested that they speak after the guests had left.

The moment all the guests left Savitri rushed to her husband and told him that Gayatri Devi had some important news to break to them. He was a very seasoned man. Small incidents did not excite him. He said, "She will call me when she wants to talk to me."

The party had ended rather early. There was nothing missing and yet all was not the same as before. The Modys were happy for their daughter but Rahul's problems kept haunting them throughout the party. Gayatri Devi too had just gone through the motions. The chief guests and the host both heaved a sigh of relief after the last guest left.

Rustom had had an elaborate discussion with Mr. Khodaiji, who was an old man and the only Parsi resident of Rasulabad. Khodaiji was of the view that Sita's entire issue had been blown out of proportion by the District Magistrate and that it would die a natural death in a short time. He was insistent that had the District Magistrate ignored the demand and taken precautionary measures, the matter would have been nipped in the bud.

Gayatri Devi was reminded that she had to speak with Savitri Rani and Mithai Lal. She excused herself and called them. Shahnaz joined her parents.

Gayatri Devi said, "I can understand Savitri's anxiety about Sita. In fact, I've been equally worried. Taking everything into account, I'm of the view that the time has come for Sita to leave Rasulabad and make her own home. I understand that the demand for banning her entry here has been engineered by miscreants and it need not be taken seriously. Rahul and Samir have identified a suitable boy for her – Gyaneshwar Singh. I approve of the match as well. He's well-groomed, well-educated and well-mannered. He hails from a very influential family. His father is a politician known for his expedience rather than his probity. Mercifully, the boy does not share the ways of his father. Rahul says that he seems to be head over heels in love with Sita. She too knows him very well and holds him in high esteem. He has been with her since Samir's death and has helped her in managing her affairs. While she hasn't said an official 'yes' so far, I think that will happen soon enough."

She looked at Savitri and asked, "Does that not make you happy?"

The news was no surprise for Savitri. Rahul had discussed the proposal with Diwan Mithai Lal and he had told her about it. She had met Gyaneshwar at Delhi and had liked him immensely. She said, "I'm supremely happy. Anything that you decide is always for the best." After a few moments she asked, "May I also come with you to Delhi?"

Gayatri Devi replied, "We're leaving tomorrow. Shahnaz would naturally like to go because her parents want to be with her. Mithai Lal and you have to be here to hold the fort." She smiled and added, "Don't worry, I'll make Sita speak with you over the phone and ask you for your blessings."

They left and Gayatri Devi found herself with Zaroo, Rustom and Shahnaz. Rustom broke the ice. He said, "Gayatri, I marvel at your sense of commitment. Even in your turbulent moments you don't lose sight of your responsibilities. Gyaneshwar is a very fine boy."

She said, "The problem is Sita. She hasn't made up her mind as yet. I think I'll ask her point blank this time."

Zaroo said, "So much has happened in such a short time and she deserves to take her own time. She's a very wise girl and I'm sure that she'll make the right choice. The fact is that she's aware of the proposal and yet she's accepting help from Gyaneshwar. Can there be a more positive signal?"

Gayatri Devi said that that was the most sensible statement she had heard all evening. She looked at Shahnaz and told her with an air of familiarity and affection, "Sweetheart, please go to your parents' room and make sure they are comfortable."

❖❖

Usually, Gayatri Devi's late husband appeared in her dreams only when she desired guidance. But that night he appeared unexpectedly. He wore his usual dignified and calm expression. She asked him, "Why did you leave me alone to face all the problems? Rahul is in trouble and so is Sita. These are the two I love the most."

He said, "You love Shahnaz no less. You're so fortunate that God has given you great capacity to love. The most enjoyable experience is to love whoever you come in contact with, because that is how you gets love back from everyone. And how have I left you? I'm always at your beck and call."

She laughed in her dream and said, "Very easy to give a sermon and simplify situations! I'm worried about Rahul. I won't be able to bear the humiliation if he's not completely exonerated. You must either save him or call me to to join you where you are."

In response, the Rai Bahadur recited,

'However much one may try,
What is destined, one can't defy.'

and then he disappeared.

The next day Gayatri Devi, Zaroo, Rustom and Shahnaz left for Delhi. Gayatri Devi and Shahnaz travelled in one car while Zaroo and Rustom returned in the car that had brought them to Rasulabad.

❖❖

Shahnaz wanted to stay with Gayatri Devi, and not go to her own house. She was so persistent that Gayatri Devi had to give in, but when their car reached the destination they found that Zaroo and Rustom had also followed them to Rahul's house. She asked Rustom, "Why don't Zaroo and you go home and relax for a while? In fact, I wanted Shahnaz to take it easy too but she insists that she's indispensible for me and I can't deny that."

He replied, "I don't think there's much time to lose and we must get cracking right away. With your permission I'd like to call Rajeshwar and find out what he can do to help us in the matter."

She said, "I appreciate your kind gesture but why have you thought of Rajeshwar? Don't you think Vinay is the one we should talk to?"

Rustom was a man of the world. He knew that a wheeler-dealer was the need of the hour because he was more likely to know the pulse of unscrupulous adversaries than a straightforward, law-abiding jurist. He said, "Vinay's knowledge is likely to be confined to the facts alone, but we need to work out the ways and means to counter the false allegations."

She saw sense in this suggestion. She said, "Alright. First let's go inside and work out our plan of action."

Noticing some activity outside, a servant opened the door and on seeing Gayatri Devi, ran out to pay his respects. Sita, who was inside the house followed him and embraced her.

Inside the house, cold drinks, water and snacks were served by the servants. Gayatri Devi asked Sita if Rahul was at home. She replied that he had gone to meet Rajeshwar. Gayatri Devi looked at Rustom meaningfully and said, "The wise seldom differ."

An hour later Rahul arrived with Rajeshwar. He looked tired but Rajeshwar was his ebullient self. Ignoring everybody present, he walked up to Gayatri Devi and said, "Good that you've come. I wanted to see you in connection with a private matter. I understand that you're the only one who can help me."

She was surprised. Rustom had told her that Rajeshwar might be able to render help in Rahul's matter, and here he was asking for her help! She said, "You have a very long life. We were just talking about you. It's a coincidence that while you say I can be of some help to you, I've come here to seek your assistance and guidance."

Rajeshwar knew well what she wanted from him. Rahul had come to him to explain his position and ask him for help, but he wanted to make the best use of the situation and ensure her support for his own ends. Primarily, he wanted her to prevail upon Sita to accept the proposal of marrying Gyaneshwar. Rajeshwar and Gyaneshwar had differences of opinion on many subjects but his love for his only son was absolute. He said, "Being of any use to you would be my privilege. Please let me know what I can do. My work can wait."

Gayatri Devi looked at Rahul and asked him if he had apprised Rajeshwar of the situation. Rajeshwar did not wait for Rahul's response. He said, "I know everything about Rahul's problems, and I'll fix everything. After a detailed discussion with him, I spoke with the concerned authority of the Bar Association and asked him to close the matter. He asked me for a small favour and I've assured him that the needful will be done. If you want, I can call him here to see you and satisfy you that nothing adverse will happen to Rahul."

On hearing this, Gayatri Devi realised that things were moving too fast for her liking. She said, "It's very kind of you to have taken so much trouble but all I seek is fair play. I do not want any fixing to be done. I have no doubt that my son is innocent but I want this verdict to come from the authorities concerned. I won't be able to live with myself if he is not acquitted publicly. I want your help reach to the truth of the matter, ."

Rajeshwar felt snubbed. Did this lady not understand how things worked? He said, "If you want to separate the chaff from the grain then I'm the wrong person to approach. I believe that the objective should be achieved, leaving the dirty work of separating the chaff from the grain to those who have the time and stomach for such pastimes. I know that Rahul has been falsely implicated and therefore I think I must come to his recue but frankly speaking, if I were to go by the charges and the evidence supporting them then my conclusions might not be free from suspicion. His adversaries have done their job very well and on the merit of the case alone, Rahul may not be able to avoid punishment. We can't let that happen and therefore, at the moment, let us focus on our objective of getting him exonerated."

Rustom was feeling uneasy at Rajeshwar's uncouth conduct. He too was aware that the case against Rahul was well made and the immediate need was to hush up the matter. But he was also aware that Gayatri Devi was not for manipulating her way out. A thought struck him that she might decline taking Rajeshwar's help. He said, "There's a lot of sense in what Rajeshwar says. Our first priority should be to close the case. The truth always comes out at the end of the day but God forbid, if something unfavourable takes place in the meantime, the harm would be irreversible."

Rahul, who had been feeling very uncomfortable all along, looked at his mother and said, "*Ma*, in any case I've been feeling very suffocated in the profession. Ethics have been thrown to the winds. The Bar and the Bench both make merry at the cost of the litigants. Lawyers want more appearances in the courts and the judges facilitate them by prolonging litigations. The system has enough loopholes to ensure that the lawyers and judges scratch each others' back with the litigants not being any the wiser. And the question of accountability does not arise. I find myself unsuited to the profession, and instead of fighting a corrupt system, I'd prefer to withdraw from the scene. That will settle everything."

Rustom decided to speak his mind. He said, "You cannot play into the hands of your detractors. They want you out because a person of your integrity and ability is a threat to the system in which they thrive. Your foremost responsibility is to prove yourself innocent in all respects. Do that first and then take your call — whether you want to continue in the profession or otherwise."

Gayatri Devi looked at Rahul questioningly but before he could say anything, Shahnaz burst out. She said, "Dad, do you realise the agony that Rahul will have to go through in the process? The summons, the interrogations and the humiliation that goes with them. His quitting would mark the end of the episode and a new world would open up before him. Human memory is short and it won't take long for people to forget."

Sita thought that the discussion was digressing from the main issue and that the nuances were not being understood. There was no doubt that the matter should be closed at the earliest, yet it had to be proved to the world that he had been falsely implicated and that he was innocent. She spoke softly, "Rahul must exonerate himself at all costs and in the true sense of the term. No amount of agony is beyond bearing to protect one's honour."

Rajeshwar got exasperated and said, "A philosophical debate is not what I had bargained for. It's not going to lead us anywhere. Everything has been fixed and the case will be dropped in a week's time." Looking at Gayatri Devi he concluded, "Madam, I hope this is what you want. Isn't it?"

She maintained a stoic silence. She concurred with Sita's views on the subject but was not sure if Rahul was willing to take on the establishment. She had no doubt that Rajeshwar would be able to have the proceedings against him stalled but that was only half the problem. The stigma would accompany him wherever he went. Then she was reminded of the point Rajeshwar and even Rustom, in his own way, had raised — that it may not be possible for him to get away entirely unscathed in the event of a showdown.

She spoke in a serene voice, "Rajeshwar, I'm grateful to you for standing by me in my moment of need. I shall never forget this act of kindness." She looked at Rahul and added, "The decision has to be yours. I'll go along with whatever you decide."

Rajeshwar had already had a very elaborate discussion on the subject with Rahul and was in no doubt about his inclinations. He said, "I was only waiting for your reaction. The fact is that I have the assurance of the Chairman of the Law Commission that the matter will be dropped. I have already told Rahul not to worry on this count any more. This calls for a celebration but I have to leave for another important appointment."

After Rajeshwar left, Gayatri Devi looked at Zaroo and Rustom and said, "How selfish of me to have detained you. It was Rustom's idea to involve Rajeshwar to sort out the problem and now it seems he was right. He has always played the mentor to Rahul."

Rustom said that they were all like family and anything done to assist one's family needed no special mention. Zaroo and he sought her permission to leave and she got up to see them off. Shahnaz too went along with her parents, promising to be back the next day.

Gayatri Devi was now alone with Rahul and Sita. She was not sure if she was happy at the way the matter had ended. She could not believe that there could be any truth in the allegations. But if Rahul was truly innocent why did he not contest them? What confused her most was his idea of quitting the profession. She was of the view that if he left the profession at this juncture it would provide grist to the propaganda mills of his adversaries. Rustom's view that the immediate problem should be solved and the truth could come out automatically over a period of time, was not acceptable to her. She thought that Shahnaz's comments were coloured because of her concern for Rahul. To her mind, Sita's observations were sound and objective.

She asked Rahul, "How has the thought of quitting the profession come to your mind? What will you achieve by doing that? Don't you think that getting the matter closed, as Rajeshwar says he can do, pronounces you guilty in the eyes of the public?"

He fumbled a bit and said, "I'm confused and therefore I have decided to leave everything to destiny. I know the law has ceased to take its normal course and I can't take this anymore. Even if I decide to fight and eventually prove my innocence, do you think I'll be able to absolve myself of this stigma? People know I have influence and resources and regardless of what method I adopt, a favourable decision in my case will be attributed to manipulation and influence. So I'm damned if I do, and damned if I don't. If I leave the profession I will at least be out of sight, and out of sight is always out of mind."

She was shocked at Rahul's statement. She said, "Does it mean that there's no way that you can rid yourself of this stigma? If that is the way it is, then we will have to reconcile to the idea that we can't ever walk with our heads held high again. A person with a clear conscience is expected to fight the evils of the society rather than run away." She heaved a deep sigh.

He was quiet. He knew his mother was really upset but he did not know how to console her.

Sita appreciated the awkwardness of the situation and to change the subject, said, "*Ma*, I have a lot to talk to you about and since there is an embargo on, my visiting Rasulabad, I may not find you and Rahul alone like this again. I've already sounded him out about my intentions regarding the properties left behind by my father but unless I have your consent, I wouldn't like to finalise anything."

Gayatri Devi was relieved at the change of topic. She was not in agreement with the plan of action that had been worked out but the decision lay with Rahul. She did notice that Sita had referred to Samir as her father, and that there was a confident gleam in the her eyes. She said, "What a coincidence! I too want to talk to you about something."

Sita said, "I think that I've been able to discover my parentage through divine help. *Amma, Babuji* and you have provided me with all that any loving and devoted parents can. If there was anything missing, it feels fulfilled now. As a gesture of gratitude, I want to donate all that has come to me by way of inheritance to charity. For this, I want your approval."

Gayatri Devi took Sita's hands into hers and said, "My child, I can imagine how much you must have suffered silently. You're right, God has been kind and any gesture in the service of humanity amounts to acknowledging His grace. You go up in my esteem, but there is a condition on which Savitri, Mithai Lal and I will give you our formal consent."

Sita assumed that she would tell her to avoid coming to Rasulabad and to engage herself with charity work in Delhi. She said, "I can see that not only have you already given your consent, you've also given the sanction on behalf of *Amma* and *Babuji*! But do tell me what you want me to do for you. I shall do anything that makes you happy."

Gayatri Devi smiled and said, "I know that of late you've been in close touch with Gyaneshwar and have been spending considerable time with him. I understand that he's a very fine boy. Your late father and Rahul had initiated the talk of his marriage with you. We find him to be very desirable and more than anything else, I understand that he's head over heels in love with you. We'll give you our consent to do what you want with your inheritance on the condition that you consent to marry Gyaneshwar."

Sita did not answer readily. Gayatri Devi said, "If you have any particular objections you can tell me."

Sita clung to her and with moist eyes said, "*Ma*, how can you all be wrong? I find Gyaneshwar very sensitive but he's always torn between his father and his values. The twain shall never meet but he's somehow managing the contracdition."

Gayatri Devi said, "That is a point in his favour. Do I then take it that you also approve of him ."

She said, "*Ma*, you've been my biggest support and I have always looked up to you for advice and guidance. But at the moment I'm a bit overwhelmed by the pace of events. I've found my natural parents and lost them in the same breath. Marriage is the last thing on my mind at the moment." And she started sobbing.

Gayatri Devi drew her close and caressing her head said, "Now that I know your mind, I'm at peace with myself. I'm glad that Gyaneshwar is in control of Samir's estate and the two of you can do what gives you the maximum satisfaction."

Rahul, who had been listening to the conversation quietly, asked her, "*Ma*, what about your satisfaction? You've been working for our happiness all your life and have got very little in return. This is my biggest regret."

She released Sita's hands and said to her son, "Your father had once told me to draw solace from whatever was available and I've abided by his advice all my life. I believe that if I deserve less I can't ask for more."

Satai, who had shifted to Rahul's house for the time being, came and announced dinner. The food was light but delicious.

Sita asked Rahul, " Why don't you fight and vindicate yourself, like you did in the case of the Enforcement Directorate? Closing the case through political aid may not send the right signals."

Rahul was surprised at her gumption to question his decision. He said, "Do you think people have absolved me of the charges framed by the Directorate? Certainly not! My clearance is still attributed to my influence. They say that I'm capable of manipulating much more important cases. This was an ordinary matter as far as I was concerned. They'll say the same even when the Bar Association matter is dropped."

Gayatri Devi quietly left for her room. Sita watched her leave and sensed her deep sadness. She realized also that Rahul had got himself into a predicament he could not easily get out of. At that moment she also realized that his concerns and ambitions were far removed from her own. His personality was too complex for her. She could never understand or even care to comprehend the compulsions that drove him. She realized she had been infatuated with Rahul's magnetism, but that infatuation was not the best basis for an enduring marriage. Her decision on marriage fell into place.

Rahul meanwhile realized that Sita had imbibed the deep idealism of his mother. While she would always be a friend, he could hardly imagine that they could enjoy a harmonious relationship as man and wife. While all along he had denied having any interest in Sita, he had felt that she was his for the asking. Suddenly he realized that he was being judged by her and was falling short.

"Could you please go to *Ma's* room and be with her, as she does not seem to be well?" he requested. Sita too felt that all was not well with Gayatri Devi and followed her to her room. Gayatri Devi was surprised to see her and asked if she wanted anything. Knowing that she would never admit that she was disturbed and unwell, Sita told her that events had made her very restless and asked if she could spend the night in her room. Both had spent many nights together in the past, when Sita was not well or when they needed to discuss something important and private. Tonight, however, Gayatri Devi wanted to be left to her own thoughts. She replied that Sita was welcome to sleep in her room but made it clear that she was in no mood to talk. Sita silently touched her feet and said, "Forgive me if I've ever hurt you in any respect. I need your blessings to emulate your example. Even a fraction of your qualities will take me far."

Gayatri Devi held Sita by her shoulders, kissed her on both cheeks and said, "You always have my blessings and I'm sure that you will spend the rest of your life pursuing the virtue of goodness. That is the greatest prayer and the greatest boon." Sita went to her room but Gayatri Devi continued to dominate her thoughts. She woke up late at night and just as a precaution went to her room to see if all was well. She peeped in and found her still asleep. She appeared to be talking to someone in her sleep. She could not hear clearly but she thought she heard her telling somebody, "The laws of nature must prevail and nature does not allow us to suffer beyond our endurance."

Sita suspected that she was talking to her late husband and left as quietly as she had come. The next morning the household woke up to find that Gayatri Devi was no more. She had bid good bye to the world in her sleep.

New Beginnings

Gyaneshwar was the first to arrive. Rajeshwar sent a message through him that he was going to see the Chairman of the Law Commission and would come only after obtaining the orders to close down the case. *Nawab Saheb* and *Begum Saheba*, along with Azhar and Nikhat arrived almost simultaneously with Rustom, Zaroo and Shahnaz. They were all shell shocked when Sita narrated the sequence of events.

Shahnaz was inconsolable. Her regret was that she did not stay back the previous night. She told Rahul that adversity always brought out the best in a person and the time had come for him show to the world his real worth. There was an endless stream of visitors from different walks of life – the politicians, the bureaucrats, the businessmen and a host of personal friends and acquaintances. They were unanimous in their observation that only saintly people died so peacefully and without any pain.

Sita and others were of the view that her cremation should take place in Rasulabad, but Rahul had his reservations about it. He was willing to take the body to Rasulabad only on the condition that Sita did not accompany them; but she was hell bent on attending the ceremony.

Rajeshwar came with the news that the proceedings against Rahul had been dropped. After handing over the order to Rahul in full public view, he occupied centre stage. When he was told about the difficulty of Sita visiting Rasulabad, he swung into action. He telephoned the District Magistrate and asked him why a matter of almost no consequence was being blown out of proportion. He told him that Sita would accompany the body of Gayatri Devi and he must make all arrangements for maintaining law and order in the town. He did not allow the Magistrate to react and hung up right away, announcing that everything had been set right. Rahul, Sita, Shahnaz, Gyaneshwar and others were very uneasy at his 'bull in the china shop' attitude, but there was very little they could do about it.

Rahul tried once again to dissuade Sita, but she said, "If I don't attend the cremation, that is an implicit declaration that there is in fact discord between the Hindus and Muslims of Rasulabad. This goes against the grain of Ma's life. I plan to visit Haji ji's family when I go to Rasulabad and try to instill some sense into them. Everyone in his family cannot be devoid of sense. Remember, they insisted on her participating in Haji ji's burial in spite of the so called tension in the community. Moreover, she was the sheet anchor of my life and the least I can do is to pay my last respects to her. I understand that the problem is limited only to Haji ji's family and I see no reason why it cannot be resolved."

Rahul said, "My childhood buddy has grown up." And he walked away to attend to the conglomeration that had gathered and to organise things.

The body was wrapped in the tricolour and placed on a flower-decked bus. Rahul, Sita and Shahnaz sat on the bus.

Gyaneshwar too was keen to go, but Rajeshwar dissuaded him on the pretext that his presence was required at Delhi. Rustom and Zaroo took the train to Rasulabad.

❖❖

Diwan Mithai Lal, Madhoji, the District Magistrate, the Superintendent of Police and the entire administration of Rasulabad were at the *Haveli* to receive the body . A raised platform with a white cover had already been erected for the body to rest in a position that people could have a last glimpse, even from a distance.

All eyes were moist when the body was taken off the bus and placed on the platform and many started wailing. People walked up to Rahul, Sita, Madhoji, Diwan Mithai Lal and other *members* of the family to offer their condolences. It was decided to keep the body in state for some time to enable the public to pay their last respects. The Police arrangement was quite visible and a close vigil had been kept on the visitors.

Zaroo, Rustom and the family of *Nawab Saheb* arrived the next morning by train. They were received at the railway station by Diwan Mithai Lal and brought to the *Haveli*.

Gayatri Devi was cremated with full state honours. Rahul, with Sita and Shahnaz standing behind him, lit the pyre and the armed constabulary fired three rounds to pay its respects to the departed soul.

While the armed Police was firing in the air, Shahnaz suddenly cried out and fell down, holding her arm in pain. Sita, who was standing next to her, immediately bent over her and used her *chunni* to stem the flow of blood. There was pandemonium in the crowd. Rahul organized a cordon around Shahnaz. There were a number of doctors in the crowd who rushed to render assistance.

The general impression was that she had been hit by one of the loose particles of the bullets fired as mark of respect but the Police which sprang into action identified a young boy, holding a country made pistol in his bandaged hand trying to escape the scene. Three policemen encircled the boy and caught him but in the scuffle he dropped the pistol a little distance away.

The doctors moved Shahnaz to the local hospital and after the necessary examination it was found that the injury was not of a serious nature. She was bleeding profusely but there was no bullet in her body. She was in complete possession of her faculties and was conversing normally. Zaroo was almost hysterical but Rustom was calmly working with Rahul and the Administration to get to the bottom of the crime. It turned out that the suspect, who had been caught by the Police, was none other than Haji ji's son, Rasheed, and the intended target of his bullet was not Shahnaz but Sita.

Rahul and Sita went to the *Haveli* where they found the Superintendent of Police and the District Magistrate sitting inside the visitor's room with Rasheed. Rahul said, "I'm Rai Bahadur Rahul, and your father was my good friend. Why is there a bandage on your right arm?"

The boy, having recognised Rahul, replied, "I was playing at the *madarsa* yesterday and a ball hit me."

Rahul asked, "Are you a sportsman?"

The boy said, "Yes, I'm the school athletic champion for the under-eighteen category."

Rahul wanted to make the boy feel comfortable. He commented, "There seems to have been a mistake. Sportsmen are very fair minded and they can't do what is being attributed to you. Did you fire at someone today during my mother's funeral? Did you fire at a woman, no less?"

The boy replied, "Yes."

When Rahul asked him why he had done so, he said, "I'm the eldest male member of my family and the lady I shot at is a symbol of shame for us. She is also responsible for my father's death. I'm sorry that I failed in my mission but I'm sure that *Allah* the merciful will punish her one day."

Rasheed seemed to have no remorse at all for what he had done. Rahul rang up Shahnaz to apprise her of the latest position. Ignoring the protests of Zaroo and the injunctions of the doctors, she left the hospital bed and arrived at the *Haveli*.

She took Rahul and Sita aside and conferred with them for a few minutes. Then she walked up to the police constable who had been deputed to keep vigil.

"Why have you tied him up with ropes?" she asked. "Nobody has seen him firing and no gun has been found on his body. The gun that has been found nearby could not have his fingerprints because his right hand is bandaged."

Sita joined Shahnaz, "The boy seems to be a minor. Please call for his guardians. He should be spared any unnecessary trauma."

The Magistrate and the Superintendent were listening and they knew that what she was saying was a part of a strategy to defuse tension They came forward and said that they had to detain him because if they had not done so, the masses would have lynched him. The boy was very happy to hear what Shahnaz and Sita had to say about him. He was convinced that *Allah* the merciful was responsible for their compassionate stance.

While untying the knots, Shahnaz said, "You must be a strong lad to be able to bear such strong ropes without flinching. Your mother is to be commended for bringing up such a brave boy."

Rasheed was non-plussed. His hatred for Sita, which was coiled inside him like a tight spring, began to dissolve in the warmth that he was receiving. The lady he had wanted to kill, and the lady he had shot instead, both seemed very different at close quarters. A feeling of remorse entered his mind and he started wondering whether he had made a terrible mistake. Feeling very alone and inadequate he began sobbing.

Shahnaz cradled his head in her arms and suggested to the Police that they let the boy go home and keep a vigil on his activities from a distance. She pointed out that in the absence of any evidence they could not convict him and he was underage anyway. Sita said that an unconditional release of the boy, *appa*rently because of her intervention, might set the thinking of the family right and help in restoring normalcy in the city. The Magistrate and Superintendent agreed, but they refused Sita's offer that she drop the boy off to his house herself. And they reiterated their request that she leave Rasulabad altogether.

❖❖

Rasheed was released and reached home with a confused mind. He found his mother and sister sobbing. They were surrounded by a few religious leaders of the city who were assuring them that they would trace Rasheed and bring him home. These so called leaders were the same ones who had spearheaded the hate campaign against Sita.

Zubeda was very excited to see Rasheed. She ran to embrace him and asked, "Where have you been? *Imam Saheb* told me that you had gone to *Malkin's* funeral and that the Police had detained you, as they suspected that you were behind the shooting. I had *Maulvee Saheb's* assurance that he would have you released, but I was very worried for you. What was the need for taking such a drastic step?" She looked at *Imam Saheb* gratefully and said, "May *Allah* the Merciful bestow upon you more and more power and influence to continue doing good to the community."

Rasheed was in a state of utter confusion. Because of Shahnaz and Sita's stance, he was no longer sure whether Sita was an evil symbolising the humiliation of his family or an apostle from *Allah* himself to save him from the tight spot he had got into. He had heard that Sita's mother had brought dishonour to the family but what he saw with his own eyes was that she had stuck her neck out to save him from prison. And he was most intrigued to see that his mother was accrediting his release to Imam *Saheb*!

He released himself from his mother's embrace and said, "*Ammi*, I have been released by the grace of *Allah* but He made Shahnaz and Sita the instruments for it. Sita behaved as if she was indeed my real sister. She told the Police that I wasn't guilty and put forth such arguments in my defence that they had to release me. *Imam Saheb* did train me to shoot with the gun that he supplied to me. He even drew up the plans for the shooting but after that he was nowhere to be seen."

Zubeda said, "My son, you have yet to learn the ways of the world. By the grace of *Allah*, *Imam Saheb* does not have to go anywhere. Sitting here he can achieve what he wants."

Imam Saheb did not say anything. He continued smiling benevolently, sipping the tea that had been made for him. With an unctuous air he declared, "Mysterious are the ways of God and not a leaf shakes without His will."

Rasheed kept quiet but he could not accept that the *Imam* had any role to play in his release. Moreover, he could not really understand the misdeed that Sita was guilty of. He was clear that her mother had committed a sin by marrying a *qafir* but what was her fault? The realisation that her mother was his aunt aroused a curious feeling inside him.

Imam Saheb patted Rasheed on his back and said patronisingly, "You have done a great job but you should move out of this house till tempers cool down. Once Sita leaves the city you may come back. Come to the mosque and stay there."

Zubeda said, "*Imam Saheb*, after the martyrdom of Rasheed's father you have come into our lives as a saviour."

Rasheed was getting increasingly uncomfortable at the way things were turning out. He had seen no hostility on the part of Shahnaz and Sita and although *Imam Saheb* was showing extreme concern for his family and its honour, he only talked of confrontation and revenge. He told his mother, "*Ammi*, it was Sita *Appa* and Shahnaz *Appa* who got me released from the clutches of the Police." He stopped suddenly, as he realised that he had made a grave mistake by referring to them as his elder sisters. "I mean Sita and Shahnaz," he corrected himself.

Imam Saheb flared up and said, "Is this how you show your gratitude to *Allah*? His ways are mysterious and they're beyond the perception of common mortals. Sita got you released because she knew that if you had not been freed, the community would have burnt the entire city and the *Haveli* would have been razed to the ground. Moreover, she has her eyes on the Assembly seat vacated by Gayatri Devi and she can't afford to incur the wrath of our community. Don't live under any illusions, I warn you!"

Rasheed mustered his courage and said, "I'm very grateful to *Allah* and to you for coming to our rescue but even by your logic, she is likely to avoid any confrontation rather than to trigger it and therefore we are safe."

Imam Saheb looked at Zubeda and said admonishingly, "I have not come here to take lessons from someone whom I should not even be talking to. If his wisdom tells him to embrace the enemy's daughter and swallow the humiliation then all I can do is to pray to the Almighty. I see no place for myself here."

He got up to leave saying, "I've launched a movement to restore the lost honour of the family and the family is keen to embrace the one who has brought about the humiliation. They deserve to spend the rest of their lives in hell."

Zubeda got panicky and got up. She beseeched him to forgive the youngster. At her urging Rasheed also apologized to the Imam. But by this time, he had stormed out leaving his half finished cup of tea.

❖❖

Madhoji was anxious about the future of the trust. Sita would have been the best person to take over after Gayatri Devi's passing but there was talk of her marriage to Gyaneshwar. Rahul, to the best of his understanding, was neither interested in social work nor cut out for it. Moreover, the scandal that he was embroiled in was the biggest deterrent to entering public life for the time being.

As for Shahnaz, he had always harboured doubts about the ability of a city-bred girl coming from a privileged background to attune herself to development work in the villages. But her calm, sensible behaviour in the wake of her shooting, her maturity in not reacting in the face of extreme provocation and her ability to strike a chord with Rasheed had set him thinking.

After the shooting, Zaroo was certain she did not want Shahnaz to stay in Rasulabad. Rustom was non-commital. He only wanted her to come away to Delhi for a few days before making a decision. He was clear that even if the security aspect could be taken care of, Shahnaz could only live and work in Rasulabad if Rahul and she decided to get married.

Zaroo, Rustom, Diwan Mithai Lal, Madhoji, Shahnaz, Sita and Rahul met at the breakfast table. The chair that Gayatri Devi occupied was conspicuously empty.

Shahnaz said with tears in her eyes, "Aunty was an institution and the legacy of an institution never dies. Believe me, I feel she's sitting right here smiling at us, telling us to follow in her footsteps."

Rahul remembered his duties as the new head of the family and asked Sita, "Where is *Savitri Ma*? Why has she not joined us?"

She replied, "I wonder if Babuji has told you that Amma and I are leaving for Delhi tomorrow morning. She is busy attending to last minute chores as after we've gone he will be alone in the house."

Rahul said, "Sita, I must apologise for making you return to Delhi so soon. The District Magistrate is insistent that you leave or else, he fears, there may be a law and order problem."

She said, "I don't want to be the cause of any suffering. By the grace of God, everything is under control so far and I'm sure that my going away will leave the communities with no excuse to fight." She laughed and continued, "I didn't know, however, that all you would work together to throw me out of here!"

Sita's comment brought some cheer to the gathering. Rahul smiled and said, "You've been looking for an excuse to leave us and go to Delhi! I only facilitated the fulfilment of your wish. Also madam, we are aware that there are certain proposals you have accepted and thus are anxious to return to Delhi.

Shahnaz said, "It's rude to talk in riddles. What is this proposal that 'madam' has accepted?"

Rahul said, "Well, we don't want her to leave Rasulabad but we sure want her to get married. Samir Uncle and I were keen that she gets married to Gyaneshwar. Our choice met the approval of Ma, Diwan Mithai Lal, and *Savitri Ma*. Then I found that Gyaneshwar was very keen too. Now Sita has consented to marry him."

Rahul said, "I'm conscious that this isn't the most apt time for announcing the good news, but Ma used to say that no time should be lost for spreading happiness."

Rustom commented, "Gyaneshwar is a very fine boy and Sita and he make a fine pair. I'm sure that they will be very happy together."

Thinking that this was an opportunity to voice his concerns, Madhoji said, "Rahul, there cannot be better news, but before Sita steps into her new role I'd like to hear what you have in mind for the trust and the various projects it has been pursuing."

Rahul said, "I'm not cut out for such work. You Madhoji are the best person to head the trust and I think Shahnaz will be able to assist you ably. If this is acceptable to Shahnaz then you can work together. As far as the Assembly seat is concerned, let the party decide whom they want to field as a candidate. I couldn't care less if the party loses."

Rustom said, "I don't think that Shahnaz is ready as yet."

Zaroo said, "She is too young and she has to settle down first. She can't live here. It was different when Gayatri was around but how can she live here alone? No, it won't work."

Rahul said, "I can assure you I didn't propose Shahnaz's name without considerable thinking. Ma was convinced of Shahnaz's devotion to her as well as to her work. The concern she had was that her parents may not quite approve of the idea of her living here."

Rustom looked confused. He was not sure if he was getting nearer to his objective of getting Rahul and Shahnaz married, but he did see a ray of hope in the new development. He said, "Everything is happening at breakneck speed. Let us sleep over the possibilities for a few days."

Sita's departure from Rasulabad was a poignant moment. Although Savitri was accompanying her to Delhi, she felt that she was leaving her home. Before leaving the *Haveli* she closeted herself in Gayatri Devi's room and remained there for almost an hour. The retainers of the *Haveli* bade goodbye to her with moist eyes, imploring her to come back soon. Besides Rustom, Zaroo, Shahnaz, Rahul and Mithai Lal, there was quite a sizeable crowd comprising the old residents of Rasulabad to see her off at the railway station. There she was her old self, meeting all those who had come to see her off. She surprised Rahul by touching his feet and saying, "No one can take Ma's place in my life but you remind me of her."

Rahul hugged her and said, "Hey buddy, what's suddenly got into you! I'm still going to come to you when I need bailing out." But he was only joking as events preceding breakfast had settled the issue of whom he would be confiding in for the rest of his life.

❖❖

Rahul had entered the long room early and found Shahnaz studying the old black and white photos of the family hung on the walls. "Who is this handsome man?" she asked pointing to a tall figure on horseback. " And why did he have to hide his face behind such a large mustache?"

"That's my greatgrandfather Rai Bahadur Ambika Prakash," Rahul replied laughing. "And his mustaches were the pride of the family."

"The family honour being strung on twenty wisps of face hair," Shahnaz was gently teasing Rahul.

"Of course," he said. " Let me see you match him. Actually, don't bother. It would spoil the pretty picture you make."

" What's this obsession with honour, sir?" asked Shahnaz. She was now close to Rahul and he caught the aroma her perfume.

"Honour is everything for us," said Rahul turning serious. " And I think I have short changed my family's most precious heirloom."

"Honour, shame, glory, name – the hero's journey, and maybe the heroine's too, if social norms permit. But what does all this have to do with living? What does it have to do with breathing? Do plants have honour? Do trees?" Shahnaz had gone back to gazing at Rai Ambika Prakash's mustaches.

"What do you mean?" he asked. He was always a little unsure when Shahnaz's emotions took flight.

"This wound of mine was caused by a boy trying to protect his family honour," she said pointing to her arm. "Sita's shooting too was an attempted 'honour' killing. The torment that gnaws at you day and night is a result of your quest to regain the family honour. Indeed, the deep hurt that Gayatri Devi lived and died with came from a sense that she must guard the family honour in the face of its growing irrelevance in a changing world."

"But Rasheed was misled when he tried to kill to protect his honour. Ma only wanted her family to live with integrity."

"But her obsession with honour, the depth of her engagement with that principle, may have been because it was the last defence she had in a world she hardly recognized. While you chose to grapple with this world, she hid behind the only armor she thought she possessed."

Rahul did not speak. He did not trust himself to be able to respond to Shahnaz's challenge adequately.

"The desire for honour is an illusion, as much as greed or expeditiousness. It is certainly better to live honourably and well, than to live dishonestly and deceitfully, but ultimately, desiring anything so obsessively, even honour, is a source of misery that is sure to spread its unnatural contagion everywhere."

Rahul gripped Shahnaz by her arms, incoherent with rage. "Don't you ever speak this way. How dare you come and psycho-analyze my family in this way? You little pipsqueak, city slicker, rich doll…" He was holding her very hard and Shahnaz winced. Then ignoring the discomfort she smiled at him.

"I love Ma," she said. "As much as you do. As much as Sita. Don't hold it against me if I remark on some things about her that I noticed. Besides, I don't know whether what I am saying is true or not. All I know is that a perfectly fine young man, Rai Bahadur Rahul, is in distress and has been for years because of something vacuous, something illusory called the 'honour of the Raibahadurs'. Rahul, you don't have to live up to your family name. You only have to live your own life the best you can."

Shahnaz at this point had clasped Rahul's face in her hands, while his grip on her was loosening. Suddenly he started sobbing.

"I have let everyone down," he said.

"You have not," said Shahnaz. You do not have the power to let anyone down except yourself. And you're too young to conclude whether you've let yourself down or not."

Rahul released her and strode up to the portrait of Rai Ambika Prasad. "Haven't I let you down?" he demanded. "Haven't I?" Then he paced around the room stopping before the portraits of all his ancestors. "And you? And you? And you?"

Shahnaz watched him smiling. There was a full minute of silence. Then suddenly Rahul started laughing. He laughed so loudly that Ram Lal who was in the kitchen came running. He saw Rahul rolling on the floor.

"How can I let down photographs?" he was shouting in

between burts of laughter. "They don't exist except in my head. How can I let anyone down except myself?"

Shahnaz was standing in a corner smiling broadly. Ram Lal closed the door and retired to the kitchen to prepare breakfast. When Zaroo and Rustam entered the breakfast room twenty minutes later Rahul and Shahnaz were at the table deep in conversation about the history of Rasulabad. Their faces were flushed with emotion but they did not have a hair out of place.

❖❖

Gyaneshwar, Rajeshwar and his wife were at the New Delhi railway station to receive Savitri Devi and Sita. Sita touched Rajeshwar and his wife's feet and they blessed her. Gyaneshwar touched Savitri Rani's feet and she hugged him. They all went to Samir Saxena's bungalow, which was now Sita's house. The house looked resplendent as Satai had spruced it up under Gyaneshwar's guidance. On entering, Sita experienced a peculiar feeling of independence and contentment. This was the house where she was born, the house where her mother had spent the last days of her life.

Zaroo and Rustom were also eager to return to Delhi. Although Rustom was in constant touch with his offices all over the country he had started feeling restless. But they did not want to leave until a decision was taken on Shahnaz's future. Their shrewd eyes could see that things were working towards bringing Rahul closer to Shahnaz. The problem was that they were both very independent in their views and a marriage between them could not happen through someone else's manipulation.

Every passing day added to their anxiety. Luckily, a few days after Sita's departure, Madhoji and Mithai Lal again broached the subject of Gayatri Devi's succession. Rahul said that he had already suggested that Madhoji and Shahnaz handle the affairs.

Shahnaz wanted to say something but Madhoji intervened. He said, "Shahnaz is immensely committed to the cause of the trust. She is adequately suited to handle the work and I will continue to guide and assist her as I've been doing in the past. This will ensure continuity in the management of the trust because I'm not in very good health and I can't do justice to the responsibility much longer."

Rustom intervened to say, "Are we not putting the cart before the horse? The basic prerequisite for contesting the Assembly election or heading the trust is that the person concerned should stay at Rasulabad. Neither Shahnaz nor Raul stays here. Also, we seem to be losing sight of the big picture. Gayatri Devi has left behind a sizeable property besides the trust and a seat in the Assembly. Rahul has to take a decision on that also."

Rahul said, "You know very well that I'm not interested in taking over either the social or political reins of my mother's establishment. I had a long chat with Shahnaz on the subject. She told me that not only was she deeply interested in the work, she was totally committed to carrying out Ma's community development work. Her only condition is that Madhoji continue guiding her as he had been doing during Ma's lifetime. She says she's not interested in politics but she's quite open to the idea of making Rasulabad her home. That solves the problem for the moment. The Assembly by elections are still a few months away. We'll cross that bridge when we come to it. If nobody is interested in contesting the seat from our side, we'll leave the choice of the candidate to the party."

Rustom, who had been listening to Rahul with rapt attention said, "My wife and I too have been discussing the subject with Shahnaz and we're glad that she has found a vocation that satisfies her. We're happy that she is happy. And in any case, stepping into Gayatri Devi's shoes is a matter of great privilege."

Rahul said, "Uncle, you have no idea what a major problem you've solved. Thank you very much."

Rustom said, "All that is very well but you shouldn't lose sight of the fact that your getting elected to the U.P. Assembly will help in ironing out your problems with the establishment. In any case, I do want to know what plans you have for yourself."

Rahul laughed and said, "I'm still a lawyer, I don't reveal everything. But unless I talk to you, my plans cannot mature."

Rustom asked him point blank, "Tell me what you've decided for yourself?"

Rahul said with a mischievous smile, "With your permission and blessings I've decided to marry Shahnaz and live here with her.'

Zaroo was speechless. Rustom said, "For me, it's like a dream come true. But have the two of you spoken to each other about it?"

Shahnaz was looking down but the lawyer in Rahul was ready with the repartee. "How could we do that without your consent and blessings?"